DISCARD

ZILLIONAIRE

A BUSTER HIGHTOWER MYSTERY

ZILLIONAIRE

GARY ALEXANDER

FIVE STAR
A part of Gale, Cengage Learning

Detroit • New York • San Francisco • New Haven, Conn • Waterville, Maine • London

GALE
CENGAGE Learning·

LIBRARY OF CONGRESS CATALOGING-IN-PUBLICATION DATA

Alexander, Gary, 1941–
    Zillionaire : a Buster Hightower mystery / Gary Alexander. —
1st ed.
        p. cm.
    ISBN-13: 978-1-4328-2534-8 (hardcover)
    ISBN-10: 1-4328-2534-8 (hardcover)
    1. Comedians—Fiction. 2. Billionaires—Fiction. 3. Heirs—Fiction. I. Title.
PS3551.L3554Z28 2011
813'.54—dc22   2011016077

First Edition. First Printing: August 2011.
Published in 2011 in conjunction with Tekno Books and Ed Gorman.

In memory of Melvin Elliott Hand

ACKNOWLEDGMENTS

Herewith, just a very few of the fine folk responsible for assembling what follows into something (hopefully) readable: Roz Greenberg, Tiffany Schofield, and Libby Sternberg.

ZILLIONAIRE: an extremely rich person.

—*New Oxford American Dictionary* (2001)

1.

December 7, 1941
Sublieutenant Saburo Taihotsu was no drinker, but in order to sleep he'd gulped three cups of sake after last evening's mess.

Following a sleepless night, he forced down a breakfast of rice and dried squid.

Soon thereafter, the young naval officer sat on the flight deck of the flagship carrier *Akagi,* strapped into his Zero fighter, eyes red, head throbbing, on the verge of throwing up.

The fleet was 220 miles north of Hawaii's most populous island, steaming at flank speed into heavy seas. *Akagi* listed ten degrees and pitched crazily. Waves curled in frothy swells, showering everything and everyone.

The fighters were the first to launch. Because the deck was crowded with airplanes behind them, their takeoff runs were uncomfortably short.

It was Saburo's turn to go. He tightened his sphincter and advanced his throttle. The air control officer dropped his flag. Saburo released his brakes and surged forward. He plunged off and settled toward the water. With the ocean lapping at his undercarriage, Saburo drew the stick into his lap and the Zero clawed upward.

He climbed to his assigned altitude, thinking that he had survived the easiest portion of his day. Saburo had once lived six months in the land of his imminent enemy. He was less eager than some of his comrades to engage them in foolhardy battle, to risk prematurely joining his ancestors.

The *Akagi* planes and those from the other carriers formed quickly. They were to be the first of two attacking waves. The Zeros circled at 14,000 feet, poised to protect the bombers layering below. One hundred and eighty-three aircraft turned southward as one.

For the next hour, the youthful sublieutenant's mind oscillated. He would, he wouldn't, he would, he wouldn't, he would, he wouldn't. Saburo tried yet again to convince himself that he wasn't a coward. He didn't fear death. He'd gladly die for his emperor. He merely despised futility and squandered lives—especially his own.

At the end of almost two weeks and 4,000 miles, it was utterly inconceivable that their great armada of carriers, battleships, destroyers, cruisers and supply ships had not been detected.

Such preposterous hubris.

They were flying into an ambush, Saburo knew. A wasteful, horrific slaughter. The Americans possessed the amazing new radar invention, and their Hawaiian bases were heavily fortified. There would be American P-40 pursuit planes out of Hickam Field, swarming like enraged hornets. And F4F Wildcats launched from the primary target, the carriers moored at Pearl Harbor. Accompanied by withering anti-aircraft fire.

Saburo pictured a sky filled with bullets and deadly puffs, artillery shells popping like theater popcorn. But these kernels would explode into shrapnel.

Movie house popcorn evoked sentimental memories from the land of their future foe. County fairs. Big band music. Fast coupes with rumble seats. Deluxe hamburgers and all the trimmings. Voluptuous, blond-haired, pale-eyed, freckle-cheeked girls, dreamboats who did things to Saburo in bed that his Japanese bride would not.

During his stay there, he had been joyously contaminated.

In 1937, Saburo had toured the United States with his industrialist father, owner of Taihotsu Iron Works™. The elder Taihotsu had hoped to establish new markets for his automotive and locomotive parts. It had been Saburo's impression that the American executives had listened to not a word as his father had described his products. They had seen only his dark skin and slanted eyes. They had seen an untrustworthy inferior, an Oriental who could not possibly grasp modern engineering and manufacturing techniques.

Furthermore, the race was indirect, warlike and inscrutable.

The Yellow Peril.

The Asiatic hordes.

His father had returned to Japan mortified and embittered. Saburo had remained and enrolled in a western university for language training before going home to enter the Imperial Navy Flight School.

Saburo loved and hated America with its intimidating vastness and infinite resources. He loved and hated the people. They could be open and generous. They could be petty and mean. They could be soft and they could be tempered steel. They were mongrelized with no heritage, no culture, and with one hundred heritages, one hundred cultures. They were honest and devious and weak and brave.

The United States of America would be a tenacious and unpredictable adversary.

When Saburo spotted the north tip of Oahu, he made his decision. He would not contribute his life to the senseless carnage.

He twisted his magneto switch from ON to RIGHT MAG-NETO to LEFT MAGNETO to OFF. He reversed the process, rotating the switch back and forth, back and forth, back and forth. He was interrupting ignition to the fourteen cylinders of his 940 horsepower, air-cooled radial engine. The tachometer needle fluttered and the stick vibrated in his hand.

A wingman furiously jabbed a finger at Saburo's cowling. Saburo innocently pressed his face against the canopy and observed black smoke issuing from his Zero's exhaust stacks. Via hand signals from plane to plane, Saburo's flight leader, Lieutenant Commander Tomeo Onishi, took note. There was, of course, radio silence.

Commander Onitsha's head swiveled. He jabbed a thumb rearward.

"No," Saburo mouthed in protest, working the magneto switch with added vigor.

The flight leader repeated his return-to-*Akagi* thumb thrust. Saburo nodded obediently, jaw grimly set. He dipped to break formation and made a 180.

He had decided none too soon. Emerald green and volcanically rugged, Oahu was sharpening into focus. If a pilot suffered mechanical trouble after landfall, he would be expected to nurse his airplane to any reasonable target and hurtle into it.

Not this hepcat.

Not today.

Saburo's tachometer needle continued to fluctuate. Vibration intensified.

He cursed. The engine should have resumed normal operation. It began clattering instead. He suspected that his shenanigans had bent a valve. Then, in a progressive reaction, another. And another. Saburo lost 200 RPMs, and the Zero started to shudder. The power plant was consuming itself.

Saburo was 150 miles from his ship. He remembered from navigation briefings another Hawaiian island the size of Oahu, so he set a westerly heading. After ten long minutes at reduced power, the northeast coast of Kauai came into view.

Smoke darkened his cockpit. Saburo shut off the engine

before it shook loose from its mounts. He unlatched the canopy. The slipstream whistled at typhoon velocity, but he was eager to breathe fresh air again.

The area appeared remote. A small, calm bay. A sandy coastline. Ranch land and verdant hills beyond. Saburo noticed rocks in the shallows, jutting above the waterline.

To extend his glide, he lowered wing flaps and kept the landing gear retracted. He banked steeply to parallel the shore. Centrifugal force pressed him into his seat. The strength of a crosswind surprised him. He kicked hard right rudder to avoid drifting into the hillside above the beach.

He had overcorrected. He was again over water and out of altitude. He raised the Zero's flaps to smooth the plane's underbelly and pancaked onto a gentle surf. A jagged rock, concealed just below the surface, sheared off his starboard wing.

The collision threw Saburo forward so violently into his shoulder harness that his collarbone snapped. The harness broke free of its flimsy brackets, and the instrument panel crushed his nose.

The rock also ruptured a gas tank as if it were tissue paper. Seawater rushing through the tear prevented a fire and saved Saburo's life.

The A6M2 Mitsubishi Zero was lightweight, agile, and fast, boasting a maximum speed of 330 MPH. Although it would be obsolete by mid-1943, on December 7, 1941, it was perhaps the best fighter in the world, the British Spitfire its only equal. The Naval General Staff had never seriously considered sacrificing the Zero's speed and maneuverability with ponderous frills such as self-sealing fuel tanks, cockpit armor, and fire extinguishing equipment.

The off-center impact had spun the Zero around. It rode the wave motion ashore, bobbing rear-end first. The tail wheel dug into the sand, and the airplane stopped.

The last thing Sublieutenant Saburo Taihotsu saw before losing consciousness was a large Caucasian woman. She climbed onto his remaining wing. As she stared down at him, the morning sun cast a halo behind her dazzlingly golden hair. He thought she was an apparition, a wraith, a creation of his cowardice and treachery.

He thought he was hallucinating.

He wasn't.

2.

Now

"I get nostalgic for the good old days, way way back, once upon a time, when my prostrate wasn't the size of a glazed doughnut," Buster Hightower said, near the end of his set. Sweating heavily, he hesitated to make quotation marks with his fingertips. "I'm what you call 'of a certain age.' "

Sporadic giggles.

"The only TV commercials I used to watch were for junk food. Now, I'm all eyes and ears when one comes on for medicine. How old I am is a military secret, but suffice to say that a lot of those commercials are aimed at my age group. Ones that'll shrink down that prostated prostrate of mine, ones that'll tune up my ticker, uncholesterol my cholesterol that's the consistency of lard, unvaricose my veins, et cetera. By the way, my birthday's today, which is why this particular topic is stuck in my noggin."

He paused for scattered "happy birthdays" and a drunk's attempt to sing the song.

"Thank you, thank you. These commercials for miracle medicines for geezers, they got me all fired up how they'll fix this and that and the other thing, how I'll live forever. Then they end up with the fine print where they tell you about the, ahem, possible side effects."

Buster ticked them off on his fingers. "Liver damage, heart ge, lung damage, kidney damage. High or low blood pres-

17

sure. Constipation, diarrhea—hey, which is it? Hallucinations, psychosis, dementia. Hoof in mouth disease—had it for years. Warts, dandruff, halitosis. The heartbreak of psoriasis."

A smattering of horselaughs fueled him. Buster was screaming now.

"Distemper, hair growth in unusual places, neuritis, neuralgia."

The bit and the response were petering out.

"Speaking of TV commercials. We watch pro football like most everyone else. What're the two things they always advertise? The two things. Beer and cars. Yeah. Beer usually comes before cars. You know why? It's a conspiracy is why. You get sloppy on all that beer and run out at halftime to buy one of those cars or SUVs they got on special. Base price, seventeen grand in great big numbers on the screen. A fantastic bargain, right? Then in tiny little numbers and letters—more quote marks—'as shown, thirty-nine-five.' Guess which one you come home with.

"Speaking of big bucks, I'm exploring the option again of forming an exploratory committee to run for president. No fooling. All you gotta do is fill out a form and have the price of a stamp to mail it in. Is this a great country or what? The thing I'm exploratorying is whether I can raise the filthy lucre to run. Haven't been able to yet, but there's next time. You know as well as I do that the bottom line of getting elected president is the bottom line.

"Speaking of even bigger bucks, how about Saburo Taihotsu, the Mongoose? The world's richest man's over ninety-two years old and they say he ain't gonna be getting much older. Quite a life Saburo's led. After he did his share of damage at Pearl Harbor, he crash-landed on another Hawaiian island, Kauai.

"He kept himself busy waging a one-man guerrilla campaign that earned him the Mongoose nickname, till he surrendered when the war ended. Yeah, I know, he did penny-ante stuff like potatoes up exhaust pipes, nails on the road to flatten tires, setting brush fires.

"But still. Almost four years on the loose and nobody laid a hand on him. Then he went home to Japan, to lead the mother of all manufacturing empires. Half the cars and trucks in this parking lot are Taihotsus. So's my girlfriend's car. Our fridge and television are Taihotsus."

Buster waved his mike and looked at the speaker beside him. "Hell's bells, this here boom box unit I'm using, it's a Taihotsu Tonemaster 2500. I tell you, you can't avoid the old boy. Now they're saying that Saburo's secretly liquidating everything and nobody knows where the bucks and yen and whatever went. Know what they're saying? Saburo Taihotsu's figured out how to take it with him. Yeah. Hey, why not? Nobody's proved different.

"I get most of my news from the supermarket checkout line," he said, not entirely kidding. "Ever read the *Weekly International Tattler* and other serious journalism they got there? You oughta. They got the straight scoop. Like how Elvis is alive and Lee Harvey Oswald had help.

"The *Tattler* says aliens beamed up all Taihotsu's moola. But what're they gonna do with it? I dunno. Maybe convert it into $20s and go to Las Vegas. Vegas, where the ATMs spit out $100s, not $20s. In that town, a $20 wouldn't get a second glance. You'd be invisible even if you had three eyeballs and antennas where your ears are.

"At this minute, Saburo's in the fetal position under the bed in a Tokyo penthouse so high up it's got its own weather, and he ain't talking to nobody about nothing. In comparison, he makes Howard Hughes seem like a normal, well-adjusted, middle-class, broke-at-the-end-of-the-month fella who carries a lunch box when he punches in on the time clock."

Chuckles.

"Jeez, 100 billion smackers Taihotsu's worth. They're doing all kinds of fun math with it. Taihotsu Tidbits, somebody called them. Like one-hundred billion one-dollar bills end to end, they'll stretch 380 times around the earth.

"Me, I'm running numbers on how many sandbags they'd fill to hide behind to fend off my creditors."

Knowing chuckles.

"Hey, speaking of a fistful of bucks, any lawyers out there? Gimme a show of hands. None? Yeah, yeah, I asked that earlier when I whipped the stale lawyer joke on you. The two hands raised then, you must have been disbarred in the last hour.

"I start out with a stale lawyer joke and finish up with a stale lawyer joke or two or four. Sorry. Union contract. So here goes. What did the lawyer name his daughter?"

Buster waited, then said, "Sue."

Giggles.

"Okay, boys and girls, since you insist, we're gonna have a bonus round. What does a lawyer use for birth control?"

Pause.

"His personality."

Buster was rewarded with howls.

"Here's one that's no joke. What's a dumb lawyer get for clients? Dumb clients is what. There was a piece in the paper last week. This bank robber slipped on his stocking mask and opened the bank's door. Except it wouldn't open. He forgot it was Saturday and banks close early on Saturday. He's rattling the door and the guy using the ATM looks over. Turns out he's a plainclothes detective. End of story."

Louder giggles.

"Whadduya have when a lawyer's buried up to his neck in sand?"

Pause.

"Not enough sand."

Mixed applause and howls.

"Lastly, where does a malpractice lawyer go when he needs a doctor?"

Silence and head shakes.

Buster shrugged. "That's not a joke. I was just wondering. Hey, you folks, you been great. Before I dismiss class, I'm giving you a homework assignment. Write a paper on how come aluminum foil's shiny on one side and dull on the other."

He waved the microphone and hoisted his beer bottle in toast to nineteen people. They were so few and scattered he could count them in the dim light as he worked. But they were putting their hands together for Buster Hightower, some even up on their feet.

He blew kisses and went backstage. Mike, manager of Snickertown Comedy Club, was waiting with, uh-oh, a sourpuss face.

Buster thrust his arms forward and made a cross with his index fingers. "I got another week, Mike. Go on. Shoo! You ain't driving a stake through my heart. Climb back in your coffin."

"Sorry, Buster, it's a wrap after tonight. What can I say? It's not your fault business is lousy. We're going on hiatus until the first of the year. Blame it on the nice weather or the rotten economy."

Mike clapped Buster's shoulders. "Cheer up. We've both been through this, big guy. You're a trouper. Look me up in January."

Buster got his jacket, thinking, yeah, I've been through it. A career comic, he had whistle-stopped from saloon to smoker to NCO club to private party to cocktail lounge to corporate function to dumpy casino, before and after comedy clubs and TV standup had come into vogue.

A tall, husky, shambling man, Buster Hightower mumbled to himself as he walked outside, "Happy flippin' birthday."

21

Today was his sixtieth.

The big six-oh.

He trudged into the parking lot and saw the four round headlights of his car flick on. Buster's 1959 Cadillac convertible fishtailed ahead, rear tires smoking. It slammed to a halt, nosediving less than fifteen feet from its owner. The top had been taken down, and the driver was wearing a plastic Richard Nixon mask. He turned toward Buster, flashed him twin V-signs, then goosed it, bounding onto the street, raising sparks as the 5,000-pound land yacht bottomed out.

Buster watched his Caddy vanish into the darkness, pumping rooster tails of exhaust smoke.

"Happy birthday to you, happy birthday, dear Buster," the comic muttered as he lurched inside to find a telephone. "Happy birthday to you."

"You left your keys in your car?" The investigating patrolman asked incredulously. "At night? *Here?*"

The Snickertown Comedy Club was not situated in Seattle's finest neighborhood. On an arterial in a DMZ between downtown and the south industrial district, Snickertown was sandwiched between discount foam rubber and wholesale leather goods. Half the comics playing the club smirkily inserted the location into their routines. The area had experienced nocturnal crime, some petty, some not so petty.

"I forgot. I was running late for my set. If that ain't a valid reason, I don't know what is."

"You don't often see anything that old on the street. Can you describe it?"

"Bright, gleaming, fire engine red. A 1959 Cadillac Eldorado convertible with a white top. A *snow*-white top. It's a mile long, has stylish tailfins, a wraparound windshield, wide whitewalls, pushbuttons on the dashboard, and more chrome than a showroom full of Toyotas.

"That baby's gorgeous, absolutely immaculate, a timeless classic with C-O-M-I-C vanity plates. It'll be impossible to miss. You'll be doing a special dragnet and assigning an elite team to my case, right?"

"Approximate value?"

Though it was Buster Hightower's only possession of value, he'd never had it appraised. It was his 401(k) and his pension, and he'd planned on cashing it in when the time came. "Priceless."

"Can you be specific?"

Buster hadn't an inkling. "Thousands and thousands and thousands."

The police officer recorded Buster's description of the stolen car as "large red older vehicle" and left the value blank.

He asked, "You said he had this mask on of who?"

"Richard Milhous Nixon, former president of the United States of America. They used to wear those masks when they demonstrated against him. You know, against Vietnam and dirty tricks he pulled to get reelected."

The officer stopped writing and stared blankly. "He was president in the old days?"

This public servant's been shaving for about five minutes, Buster thought. "Long long ago. Ever hear of Watergate?"

"Oh yeah. Now I remember. Nixon was the peanut farmer."

Buster sighed and said, "It was like he was waiting for me before he peeled out, like he was making a statement."

"Sounds personal. Do you have any enemies?"

Buster's mortality suddenly weighed on him, as if a gorilla had climbed on piggyback and hung a 500-pound albatross around his neck.

"Anybody my age has made an enemy or three, son, and I am a Seattle boy, born and raised. But nobody recently, to the best of my recollection, has been desiring a chunk of my hide."

The young officer leaned closer to Buster and sniffed. "Mr. Hightower, have you been drinking?"

"Of course I been drinking," said an exasperated Buster. "My audiences drink like fish. It'd be impolite not to. Downright rude. Please find my car before it gets hurt. Please. Believe me, it'll be easy to spot."

"You're a comedian?"

"Guilty."

"Like Seinfeld?"

"No, not like Seinfeld. Jer, laughmeisters like him and the newer big-timers, they don't travel to gigs in a '59 Cad, irregardless how cherry it is. They go first-class air and private jet and stretch limo. They stay in the best hotels, in suites up so high they have views into the next time zone. Guys like them, they have champagne waiting and flowers and chocolates on their pillow and—"

"Say something funny."

"Would I ask you to catch criminals when you're off duty? To shoot a crook just to entertain me?"

"Come on."

Buster Hightower's trademark was his ranting and raving, a maniacal outrage over politics and other infinitesimally small things. His routine contained neither cruelty nor obscenity. You want the f-word, he'd tell them, go in the can and read what's scratched on the wall above the urinal. No misogyny, no homophobia, no racism, no toilet bowl humor for this boy. Never had, never would. Consequently, his appeal was seriously curtailed.

"Will a stale lawyer joke do?"

"No way. I hate those things. I'm going to college part time and on to law school when I get my degree."

A truly sick individual, Buster thought.

"Okay, then. How come aluminum foil's shiny on one side and dull on the other?"

The police officer glanced up from his clipboard. "That's funny?"

3.

Carla Chance shared her townhouse condominium with Buster Hightower. Their unit contained so many black balloons, it looked to Buster like it had the bubonic plague. For her man's birthday dinner, Carla had fixed his favorites: rare prime rib and baked potato, hold the veggies; chocolate cake; chocolate ice cream; and his favorite beer, which was anything cold. It was much cheaper than eating out, she'd said, and far more intimate.

Buster ate and drank well, but he was not in a celebratory mood. He'd been grumpy from the second he arrived by taxi, and his disposition had improved little. Finished with dinner, greasy napkin still tucked under his chins, he paced the room, complaining about life's injustices. How there was always a banana peel on the sidewalk in front of him, a piano ready to drop out of a window. How the fickle finger of fate constantly thrust its middle digit in his face when it wasn't checking out his prostate gland.

"For Heaven's sake, quit your bellyaching and keep your voice down. This isn't the first job you've lost," Carla said, covering her ears. "You've scared the cats half to death. They're hiding under the bed. The neighbors will be pounding on the walls again. Even with good insulation, we can't hold in a 100-decibel foghorn. An ongoing tantrum is not going to get your hunk of junk back for you."

"Not junk, Carla. An ancient treasure, a rare artifact, an automotive Dead Sea Scroll, transportation fit for the gods,"

Buster said, quieter, though continuing to pace. "Just cuz you can't insure it, you think it's got no value. You, who write life insurance on kamikaze pilots. Business interruption coverage on hit men and arsonists. Group life on the Seventh Cavalry. Hull insurance on the *Titanic*."

"Buster."

"Lumberyards next door to fireworks factories. Opium farmers. Drag racers. Contestants in hot dog eating contests."

"Buster, Buster, Buster."

"Motorcycle gangs. Axe murderers. Asbestos miners. Cliff divers. Carnival sword swallowers. Fire eaters. Those loonies they shoot out of a cannon at the circus."

"Buster, it's *you* I can't insure. The jalopy of yours, too, but you're the main issue. All your tickets. All your accidents, rear-ending people while you're distracted rehearsing a bit in the car."

"Hey, my license's been reinstated," said the comic.

"Oh, that'll qualify you for safe driver of the year."

"I'm not the only guy on the road who's got a lead foot."

A good point, she thought, but not nearly good enough.

Carla Chance was an insurance broker, owner of the aptly named Last Chance Insurance Agency. Buster had seen her Yellow Pages ad: LAST CHANCE INSURANCE AGENCY. TICKETS? ACCIDENTS? DUI? NO PRIOR OR CANCELLED INSURANCE? SUSPENDED LICENSE? NO PROBLEM!

Buster had gone to her office to seek an automobile policy for himself and his '59 Cadillac. As elsewhere, coverage was denied. His request for a date was not. A confirmed bachelorette, Carla wouldn't have married him if you held a gun to her head, but he did win her heart. For three years, they'd lived in her condo in Kent, a city of 85,000, which was twenty miles south of Seattle.

"You're uninsurable, Buster. How often do I have to repeat this? You have the world's worst driving record and your car's older than Methuselah."

"You're almost as compassionate and understanding as that Hitler Youth cop who took my crime report. He's going to law school, you know. Doesn't that tell you something about his character?"

"Stop whining."

"I'm not whining," Buster whined.

"The policeman was doing his job."

"The cop was right on one count. It has got to be personal. The rancid putz, the sadistic maniac, he took my favorite possession in the whole wide world and rubbed my nose in it."

Carla pouted. "You said I was your favorite possession."

"Yeah. And you said 'possession' was sexist and chauvinistic. You threatened to knock me flat on my oink-oink butt."

"I was teasing."

"Teasing with a clenched fist."

Carla Chance was Rubenesque. Two years older than Buster and one inch shorter at six feet, she dressed tightly in primary colors. They were a noticeable couple.

She said, "So what's with the Nixon angle?"

"Yeah, the mask bothers me too."

"Somebody checked the election records and found out you voted for him?"

"Impossible. I haven't voted in my entire life."

"You sliced and diced him in a set once upon a time, you've told me."

"Everybody and his brother did Tricky Dick. Did him with the gloves off. Remember in the debate with JFK and when he'd tell a whopper, his upper lip would sweat? I'd carry a water pistol and give mine a little squirt when I'd quote him. That was a kazillion years ago. I got a soft spot in my heart for Watergate. I ever tell you that?"

"Only six hundred and twelve times. And the soft spot's in your skull."

"Saturday, June 17, 1972. The break-in coincided with my break-in to the profession. It was opening night of my first long gig. A Holiday Inn in Toledo," Buster said. "I played that joint for sixteen weeks and saved up the dinero to buy the Caddy Eldo. The car was old then. Now it's a collectible, an investment."

"So somebody's having fun with you. Perhaps your ex-wives, perhaps not. You didn't indicate that they had senses of humor or were history buffs that waited until your birthday to torment you."

"They were grouchy," Buster said. "And none of them ever remembered my birthday."

"Well, you're no barrel of laughs yourself right now. You're depressing me on what should be a happy occasion, car theft or not. Say a funny, Buster. Crack a joke. Please. I'll laugh. You'll laugh. It'll be contagious."

Buster sat heavily in his easy chair. "If I was a plumber, you want I should come home from a hard day at work and take apart the flippin' sink and overhaul the garbage disposal?"

"I give up. Think. Who's got it in for you?"

"Nobody. I'm not saying everyone loves Buster, but I can't think of who brutally and viciously disloves me. Without my pride and joy, how'd I gonna get to work?"

"You're unemployed again, remember? I really am sorry, Buster."

Buster flinched at the "again." "Lucky me."

"Now that you're sixty, you could incorporate a stronger oldster gimmick," Carla suggested. "How in your golden years, you have more nose and ear fuzz than hair on the top of your head. Bad hearing, worse eyesight. Memory loss, weight gain.

29

Itchy support hose. You scratch a lot anyway."

Buster shook his head. "Nah. I ain't ready to play the geezer card on a regular basis. Not quite yet. On my birthday tonight, that was a one-shot deal."

Standing behind him, Carla kneaded his shoulders. "Have I ever said you could get your insurance license and come to work with me? I'd prep you on the test."

"Only six hundred and thirteen times."

"Do your bit in living rooms. Loosen them up. You're a natural salesperson. Have I told you what the commission is on a two-hundred-fifty-thousand dollar whole life policy?"

"Yeah, yeah, yeah."

Carla came around and nestled on his lap, running her hands through his graying mad-scientist mop. She fed him beer from his bottle as if he were an infant.

"You're also the sweetest guy in the world. So who stole your car?"

Buster blushed and shrugged.

Carla planted a wet kiss on him and trilled, "Oh by the way, happy birthday to you, happy birthday dear Buster, et cetera, et cetera, blah blah blah, happy birthday to you."

She handed him two envelopes. One was from her, lavender in color and potently perfumed. The other was a plain business envelope with no return address.

"Open mine first."

"Thanks, kiddo," Buster said, sniffing it. "Who else remembered my birthday?"

"I don't know. It was left on the stoop this afternoon."

Buster held the mystery envelope up to the light. "How do you tell if it's a letter bomb?"

"We could soak it in the bathtub."

"We'll live dangerously." Buster tore open Carla's envelope. "Woo-ee!"

She had bought the card at an adult bookstore. It made extravagant promises in explicit language and included helpful illustrations.

"Let's see your secret admirer top that."

Buster tentatively removed a folded letter. The text was words clipped from magazines, then photocopied: BE PREPARED TO PAY BIG RANSOM. MESS WITH US AND YOUR CAR WILL BE RETURNED TO YOU ONE PIECE AT A TIME. WE WILL BE IN CONTACT.

Buster gasped. "You mean like where they chop off an ear and mail it to you?"

"Car thieves can be a cruel breed," Carla said. "I have policyholders who are car thieves, but not weird like this."

"It'd be a tailfin or a slab of chrome, the perverts."

"Don't whimper," Carla said. "They can't be serious."

"They knew in advance they were gonna kidna—steal my car." Buster said, up and pacing. "They obviously know me. They gotta know I'm not exactly rolling in dough."

"Buster, they didn't specify what the ransom is."

He was speechless. They hadn't.

They jumped at a knock at the door.

Buster carefully opened it to a blond man of partial Asian extraction.

"Uncle Buster?"

Uncle Buster? Do I have an illegitimate cousin, wondered the thrice-married, childless comic.

"Huh?"

Carla pushed by Buster and threw out her arms.

"Rob?"

The visitor threw out his.

"Aunt Carla!"

4.

Seated in Carla's and Buster's living room, Rob Weather declined a slice of the comic's birthday cake. He did accept beer, which he drank thirstily.

Several years ago, Carla had gotten on a genealogy kick. Getting no younger, Carla had craved relatives, blood ties, a sense of family. She had no siblings, no living parents, no aunts or uncles or cousins. Buster coming into her life had been no help. His kin consisted of an older brother and a younger sister he rarely saw.

She had traced her only known relation, the great grandson of the second cousin of her grandfather, by the name of Robin Chance (Rob) Weather.

Maybe he was kin, maybe not. There were gaping holes in her research, but Rob had welcomed her overture. Neither party cared about small technicalities. They had become family and that was that.

Because of their age difference and diluted gene pool, aunt-to-nephew had seemed more comfortable to them than, as Buster put it, seventh cousin-to-seventh cousin. Rob and Carla had maintained telephone contact and exchanged Christmas cards, good enough for both of them.

Apparently until now. Carla knew little of Rob other than that he was in television news. Since he'd landed on her stoop like an orphan, she rightfully requested the life and times of Robin Chance Weather.

"Have you guys got a minute?" Rob said.

"Fire when ready," Buster said.

"Okay," said their surprise visitor, who then cleared his throat. "I'll do it as if a documentary voiceover. If you own a TV and have lived in Terre Haute, Ann Arbor, Dubuque, Topeka, Grand Rapids, Cedar Rapids, Billings, Pottstown, Utica, Boise, Fresno or Sioux Falls, you may've seen Rob Weather.

"He's the reporter you see during the blizzard on the freeway overpass, commenting on the real-life bumper cars below," Rob Weather continued. "He gets to the scene of the flattened trailer park while the twister's still furrowing. He's the reporter in waders in the record downpour as residents row along Main Street."

"What do they have you doing when the weather's nice?" Buster asked. "You got a terrific anchorman voice, you know."

Carla handed Rob a fresh brew, which he didn't waste time getting after. She said, "You're the expert on presentations, dear, but I'd prefer the first person. The other way's remote and we are anything but now."

Could be him and I are in the same clan too, Buster thought; we share the beer gene.

"Thanks, Aunt Carla. I don't normally hit the sauce like this. When it's nice out, I cover treed cats rescued by volunteer fire departments. I do sinkholes. I do little old ladies who mistake the gas for the brake pedal and drive through store windows.

"Now and again, they let me do fluff-serious studio pieces. You know, pieces that are dumbed down even more than usual. Like which household appliances use the most juice. Oven, clothes dryer. Why you shouldn't leave your pet in the car on a hot summer day. Overheating, death."

"You're speaking in the present tense," Carla said. "But I'm hearing past."

Rob Weather nodded and paused, letting the beer settle.

Buster and Carla attempted to avoid staring at Rob, especially at his hair. He had an outdoorsy ruddiness they assumed came from being posted in the elements. Dark, multiracial eyes contradicted his incandescent blond hair. He was wiry and looked fit, but lines were etching his features. He was almost handsome and mildly exotic.

"It started with Kelli, in Sioux Falls, my last stop in two regards. Kelli's my ex-girlfriend. Kelli's a babe. She's younger than I am. A buddy at my last station said I should've known I was in for trouble because in Kelli's signature, she dots the 'i' with a bubble. I didn't get what he was telling me. I do now."

Buster and Carla looked at each other, visualizing Kelli with the bubbled "i." Big hair, big in other important areas, but not between the ears.

"One dark and stormy night, when I dragged myself home after hours of covering sleet–hail–snow that paralyzed three counties, I asked her if she'd caught it and me on the six o'clock or the eleven. She said no. She was watching a Britney Spears retrospective. She was glued to the top-of-the-line fifty-two-inch Taihotsu Expansiva™ HDTV we'd just paid off, the sound cranked way up.

"Trying to speak above that noise, I told her that Phil, my cameraman, quit. Eyes on the screen, she said, too bad, but didn't even ask why. That was the formal beginning of our end. Kelli's thirtieth birthday was coming up and the prospect had made her sullen and crabby and totally self-absorbed. To her, age thirty was of the magnitude of an asteroid closing in on the Earth. I'm ten years older, so I guess I hadn't been displaying the proper sympathy.

"Anyway, I told her that while we were out there, Phil slipped and fell on ice. There was some language to edit out. This was the last straw for Phil. Our pool vehicle was a Taihotsu Himalaya™ SUV with a hundred and two thousand miles and bald tires. You could see whiskers from the steel belts. We were sliding all over the place.

"When we got back to the station, the news director said we had four-wheel-drive, so what was the problem. Phil gave his resignation, as in *right now,* sparing no words. I thought he was going to throw his camera through a window.

"Then I told Kelli I wanted to leave too. I wanted a sabbatical. It just blurted out, like something expelled in a Heimlich maneuver.

"I finally had her attention. She muted Britney and asked what exactly a sabbatical was. I told her it was similar to a long vacation, to do new things. For me, seeing the Yucatán, the Maya ruins in Mexico and Guatemala, something I really wanted to do. With her. She'd known. I'd raved about the Yucatán for a long time, how an incredibly advanced civilization suddenly fell apart.

"Tikal in Guatemala is the ultimate. Its temples, its grounds, the surrounding jungles, the North Acropolis, the Great Plaza, the Lost World complex, the many other complexes, the wildlife, you name it. Tikal is said to be simply amazing, breathtaking. And I can now attest that it is, by the way.

"Perhaps it was a midlife crisis that began with daydreaming about fantastic places, but it was a trip I desperately had to take. I've bounced around in my career, but I hadn't really been anywhere significant, hadn't done or seen a thing. I'd read my share of travel articles and watched plenty of travelogues. Tikal was in the top five for me, worldwide.

"Kelli didn't hear me. She asked again what a sabbatical was. I had to admit that a sabbatical was longer than a vacation, more like a leave of absence without a job to come home to. She reminded me that I'd changed jobs twice in the short time we'd known each other. Once voluntarily, once not. It's the nature of the profession."

"Where'd you kids meet?" Carla asked.

"In a salon, where she cut my hair. I think she fell for *it*, not me. People have told me it's the color of a Krugerrand. I saw you guys looking. Everyone does. It is real.

"After we moved in together, Kelli quit her job and became a freelance grooming and fashion consultant. She does research by watching celebrities on TV. As far as I know, she's still awaiting her first client."

"Consultants," Buster said. "I've done bits on consultants and their gobblygook. And their reports the size of a paving block and their invoices that'd choke a CPA."

"Buster," Carla said.

"I love their lingo. Trend forward. Push the envelope. Bandwidth. Paradigm shift. They're a bottomless pit of material."

"Buster," Carla said.

"They're a mother lode of a comic's cornucopia."

"Buster."

"Land of milk and honey. End of the rainbow."

"Buster!"

Rob smiled and said, "I agree with you, Uncle Buster. Kelli called me a dreamer and a daydreamer, like they were four-letter words. She used to think I was being cute, but didn't anymore. She refused to discuss my wishes. I hoped she'd cool off and we could face the subject rationally. She knew of my interests, how passionate I was on them, and that we had savings adequate for such a trip. She asked if this had to do with me thinking I was being followed."

Buster and Carla's eyes widened.

"Well, I *was* being followed."

Carla said, "By whom?"

"Beats me. Kelli had said to call the cops. And tell them what? I never caught them in the act. You know how you know you're being stared at? You turn around and there's nobody there."

"How long did this go on?" Carla said.

"Two or three months. Kelli said she'd had enough. She made consecutive appointments for me with a counselor on midlife crises and a shrink who specialized in treating paranoid schizophrenia and delusions. As far as I was concerned, that was a seminal moment in what remained of our relationship. I skipped the appointments and went to a travel agent instead. I diagnosed myself as being beyond a cure. If male menopause had clobbered me like a virus, so be it.

"I got home one evening not long thereafter and noticed some anomalies. Clean rectangles on the wall where pictures had hung. Dust kittens the size of cats where the bed had been. Kelli wasn't into housekeeping.

"In a circular impression in the living room carpeting where a floor lamp had been was the bill from a moving company. The biggest stunner was her efficiency. She may've had help—but I didn't want to go there and still don't.

"On the subject of paranoia—much earlier, before my trip—in an unmarked envelope I found slipped under our door, was this."

Rob dug a piece of paper out of a pocket. It was translucent white, as thick as a playing card and twice the size. Written on it, in what appeared to be shaky calligraphy, was: 12231823922111223136141522.

Buster and Carla examined it.

"Pricey stock," Carla said. "A puzzle, a password? From whom?"

Rob Weather shook his head. "Haven't the foggiest, Aunt Carla. I've played with it. There are twenty-six digits. The alphabet has twenty-six letters, so I've taken the alphanumeric approach. Zilch."

"Could be derived from planetary alignments and/or chicken entrails," Buster offered.

"True. All I know is that my life changed then, in more ways than just being on my own."

"How?" Buster asked.

"I took my dream trip. It was incredible, except that I continued to be monitored throughout."

Carla said, "Monitored as opposed to followed?"

"I guess by monitored I mean followed more intensely than previously."

"Catch 'em in the act then?" Buster asked.

"No, Uncle Buster. I just know they were there. Without a shadow of a doubt."

"How?"

"Clothes in my suitcase were tidied. I squeeze toothpaste tubes in the middle. Somebody had rolled it up from the end. Little gestures like that."

The "Uncle" was growing on Buster. He was being treated like a trusted relative. "Flippin' neatniks, babysitting spies who don't steal. That's sick, man. That's super scary."

Rob laughed. "It's beyond unusual too. Also weird is that they seem to have disappeared since I returned to the States."

Buster asked, "In case this becomes a big deal, who besides us knows of that card?"

"Phil. I showed it to him to kill time between spinouts and nine-car rear-enders. It was a moment before he slipped and fell, so he's probably forgotten."

"Who else? Anybody get a good peek at it?"

Rob thought for a moment. "Kelli, who shrugged it off. She was incurious. She thought it's been given to us by mistake. Aside from her, my seatmate on the Cancun-to-Dallas leg of the flight back. A chiropractor or a periodontist, I think. An obnoxious, nosy character who wouldn't shut up. I had the card out, fiddling with it. He asked what it was. I was vague, but he copied the string on napkins and played with it too. He's by now tossed the napkins and forgotten about it. He gave me his business card and I've tossed it too."

"What are your plans, Rob?" Carla asked.

"I haven't any plans in TV news. Or, rather, TV news has none for me. I turned forty in February. For a field reporter who has no chance at an anchor chair, forty might as well be ninety-five, like in dog and cat years. I'm lacking the avuncular qualities that'd let me age gracefully in this game. I can't remember how many times I've been asked to dye my hair. They unanimously specify black with subtle streaks of gray.

"The time I did that would be the time I degrade from lightweight journalist to talking haircut. I said thanks but no thanks. So I've got a reputation as a troublemaker too.

"What are my plans in general, Aunt Carla?" He got up. "I was in Yucatán, Mexico, forty-eight hours ago. I have no plans, no destination. I did want to meet you before I figured out the rest of my life. If you like, call it a panic attack."

Rob might not have plans for himself, but Carla Chance did have some for him, however impromptu. An inveterate matchmaker, she thought of Sarah Hilyer in the unit across the way. Sarah was a little older than Rob and attractive too. Sarah was going through a hard time. Her mother had just passed away. So it surely wouldn't hurt to introduce her to a witty, attractive man. Never-married Sarah had just turned forty-eight, her biological clock tick-tick-ticking, change of life close at hand. If they hit it off, at the very least, their minds would be distracted from their separate woes.

She sprang to her feet and ordered, "Robin Chance Weather, sit back down and finish your beer. And the next one. You're not going out into the night in your frame of mind."

"Aunt Carla—"

"Sit!"

Robin Chance Weather sat.

Buster got up and brought Rob the ransom note from the kitchen divider. He handed it to him and told the carnapping, Nixon mask story.

"Speaking of weirdness on paper snuck under doors. Whadduya think, Rob?"

"Wow, Uncle Buster, your 1959 Caddy sounds like a classic."

Buster looked at Carla. "See?"

As Carla rolled her eyes, Rob asked, "Did you offend somebody in a show?"

"I try to offend in every set," Buster said sincerely. "I'm an equal opportunity offender. If that's what happened, the suspects number in the hundreds and thousands."

"How does Richard Nixon fit in?"

Buster shook his head. "I didn't hate him like everybody else did. None of us in the business did. The Trickster was a cash cow, him and his merry band. A license to print money. Haldeman, Erlichman. That missing eighteen minutes on the tape. If Dick had been on meds for his paranoia, us stand-up comics, we'd all of been screwed out of topnotch material."

He sighed. "Nixon makes me nostalgic."

Rob said, "You beginning your career on the same day as Watergate and the thief wearing a Nixon mask sounds like too much of a coincidence."

Carla said, "We have to agree."

"Uncle Buster, do you always leave your keys in the ignition?"

"It ain't a habit like heroin, but it's been known to happen. When I run late, I don't think of every little detail."

"You said this ransom note was left hours before you performed," Rob said. "That indicates premeditation and knowledge of your routine and your habits."

Carla beamed. "My nephew, the investigative reporter."

Rob asked, "Wouldn't a car like that be hard to hide?"

Buster said, "You'd think so. It's not a tin can like your Aunt Carla's Taihotsu Commute™ hatchback."

Carla rolled her eyes again. "I get thirty miles per gallon, *city.* Rob, I'm putting fresh sheets on the futon for you in the spare bedroom."

"Tell ya what," Buster said. "You solve this note and lead the cops to the rancid car-abusing ghoul, I'll undecipher your cipher."

They clinked bottles, sealing their commitment to the impossible tasks.

5.

Ninety-three floors in the air, Saburo Taihotsu gazed into the Tokyo night. When he had been able to walk without such difficulty, he enjoyed skirting his penthouse perimeter and counting lights in the skyline constellation that belonged to him. Hundreds and thousands of them.

This evening's panorama was neither aesthetically pleasing nor personally gratifying. The endlessly twinkling vastness had become merely that. Self-satisfaction ceased eliciting pleasure.

He was a dead man.

Gripping his walker, Saburo Taihotsu slowly reversed direction and inched back to bed in a head-bowed stoop. Saburo deemed his whipped-dog posture appropriate, at long last a just reward for the sham Mongoose legend. He had not created it, but he had allowed it to perpetuate. He was suffering retribution for soiling the Code of Bushido, for being more *gaijin* than Japanese.

Every joint aching, Saburo crawled under the covers a moment before a soft gong sounded. With a touch of a button on his nightstand, the richest person on the planet granted entry to one of few permitted access.

A robust Caucasian woman in her late twenties on roller skates wheeled in a cart laden with food, utensils and a propane grill. The woman stood six feet tall. She could have been carved into the prow of a Viking ship.

"Hiya, toots," she said in European-accented, Americancolloquial English. "What'll it be tonight, hon?"

Saburo raspingly ordered the usual. "A deluxe burger, please."

As Taihotsu's executive chef, her sole duty was to make these rarer and rarer visits. Chewing gum ferociously, she withdrew a stub pencil from vividly golden hair stacked in a bouffant. She licked the pencil's point and poised it at a vintage order pad. "Cheese?"

Saburo nodded.

"All the trimmings?"

Saburo nodded.

"Ain't you the gourmet today? Onions?"

Saburo shook his head.

She snapped her gum and grinned suggestively. "Must have a date, huh?"

Saburo smelled Juicy Fruit. He smiled.

The woman tore off the top sheet and placed it on the cart. She tucked the pad with the carbon copy into her white patent leather belt and lit the burner. She waited for the grill to heat and dropped on a ground beef patty. It sizzled exquisitely.

As the meat seared and smoked, she opened a bun and toasted both halves beside the patty. Then she smeared mayonnaise on one bun half, a mustard-catsup mixture on the other. She layered shredded lettuce, tomato and pickles on the mayonnaise half.

Her gum popping, she winked lewdly. "No onion? Right, hon?"

Saburo shook his head.

"She must be some hot tamale, huh? A real dish."

Saburo smiled again.

The executive chef wore his idealized conception of a mid-twentieth-century American carhop uniform. The neckline of the silky white blouse dove below her cleavage, and the pleated navy skirt stopped where her long, long legs started. An undersized sailor cap and the high-boot skates completed the outfit.

Taihotsu's fantastical carhop flipped the patty and bent at the waist to bring napkins from the cart's lowest shelf. She hesitated in a jackknife, affording Saburo a point-blank view of the gilded tuft between her legs. His uniform design had omitted underwear.

This woman approximated the dimensions and hair coloration of Saburo's Marie, plus abundant glamour.

Marie, his savior, protector, lover.

Marie had essentially been a hermit, who'd sheltered him for her needs and for his. After his watery Kauai landing, she had patiently waited for him to regain consciousness. Then she'd carefully assisted him from the cockpit and laid him on the sand.

Before she'd half walked and half carried him inland, Marie had gone into the water and secured a rope to the smaller, lighter pieces of wreckage. She'd tied the other end to the horse she'd ridden onto the beach and pulled the parts free enough to disperse in the breakers.

At her isolated ranch, Marie had set Saburo's nose and fabricated a cast and sling for his collarbone. She had no radio and bought no newspapers. In the first days with her, Saburo expressed curiosity about the raid and the war that had surely ensued. When Marie made infrequent trips to a general store, she'd returned with verbal reports of a languid stalemate.

He'd accepted what she did and did not tell him, distortions of fact he later knew she had concocted to serve his needs and hers. Marie had a gift for telling him what he wanted to hear. Why not bring home a newspaper now and then? he'd asked. Any change whatsoever in her eccentric routine could arouse suspicion, she'd explained; people were paranoid.

Marie had told Saburo that it was no surprise that there had been declarations of war after the abortive attack on Pearl Harbor, in which less than half of *Akagi*'s aircraft returned to the ship. There were constant rumors of negotiations, she'd said. While the western Pacific became a Japanese lake, the conflict had decelerated because of the vast distances between islands. It was sleepy and indecisive, like Germany's Sitzkrieg or Phony War of the 1939–1940 winter and spring. Since no Japanese troops landed on Kauai, this had seemed plausible to him.

Had the Pearl Harbor operation been a success, an amphibious invasion would have logically followed. This confirmed that the attack was the bloody disaster Saburo predicted. Otherwise, where was the Imperial Administration?

Lest he be tempted to stray, Marie had warned that fifth columnists were being shot on sight and all Asians were suspect. In his case, they might, as she'd expressed it, hold an impromptu necktie party. And Lord only knows what they'd do to her.

Days and weeks as a fugitive evolved into months and years as a kept man and farmhand, a house pet. Thanks to his faintheartedness, thanks to his domineering Marie, and thanks to his time in the Inscrutable West, he had been joyously contaminated.

Then one day the war was over. Marie had delivered the news in tears. She'd spoken of bombs dropped on Japan. They were made of uranium and were too horrific to fathom.

Marie and Saburo had known that the end of the war was the end of Marie and Saburo. They knew what they had to do. At nighttime, after a day of nonstop lovemaking, Saburo had ridden in the back of her truck under a bed of hay. At the southeast end of the island, he'd crawled out, and they'd had their last kiss. The next morning, in the town of Lihue, he'd surrendered at a filling station.

Saburo hadn't known until after the war that some of his

Zero wreckage had been found by local authorities and a hunt for him had been ongoing. Sublieutenant Taihotsu had also been unaware that he had become known as the Mongoose, after the bold and ferocious predator. The mongoose mammal was renowned for its willingness to confront the cobra and any other venomous snake. This two-legged variety had been no less indomitable.

A silly rumor had bizarrely escalated. The Mongoose fable had grown as they'd combed Kauai for him, blaming him for unsolved vandalism and petty crime. The Mongoose had brazenly confronted an entire island, waging a largely symbolic, one-man guerrilla campaign.

Saburo had been bewildered by the relief his surrender had caused. At long last, the Mongoose was in custody!

Saburo Taihotsu's executive chef straightened up and expertly flipped the patty. Then she blanketed it with an American cheese slice. When the cheese melted to adhesion, she placed the patty on a bun half. She folded the top on, cut it down the middle, and secured the sections with decorative toothpicks. She sprinkled potato chips in an artistic semicircle and presented the finished plate.

Saburo Taihotsu nodded his satisfaction. Alas, what remained of his alimentary canal could not accept this gastronomic challenge. For all practical purposes, the surgeons had disemboweled him. His nutrition was pharmacological.

"Will you eat later?"

"Yes. Thank you."

"Thank you, sir."

She curtseyed and wheeled out the cart and its contents.

Saburo Taihotsu felt not the slightest stirring. Depravity provided no joy.

He was a dead man.

He dimmed the lights and stared at the ceiling.

He had procrastinated seeking out Marie until the doctors would no longer make eye contact. He worried in his younger years whether she would betray him. Of course she would be betraying herself too, harboring an enemy, a Day of Infamy devil at that, the cunning and intrepid Mongoose. Or so he had rationalized.

Saburo loathed himself for loving her almost as much as he loathed himself for his cowardice. He loathed himself for his sheer dependence and, ultimately, his abandonment of her. He loathed himself for not seeking her out until recently, when he had scant time to do so.

Subtle, fragmented investigations revealed that Marie Blanchard had been dead in excess of half a century. He learned too that the daughter he had not known existed had died in an automobile crash years ago, she and her wastrel husband. Through his best calculation, Saburo's daughter had been conceived three weeks before Douglas MacArthur steamed into Tokyo Bay.

Douglas.

For all of his genius and indomitable will, Douglas had been so full of pretension and paradoxes. So willing to perpetuate the myth, to elevate an unworthy Saburo. Yet Douglas had court-marshaled and hanged Tomoyuki Yamashita, the Tiger of Malaya, a field commander superior to Douglas himself in many aspects.

Forget his imperiousness, his blind spots, his contradictions, Douglas had been a prophet. A visionary and a Washington, D.C., pariah, Douglas had realized before there was a Marshall Plan for Europe that there would be no counterpart for Japan.

"You and I and what you represent and the industriousness of the Japanese people, Saburo," Douglas would tell him. "We shall pull the nation up by its bootstraps."

Saburo Taihotsu had been summoned to Douglas's first office in postwar Japan, the New Grand Hotel in Yokohama. Amazingly, the New Grand had survived the B-29 bombings.

Saburo acquiesced without objection, as if he'd had a choice. He had been a captive at loose ends and numb with grief. His prewar Japanese wife and daughter, fearful after the early-1945 Tokyo fire bombings, had moved to live with Nagasaki relatives, only to be vaporized.

The military brass had sent a DeSoto sedan to the stockade for him. Flies and mosquitoes could not get through the closed windows, but the stench did. As the sedan driver had slalomed through rubble, Saburo had thought of what he'd heard just this morning, that *everyone* in Tokyo had head lice. He'd looked out at lazy creeks of shit and piss, of typhoid and cholera. There were few operative vehicles and no electricity.

If Saburo had remained a warrior and survived aerial combat, he would have been rewarded with this. He'd heard tales of kamikaze volunteers late in the war. There had even been a rocket-powered kamikaze aircraft named the Okha (cherry blossom) that was dropped from bombers. One such pilot should have been him, he thought. Boring in on American carriers ten degrees steeper than vertical (ha ha), screaming "banzai."

Not this hepcat.

Across a desk from General of the Army Douglas MacArthur, whom some Japanese had already been calling Emperor MacArthur, Saburo had looked out the window at the burned and flattened landscape around them.

Douglas had begun by stating that he wanted no repetition of the hardscrabble scenario in Japan that afflicted Germany following World War I, the desperate vacuum that had produced Adolf Hitler.

Saburo had coyly replied, "How may I be of assistance, sir?"

"Your daring is a symbol of resourcefulness. Your family has an industrial base that isn't totally destroyed and you have lived in the United States. You aren't alone. Facilitating Japan's manufacturing base is an utmost priority, but Taihotsu Iron Works is a priority among priorities, it and what it shall spawn."

If Douglas had been as affected as he by Japan's vulnerability, so be it. They'd had their reasons for using each other: to attain their goals, to succeed. Indeed, aided by Douglas's subtle favoritism, Saburo had done his share to pull Japan "up by the bootstraps." The fabled Mongoose, the "symbol," had enriched himself beyond comprehension in the process.

The fable of Sublieutenant Saburo Taihotsu, the Mongoose, living on pilfered pineapples and raw fish, fanatically fighting alone by whatever means possible. The myth had portrayed him crashing *after* the attack was absurd and the most shameful of the apocrypha he had permitted to endure.

In actuality, he'd nestled in Marie's lush and half-mad bosom, fed and kept like a tamed wild creature.

Saburo now lay swaddled, breathing aromatic fumes of incinerated cow, eyes misted from other than the airborne carcinogens.

He awoke at an undetermined hour, knowing something was badly wrong. His amazon carhop had been too stimulating, a foolhardy excess.

Saburo edged close to the pharmacy on his nightstand. Despite warnings that the medication regimen was crucial, he had swallowed his last pill and spoonful of syrup. Respiration was increasingly labored. His extremities tingled.

Rising partially upright, he feebly swiped at the phalanx of bottles. They clattered to the carpet. The pitiful gesture was the most honorable facsimile of hara-kiri he could muster. There would be no further deterioration. There would be no bedpans and IV tubes for the Mongoose.

Perhaps sensing this occurrence, Saburo had instructed that he not be disturbed for the rest of the day. He knew that an insecure and greedy battalion of acolytes hovered downstairs. His organizational chart had been likened to a bowl of noodles.

He had no trusted aides, no confidants. Saburo conducted fewer meetings than an espionage cell. Only his executive chef knew any of his secrets. In the preceding weeks, his last orders had been fulfilled, microcompartmentized, particle by particle, accomplished by a diffused and unknowing chain of command.

Those minions had immediately been assigned other duties in other locales, paid bonuses that ensured eternal silence on the matter and contracts with non-compliance clauses (i.e., careless talk) that came with severe financial penalties, not the least of which were loss of employment and a withering fitness report.

With some effort, Saburo reached for a calligraphic pen and a sheet of handmade parchment paper. He shakily drew 122318--------------141522. Twelve numbers and 14 dashes. Twenty-six, the sum of the English-language alphabet, two tantalizing rows of numbers separated by a chasm. It was a puzzle that would not be terribly difficult to decipher if one possessed the full twenty-six numerals, but nigh impossible if one did not.

How Saburo missed Marie.

How he wished he had known their offspring and the offspring's offspring.

Saburo Taihotsu's blood pumped within a stranger.

There was nobody else.

He knew that speculation would renew about the bags burned in the smelting furnaces, plentiful theories on the contents, and assessments of the depth of the old man's madness, his crazed scheme to move to the next world with his fortune. He also knew that his misdirection would be temporary. In the quest for his $100 billion, events would accelerate.

Saburo had endeavored to liquidate responsibly. He had ensured contractually with the piecemeal buyers of his conglomerate that no jobs would be lost. Via this subterfuge, his enormous shame would die with him. A stranger would have a sporting chance for the proceeds, he and maybe a lady love. He had enhanced the probability of the latter, but had by no means guaranteed it.

Saburo believed that he had achieved a balance.

The fearless Mongoose as a despicable coward. Should that come to light, he would be unable to rest even after worms and decay reduced him to bones and dust.

Saburo extinguished the room lights.

He drifted into a dreamy recall of Kauai. In the subtropical climate, Marie had raised two crops a year of anything she chose to grow. A city boy, Saburo had never worked so hard in his life. At her side and by himself, he tended the cattle and the fields. In his imperfect reminiscence, he had never been happier.

He is alone on this day, hoeing tomatoes, uprooting weeds and aerating the rich, red earth. He hears an airplane. Whenever an aircraft or a vehicle on the potholed road from the highway passes, he takes cover. This is a low crop of salad greens. The nearest concealment is a shed fifty meters away. The plane is extraordinarily fast. It wheels steeply over the water.

He sees the red sun insignia. It sets a course straight at him, in a shallow dive, gaining speed. He has nowhere to go. He sees the muzzle flare of the fuselage-mounted 7.7-millimeter machine guns, and of the wing-mounted twenty-millimeter cannons. Tall grass flies in clumps. Fence rails explode. The soil furrows, clods flying like shrapnel. The plane is a Mitsubishi A6M2 Zero. He knows who the pilot is, who it must be. Sublieutenant Saburo Taihotsu has just enough time to lock his heels and salute Sublieutenant Saburo Taihotsu.

6.

Robin Chance (Rob) Weather focused on a tumor the size of a locomotive. It was a wall hanging, a print not dissimilar to those Aunt Carla had downstairs. He was no art expert, but it had to be a Salvador Dalí. Had to.

He'd awakened on the rolled-out futon to two sets of iridescent almond eyes, one pair to the left of his legs, the other to the right. As she'd tucked him in, Aunt Carla had mentioned OC1 and OC2, their plump orange cats, their names shortened from the formal Orange Cat One and Orange Cat Two.

She'd said the futon room, as they called their second bedroom, was their bailiwick. But not to worry. They were harmless, just a couple of cuddly, overstuffed teddy bears, lazy old hound dogs in pussycat clothing.

Rob Weather had had no pets in childhood. His father, Richard (Dick) Weather, had claimed allergies, without a doubt another lie. In adulthood, Rob was an electronic nomad, so it'd be unfair to an animal.

As OC1 and OC2 continued staring at him, Rob wondered if you owned a cat or if the cat owned you. It was said that a dog was man's best friend and that a cat had "staff."

"Kitty, kitty," he said, wishing that they'd purr.

After Tikal, Rob had contemplated an interim of wandering, drifting here and there, when he'd considered making a cold call on Aunt Carla Chance. He had nobody else. He'd mulled it in the air, on the hop home from Yucatán Mexico, the leg between Cancun and Dallas. His initial intent had been to return home to Sioux Falls by regional carrier puddle-jumpers.

But what was "home"? Where was "home"? It struck him as the plane made its final approach to Dallas–Fort Worth International Airport that he had no home, never had one since a turbulent childhood and youth.

By the time tires squealed onto the runway, he couldn't wait to get away from his seatmate, that obnoxious chiropractor or proctologist or whatever he was. But to where? There was no job waiting in Sioux Falls, no Kelli.

As the thrust reversers had been deployed, he'd decided, yes, he absolutely would divert to Seattle, as he'd thought out loud to the seatmate—more information coaxed out of him than he'd cared to give—to visit his distant, distant aunt, to barge in unannounced on the nice lady who had contacted him through a genealogical search.

The nice lady who had so graciously taken him in called from the hallway, "Anybody ready for breakfast?"

Rob supposed that the call was for him, but OC1 and OC2 were off the bed in an instant, crying at the door.

Carla Chance, the only gainfully employed person in the trio, set out for work. Buster and Rob left in the car Rob had picked up at the airport, a Taihotsu Wayfarer™, a darling of rental fleets. It was a midsized, white-bread four-door sedan with plenty of room, trunk space, and decent fuel economy.

First stop was the library to make a copy of the ransom note, then to the Kent Police Department with the original and the incident report case number, where Buster asked if they could please forward it to the Seattle P.D. detective handling the crime ASAP and did they think the dicks up there had any automotive kidnapping experience involving priceless steel and glass and leather?

They said that they would forward the material and that they were sure the detectives had the right experience for the job. Rob thought he saw one wink at another, probably thinking that Mr. Hightower had seen too many bad movies and had fabricated the note himself to get better service, not to mention jumpstart his career.

One suggested that the vehicle was long gone, en route to a collector on the opposite coast. They did say that they'd alerted classic car dealers in the region. Insurance should cover the loss, no sweat, an officer volunteered.

Yeah, right, Buster thought, trudging out.

In the Wayfarer, he directed Rob up the hill toward Last Chance Insurance Agency, to show him Carla's business.

"I made those gendarmes' day, gave them something to yuk-yuk about at the water cooler. They're real narrow-minded about the use of the word kidnapping, is what these public servants are."

To change the subject, Rob said, "Aunt Carla has a lot of interesting art on the walls."

"I guess interesting is one word for it. They're all by those Spanish artists of hers. She took a vacation to Spain and fell head over heels for their paintings. This was before we met. Her favorites are the pictures that don't look like anything. Those artists, they were anarchiological bomb throwers and communists. That is a fact.

"The ones that do look like something, they give me nightmares. Like that Goya guy. In our bedroom, there's a Goya picture of guys executing other guys in a firing squad. I gotta wonder if it's a message to me that bad things will happen if I get caught pulling hanky-panky, which I wouldn't."

"She just likes that kind of art, Uncle Buster. She's not alone."

"The world's a crazy place and that crazy artist art, I think that's what they call the category. That guy Dalí, he's the daffiest, him and his melting wristwatches and naked ladies floating in midair and whatnot."

"Uncle Buster, I'll check the local TV stations, see if there's anybody I know. I've gotten around. Most of them have been around. We're all gypsies. If we're lucky, I'll come across a former colleague who can arrange an on-air interview with you. There's a great human interest angle, you know. Your exotic car and the ransom note, and you being, an, uh, a—"

"Unemployed comic."

Rob hesitated, wishing he had the sentence back. "Yeah."

"Now and then, when Carla isn't bugging me about going to work for her, sitting in folks' living rooms with a briefcase, pestering them about buying life insurance, she bugs me about getting an agent. I tell her, I can't get an agent. Agents get fifteen percent. I'd be pocket change. Fifteen percent of pocket change is pocket lint."

"It must be glamorous, though, traveling to different venues to perform to crowds."

"I don't know if crowds is the right word, unless you can fit a crowd into a closet."

"But you go places."

"Last place I went on the road at was the Grim Reaper Death House in St. Mausoleum, California."

"You're putting me on."

"Actually the Glen Leeper Senior Center in St. Wherever, something like that. They'd named it for Mr. Leeper, who left everything to the center when he croaked. It was an easy gig if you didn't mind the snoring in the wheelchairs."

"How did you get started as a comic?"

"Algebra."

"What?"

"Yeah," Buster said. "I walked out of algebra class one day and never returned. Ever use algebra for anything, Rob?"

"Not that I recall."

"Me neither. I couldn't figure why it was so important what x equaled. Far as I knew, x is in between w and y in the alphabet. That's all you gotta know. Maybe algebra's the key to your weird card, but don't hold your breath.

"After high school, I knew college was out of the question. Colleges have got the mother of all nasty algebra courses, plus other really hard and useless stuff. I drifted from place to place, job to job. Butcher, baker, candlestick maker."

Rob laughed and shook his head.

"No foolin'. I dated this hippie girl who made candles she sold at flea markets. I helped her, melting the wax.

"One night I was tending bar, filling in for a friend who was sick. This drunk I'd overserved said I was funny. Hilarious was his wording and he had trouble saying it. A nearby tavern was having a comedy competition and he said I needed to enter it, so I did. And won. Unfortunately for civilization, the rest is history. You?"

Rob said, "After a degree in journalism, I applied at newspapers. I had this notion that print was the only pure medium. I still do if you want to know the truth, even more so now that papers are dying."

"Yeah, dropping like flies," Buster said. "A Seattle paper that'd been around since the 1800s bit the dust. The *Seattle Post-Intelligencer,* it was called. They cut way back. Don't print it anymore. Just do an online edition you gotta stare at a computer screen to read. Lots of talented folks, a helluva lot more talented at what they did than me or any other comic I know at what we do, they're in the unemployment line."

"I don't like what that says where society is headed, but I'll stop there before I'm on my soapbox for two hours," Rob said. "The papers paid less than lousy, but I didn't care. Entry-level wasn't much above minimum wage, even if there was an opening, which there wasn't when I was sending out résumés. Most of the prime slots, the political beats and the columns, were well tenured.

"I happened into a TV station and it went from there. They liked my voice and my appearance. Those were the prime qualifiers. I heard secondhand that I was a little different without being freakish, a good fit for the field, but not quite the visuals for an anchor slot. I am, of course, talking about my mixed race and my hair."

"Which you could of anti-bleached."

"Hair coloring was mentioned more times than I can remember. No way. It's in my heritage, whatever it might precisely be."

They were on Kent's East Hill. Buster said, "Yeah, your heritage. We were kinda sorta curious, your Aunt Carla and me."

"The blond hair skipped a generation. An anomaly, as they say. Genetically, it's extremely rare. My mother was a normal-appearing, half-Japanese woman. Her unmarried mother, also a blonde Caucasian, as rumors have it, who lived in Hawaii, died when Mother was three. I'm an only child with no other living relatives that I'm aware of. My parents died in a car crash. My father was driving and he'd had a few more than a few too many. Not that my mother was a teetotaler.

"After that, I was raised by foster families. Aunt Carla and I talked about genealogy, which gave me new impetus to look into what I'd been avoiding. There was so much secrecy and ignorance, that in retrospect I dreaded what I'd find. I had no need to worry. I hit a dead end and left it at that. Just one generation and I hit a brick wall."

"Don't you care?"

"I used to."

"Like somebody went to mucho trouble to keep you in the dark?"

Rob shrugged. "I don't know."

"Here we are," Buster said, pulling into a strip mall. "Carla's between the teriyaki and the dry cleaners. She says I'm two hundred times more likely to go into the teriyaki than the cleaners."

"Is she correct?" Rob asked as they parked.

"Nothing hurts more than the truth," Buster said, climbing out.

They walked into a large outer office, with a smaller private office off to a side, where Carla was on the phone, waving to them.

"She does a lot of telephone business. I bet she's got a live one on the hook. C'mere."

He led Rob to the framed Yellow Pages ad behind her main desk:

LAST CHANCE INSURANCE AGENCY.
TICKETS? ACCIDENTS? DUI?
NO PRIOR OR CANCELLED INSURANCE? SUS-
PENDED LICENSE?
NO PROBLEM!

Rob asked, "She can insure anyone?"

"With one major exception," Buster said, sighing. "This is an insurance sales professional who writes for companies like Mayhem Mutual, Little Bighorn Life, Angst Auto and Home, Catastrophe Property and Casualty, St. Carcinoma Health Plans, Precarious Insurance Group. These outfits have home offices in third-floor walkups and in the shadow of grain silos and on offshore barges. They're very flexible."

He looked at Carla. "Or maybe she ain't on with a new victim. Could be she's taking a car crash claim from a customer in the drunk tank."

They sat at an adjacent desk, a computer between them.

"Would Aunt Carla mind if I checked my email?"

"You're one of those, huh?" Buster said good-naturedly.

"One of what?" he replied, typing on the keyboard.

"Computer nuts who can't be away from one or you go through withdrawal. They're everywhere these days."

"Computers are part of our fabric, Uncle Buster."

"Got an Internet miracle for those numbers on your card? Something you can go to and say presto?"

"Sorry, but I'll also check local station websites for a smaller miracle."

"My baby weighs two-and-a-half tons. Not small."

"A conspicuous two-and-a-half tons, Uncle Buster. It works to our advantage."

Carla was just hanging up with their good friend and neighbor, Sarah Hilyer. Not only was Sarah an eligible bachelorette, she was a community college math instructor. The silly card with the numbers was a perfect opening. Blindfolded, Sarah could solve the puzzle lickety-split.

It would have to wait, though, for her mother's funeral. Carla would attend. Buster, who didn't know Sarah's mother, probably wouldn't.

She walked in to Rob at the keyboard, on the MSN homepage. Buster, looking on, said, "Well, I'll be damned."

"What?" she asked.

"Saburo Taihotsu just died."

7.

Earlier in the week, prior to landing on his Aunt Carla's doorstep, Robin Chance (Rob) Weather's seatmate on the Cancun–Dallas leg of his flight back from his dream trip, the "chiropractor or proctologist" was, in fact, Dr. J.D. (Wally) Stockwall, DDS, sole proprietor of a marginal orthodontics practice.

Whenever asked the location of his clinic, Dr. Stockwall invariably replied "in the Beverly Hills vicinity." In reality, he shared a half-occupied strip mall near Van Nuys with a dry cleaner, a dollar store, a payday loan outfit, and a nail salon. Varnishes and cleaning solvents had permanently seared his nostrils, the odors as imprinted in his mind as his chronic money woes. He owed two months back rent on his 600 square feet.

To enlist patients, Wally exploited parental guilt, projecting dreary lives for the dentally misaligned. Bucky Beaver had no chance in this hard, cruel world. Dr. Stockwall tended to oversell, repelling more prospects than he persuaded. There were substantial voids on his appointment calendar.

Wally's investments were speculative and desperate, in the desert waterfront genre. He was the only known victim with more than an eighth-grade education to be suckered *twice* by the Nigerian 419 scam. The letters were so convincing.

If his losing streak continued, he'd be bending wire inside zit-faced mouths forever. He had approached a nameless Las Vegas–based financial aid company he'd heard of through the grapevine of colleagues also stricken by an interminable run of ill fortune. It specialized exclusively in lending to professionals who found themselves in a cash-flow pinch and no conventional options.

The firm's representative who'd visited Dr. Stockwall identified himself as Mr. Little, Western States Regional Vice-President and Debt Counselor. Little was a misnomer, for he was a knuckle-dragging, semiliterate giant who should have become extinct during the Ice Age. He was also Wally's last resort.

Mr. Little had issued him the loan from a roll in his pocket, no paperwork required, and said that his full name was Jerome (Chicken) Little. The interest rate was in a range between a high-risk credit card and the Mob.

"Wanna know why the Chicken?" the loan executive had asked with a snaggle-toothed smile.

Mr. Little smelled like a landfill. Wally had said no, he didn't know. Not saying that he genuinely and sincerely did not want to know.

"Cuz if you welsh on me and Mr. Smith, my boss, when I'm fucking done, you'll look like the sky's fallen on you."

Little had referred to the mysterious Mr. Smith respectfully, bordering on reverential. Dr. Stockwall shuddered at the recollection. Surely this Mr. Smith wore the most ironic of pseudonyms. He had to be another primordial brute, a Tony Soprano–Godzilla hybrid named Vittorio Smitholini or whatnot, who had worked his way up the Mafia's corporate ladder via his skill with an ice pick.

Wally was in arrears to the world's most terrifying lending institution. He *knew* it was and he knew he deserved better. A published survey showed that self-employed orthodontists averaged $350,000 per year. It was a taunting statistic that made him want to weep. He gripped and twisted his newspaper so hard that it tore.

Sally Jo, his wife, had nagged Wally into this sun and fun vacation. The only way he could conceal that they couldn't afford the trip was to take it, although in a perverse sense they could. Dr. Stockwall's malpractice carrier had abruptly canceled him.

Termination was instigated by an incident that had prompted an obscenely slanted and exaggerated article in a professional journal titled "Orthodontics and Gangrene: A Link?" Unbeknownst to Sally Jo Stockwall, they spent this month's premium in Cancun.

There had been, too, the rather insistent nitpicking by state dental examiners. Among the minutiae, they'd objected to his use of recycled braces and bands in new patients, an economy many of his colleagues employed. So why was *he* singled out for harassment?

The Stockwalls' cut-rate seats were not together. Supremely irritated, Sally Jo sat in a back row, across from the lavatory, wedged between the window and an exceptionally large person. Wally felt her daggers stinging his neck and ordered another wine from a passing stewardess who tried in vain to ignore him. The dreadfully resinous cabernet they sold in little bottles on this flying tramp steamer would have to do.

He stared yet again at the headline of his damaged newspaper: WORLD'S RICHEST MAN ON DEATHBED? DISPOSITION OF ASSETS UNKNOWN. DID HE TAKE IT WITH HIM?

Wally looked at his stainless steel Taihotsu DigiChron™ watch, thinking of the profits Taihotsu's corporations raked in. Saburo Taihotsu, the Mongoose, was a Jap Howard Hughes and then some. A lucky opportunist, a man with his finger in a multitude of lucrative pies, Taihotsu had gained notoriety as a World War II guerrilla fighter hero extraordinaire, on *their* side, for crying out loud, on *our* Hawaiian soil. You had to grudgingly admire his moxie, though, his élan. MacArthur had loved the little guy.

An accidental multibillionaire, a zillionaire, Taihotsu had ridden the postwar boom.

Dr. Wally Stockwall, a man of science, a healer, a facilitator of glorious smiles, struggled.

He sighed at the gross unfairness of it all. Forty years old and he could not once catch a break.

The consensus guesstimate of Taihotsu's missing fortune was $100 billion. How much was that conceptually, spatially? Here, on the next page. A "Taihotsu Tidbit," they were calling them. If you laid 100,000,000,000 one-dollar bills end to end, they would coil 380 times around planet Earth. Wally pictured a gigantic ball of green yarn.

$100,000,000,000.

Lord God Almighty!

Or at the current exchange rate: ¥10,000,000,000,000,000. In yen, Taihotsu was a multitrillionaire. Wally could not imagine.

Wally had taken sidelong glances at the unfriendly oddball seated next to him. He looked vaguely familiar. His bleached blond hair was an obvious dye job, though he seemed too old for such nonsense. The frosting and peroxiding they were doing to their hair these days was kid stuff. At least he didn't have visible tattoos and earrings all over his face. He wasn't swishy either. He was, if anything, a peculiar contradiction.

Blondie wasn't genial. From the moment they'd taken off, he'd studied a strange piece of paper with a long string of numbers on it. It would be helpful if he'd agree to change seats with Sally Jo. If Wally didn't extinguish her slow burn soon, he'd be living with it indefinitely.

There *was* something familiar about Blondie.

"Excuse me. You look awfully familiar."

Wally's seatmate pretended not to hear.

"Seriously," he said. "I've seen you."

That elicited a tight smile and a nod.

Snapping his fingers, Wally said, "Somewhere, some place. Where, where, where? I've seen you."

"You may have."

"I may have?"

"An educated guess."

"Aha! You're famous."

"Not exactly."

"Akin to not exactly pregnant?"

Blondie smiled. "I've had my fifteen minutes."

"On television?"

He fluttered a hand. "Yes. A visual fifteen minutes."

"Please share your quarter hour of renown with me."

"In a former life I worked as a TV news reporter."

"Where? New York? San Francisco?"

"In smaller markets."

"Ever Idaho?"

"Boise."

"I knew it. I have a cousin in Nampa. We were visiting. The earthen dam that broke. *You* covered the story."

"I did."

"It stuck in my mind because I wondered what prevented you from being electrocuted by your microphone or drowning."

"Low voltage, and in swift currents, it's all about the proper gear and how you set your feet parallel to the flow."

"Speaking of news, isn't this Saburo Taihotsu business extraordinary?"

"Yes, it is."

"He was a phenomenon. At near-death, Taihotsu revealed a new facet, a funny bone."

"Oh? I haven't kept up."

Wally said, "They can't locate Saburo Taihotsu's assets. Even that penthouse he's holed up in is no longer his. He'd sold it and is living there on a grace period. He'd divested his empire in bite-sized chunks, unnoticed, apparently into cash. They know that much."

"I haven't kept up on the details."

Wally thought the indifference odd for a media sort, but, well, the oddball blond worked in Podunk markets, where grain and feed prices ruled the airwaves.

Wally opened his newspaper to side-by-side photographs of Saburo Taihotsu, one circa 1941. In uniform and leather aviator helmet, arms folded in front of his Zero fighter plane, he was callow and grim.

In the other, upon his capture on Kauai in 1945, he was raggedy, but seemingly well fed and defiant, living off the land and wreaking havoc in small ways, just enough deviltry to keep us on our toes. The legendary Mongoose.

"They're recapping common knowledge," Wally said. "On the way back to his carrier after Pearl Harbor, where he shot down two of our planes, Taihotsu had engine trouble. He crashed off a remote coast of Kauai. Pieces of the plane were found, but not the pilot, who they assumed perished. The islands weren't wall-to-wall tourism in that era. There were wide-open spaces. Taihotsu lived off the land right under everyone's noses for upwards of four years, until he surrendered soon after VJ Day. His derring-do caused little harm. Fires and various low-rent mischief. No reports of injuries or deaths. Taihotsu was a resourceful saboteur. You have to give him bonus points for that. He earned his Mongoose nickname."

"He was a remarkable man," Blondie said.

"He was, and it gets curioser and curioser. He'd lived in our country briefly before the war. He had a handle on our tastes. He was savvy. He was a lady's man after the war too, making up for lost time. Like Howard Hughes, he was hot to trot for starlets, white girls predominantly, leaning toward big leggy blonds, not that I'm casting racial aspersions. He smothered them with money and what money buys. Nothing's wrong with that, in my opinion. More power to him.

"In his dotage, Taihotsu turned into a fruitcake and a loner and then a hermit, but he never lost his knack for delegating authority. He was a crafty old boy. None of his hundreds of top lackeys had much individual clout and they never knew what their counterparts were doing. His organizational chart has been described as a large pot of spaghetti flung against a wall and then running onto the floor. His minions liquidated assets piecemeal into cash, none realizing they were participants in a scheme to zero out. They believed they were diversifying. At Taihotsu's headquarters, if you became too nosy or attempted to form an alliance with fellow bigwigs, you were gone."

Wally tapped the rumpled headline. "Rumors are flying. They're saying that sealed pouches were periodically removed from Taihotsu's suite to one of his steel mills, an oldie, and his family's original Taihotsu Iron Works plant that we didn't get around to bombing into rubble during the war. They say it's an obsolete money-loser he kept open out of nostalgia, to throw it in our faces that we shunned his daddy when they visited the U.S. in the late 1930s.

"The pouches were tossed into the furnaces, burned to a cinder, less than a cinder. Are you thinking what I'm thinking was in those bags? What a lot of people are. A hundred billion dollars, plus or minus the annual budget of three large states. Money to burn. Isn't that insane?"

Incredibly, his seatmate yawned.

Wally stopped talking and introduced himself to the goofball by presenting his card: DR. J.D. (WALLY) STOCKWALL, Gentle Caring Orthodontics.

"I'm Dr. Stockwall."

"Rob Weather."

"In my Beverly Hills–area clinic, Rob, I've aligned the teeth of the stars," he lied. "Please don't ask who. It falls under doctor–patient privilege."

"Okay, I won't."

Disappointed that Blondie didn't beg for names, Wally asked this Rob Weather if he could get him a drink, dutch treat, mind you.

"No thanks."

Wally jabbed the call button and said, "So what brought you to Mexico? Vacation?"

Rob Weather hesitantly mentioned his sabbatical. Wally extracted the full story as if a recalcitrant molar.

"I am sorry about your relationship with your lady," Wally said, thinking that she was a perceptive girl.

"She thinks I'm having a midlife crisis or I've gone totally mad. I'm headed on to Seattle to drop in on an aunt I have in Kent, near Seattle."

"Where?"

"Kent. It's twenty miles south of Seattle."

"You have to do what you have to do. Bravo."

"It's probably for the best."

"Did you and your lady friends have children?"

"No. You?"

"Likewise." A Sally Jo complaint not oft heard lately, thank goodness.

Blondie's mouth fascinated him as much as his head of hair. He'd been born with extraordinarily straight teeth or he'd had topnotch work done. For TV news, it'll have to be one or the other. Wally wouldn't be surprised if the major market stations had dental hygienists on staff along with the hair and makeup drones.

Gary Alexander

Stockwall took a eugenic view of jaw structure. The maxillary prominence and attendant irregularities of the swarthier races no orthodontist could completely correct were absent. Rob's eyes threw him, though. They were brown, a pinch of Oriental in them. Blondie's genes had caromed through the generations.

"I felt I needed to do this," Rob added. "To make a change instead of waiting for a news director to."

As far as Wally Stockwall was concerned, this Rob Weather clown had had everything going for him. He enjoyed minor celebrity and glamour, a livable salary, and a steady gal. He had a future. But he'd flushed it down the toilet for his "sabbatical." To Wally Stockwall, this was light-years beyond comprehension.

He said, "More power to you. What's that?" He pointed to the slip of paper in Rob's hands.

"Beats me," Rob said, handing it to him. "It came in the mail to me anonymously."

"Unusual and doubtlessly expensive stock," Wally said. "A secret code?"

Rob shrugged. "I've been fiddling with it and fiddling with it. No light bulbs come on."

Wally decided against asking Rob to switch places with Sally Jo. This innocuous interaction was preferable to high-voltage tension.

"Mind if I give it a whirl?"

"Be my guest."

Wally Stockwall sipped his wine and shuddered.

"Unctuous, nonexistent fruit, and so chewy you need a knife and fork."

Blondie forced a smile.

Wally looked at the numbers: 12231823922111223136141522.

He copied them onto a napkin he'd gotten with his meal—a bag of peanuts, hickory-smoke flavored.

The numbers spilled over from one napkin to another.

The appropriately inscrutable puzzle temporarily diverted attention from Wally's problems.

8.

Sarah Ann Hilyer, unknowingly in Carla Chance's matchmaking crosshairs, fought an urge to count the house.

Sarah had already observed that her mother received more visitors in death than in her final years of life, and they continued to stream in after she had taken her seat. Who were all these people? She vaguely recognized some as Mother's former students who had kept in loose contact after she'd retired from the university decades ago. Others were octogenarians. Had they once upon a time bounced Sarah on a knee?

Sarah sat front row center, marveling at the flowers on the dais flanking the young minister. The memorial service smelled like a florist shop. Such generosity. She hoped there were addresses in the guest book for thank-you notes.

Mother hadn't been religious, hadn't attended church in years but for the obligatory Christmas Eve and Easter Sunday. On paper she was a member in good standing of the Lutheran church that supplied this associate pastor who was preparing to speak.

A few days ago, it'd been just Sarah, Mother and the crematorium staff. Early in the disease, when she was usually lucid, her mother had expressed her wishes that there be no funeral, no fuss. Julia Hilyer had been embarrassed by what she was becoming.

Today's sendoff technically was not a funeral. Sarah realized she was fudging. She didn't give a hoot. Mother deserved this

70

tribute. Mother and daughter were agnostic, but Sarah Hilyer believed that Julia Hilyer should have this event on her afterlife résumé, a religious touch. It certainly couldn't hurt.

Reverend Magnuson was a plump, devout young man with the blush of one freshly shaven. He wore a blue suit, white shirt, narrow tie, and his receding hair short.

Reading from the clipped chronological bio Sarah had provided, he struggled to insert anecdotes. Julia Hilyer was an accomplished woman, a wife and mother, an independent woman before that term came into vogue, a model citizen, a dedicated educator, an activist whenever conscience dictated, an adventurous hobbyist in her younger days, a hiker and private pilot.

Sarah had opted for no puffery, as her unpretentious mother would have wanted. She couldn't help but smile, though. He was making her mother sound like Amelia Earhart, despite Julia's hobbies coming after widowhood in her forties.

Out of material, Reverend Magnuson looked up and winged it, relating how Julia brought cookies to a bake sale, how her oatmeal-and-raisin were legendary. He must have confused her with someone else, bless his heart. Sarah Hilyer's mother hadn't baked in eons.

Sarah's attention drifted to the surroundings. This chapel at Taihotsu-Forest Park Cemetery was either new or had been refurbished, virtually overnight, the result of acquisition by the Japanese conglomerate. She smelled paint and carpeting. The stained glass windows, vertical slivers of light, rose on textured beige walls to an open-beamed ceiling. The glass itself was nonrepresentational, colorful shards joined by road maps of lead. There were no angels or other ecclesiastical frippery. The chapel was an abstract piety designed not to offend.

At home, a pewter urn contained her mother's ashes. It was in the front coat closet, and Sarah debated what to do with it.

Mother stated a preference for the cremation process, but no special instructions whether to display or not to display, or to scatter at sea or from a light airplane. She had merely requested an alternative to "decaying in the ground, a smorgasbord for worms."

Reverend Magnuson segued to a Bible passage, a parable on the seamlessness of life and death, then to a prayer. Half listening, Sarah surprised herself by wetting a tissue. The months and months of advanced Alzheimer's and the inevitable end had wrung the ducts dry. Sarah's thoughts wandered from his words to those people present she and her mother knew, friends and neighbors and school colleagues. Sarah was an only child, and her mother, widowed young, had outlived the majority of her family and social circle.

At the end, her mother had not recognized Sarah, but recalled her daughter's early childhood pets in exquisite detail. Not two weeks ago, she had gone on and on about Tabby and Frosty, cats whom Sarah had long forgotten, let alone their names.

Julia Hilyer survived until last Thursday, Sarah's forty-eighth birthday.

That coincidence required another tissue. Sarah's best chums and colleagues from the college, Amy Hodges and Sylvia Johnson, flanked her on the pew, giving her gentle forearm pats of support. Carla Chance, her buddy across the street in the condo complex, sat beside Amy. Sarah and Carla had ridden here together, the latter saying nothing unless spoken to, an uncommon occurrence. Sarah felt guilty for not hearing the ending eulogy through her sobs. She was weeping for herself as much as for her mother.

Outside, after saying her thank-yous, pretending to remember those she didn't, the pats became hugs, and Amy, chairman of the mathematics department at Southwest Seattle Community College, said, "Take the time off you need."

"It's midterm," Sarah protested.

"You've graded the exams?"

"Just finished."

"There you go. That makes you slightly less indispensable than normal. Anyway, you've been part time since Julia needed so great an amount of you, with just two courses. I'd like to take a short fling at your Math 230."

Unlike many community colleges, SWSCC's math department went further than offering ticket-punch credits for transfer to four-year schools. The courses were unconventional, demanding and provocative. Most sections had a waiting list.

"Math 230, Differential Equations, glazes half my students' eyes. The other half is three lessons ahead," she protested again. "You'll be ready to scream in five minutes."

"It can't be worse than my endless calculus sessions. I'd really like a stab at it."

Sarah smiled, knowing she really didn't. "Thank you."

Sylvia said, "I ought to be able to handle your Elements of Statistics. Where are you there?"

"Sampling theory."

"On what?"

"We're early. An overview of volume rendering."

"Be in no hurry to return, Sarah," Sylvia said. "It'll be a blast to teach. Besides, I need to bone up on probability. John and I are going to Vegas on the quarter break. There's a roulette wheel with my name on it."

"It's named Sucker," Amy said.

Sarah laughed. "I'll sleep on it and give you an answer tomorrow. I'll take a week at most."

"How can you escape in a *week?* You'll take two, girl."

"Ten days tops," Sarah said, aware that she wouldn't last that long. She'd drive to the ocean for a solitary, extended weekend. She'd be back in her classroom by Wednesday.

It was at Carla's car that Sarah saw Neil Jasons lumbering toward her. She had been waiting for Carla, who'd stopped to talk to somebody she knew.

"I didn't get a chance to extend my heartfelt condolences, Sarah."

She hadn't expected Neil at the service. They said hello on campus, occasionally chatted in the faculty lounge, but weren't particularly close.

A resentfully unpublished short story writer and novelist, Neil Jasons taught creative writing at SWSCC and said in all seriousness that he chaired the Creative Writing Department. It was a department of one.

Gossip had it that Neil Jasons wrote unintentionally bad Hemingway, worse Hemingway than the bad Hemingway entered in the Bad Hemingway Contests. He was Sarah's age, heavy and disheveled. Neil always dressed carelessly—scuffed penny loafers, stained tie askew, woolly jacket and, no fooling, leather elbow patches.

His hug was a bit overlong.

"Thank you, Neil."

"Listen," he said, glancing at his watch. "I canceled my sections. I wasn't sure of the service's length. Permit me to buy you a cup of coffee."

Well, Sarah was not looking forward to going home, sorting through medical and home care bills, and the nursing home statements of the past months when there was no other choice, calculating what was covered by insurance and what she owed. Sarah had procrastinated, sure that the bottom line would be depressing.

Sifting through her mother's things too, that would be worse. Deciding what to discard, what should go to charity, what to keep.

Carla arrived. "Sorry. A policyholder dumped me. Her driving record improved from abysmal to terrible, so she moved along to bigger and better things."

Sarah introduced her to Neil Jasons. Carla saw three's-a-crowd written all over his pasty face.

"Neil asked me to coffee."

"I can run you home afterward too," he inserted quickly.

Uncertain, Sarah didn't answer.

"Then it's settled," Jasons said.

"Not a problem," Carla said. "I'll catch you later."

In Neil's dented Taihotsu Zinger™ coupe, Sarah assumed Neil had a favorite nearby coffee shop. After all, this was Seattle. But he drove and drove, through residential neighborhoods and across arterials. She wasn't comfortable with this but didn't protest.

On the old highway north of the airport, Neil parked at a sports bar. There were satellite dishes on the roof and neon beer signs galore. The siding could use paint.

Shambling around to open her car door, he said, "Don't be deceived by first impressions. The resident mixologist is a java genius. He does it all."

Neil Jasons led her inside to televisions here, there and everywhere. A clientele of twenty-something men wearing team jerseys ate hamburgers and drank beer, viewing hockey and basketball playoff highlights. Bread and circus, Sarah thought.

Neil steered her to the darkest corner in the dark, loud bar. Sarah ordered the promised coffee, black.

"I am cognizant that this is an overwhelming period of mixed emotions for you, Sarah," Neil said, staring sincerely across the booth at her. "A potpourri of intense feelings. You are grieving, while concomitantly free of an enormous burden."

She didn't especially like the way he put it, but Neil was absolutely on the mark. She was spared the obligation to reply, to justify, by the prompt arrival of their drinks. Neil's coffee was a martini. It came in a fat tumbler with an olive. The bartender evidently knew him and his preference.

Sarah sipped java that didn't live up to the billing.

"I admire your dedication," Neil went on, hoisting a toast as he chewed his olive. "Subordinating your personal life in behalf of your mother's. The level of commitment is akin to creating literature. I trust that your resolve was appreciated more than mine has been."

Neil Jasons drained his glass and waved it like a semaphore for a refill.

Aware that she sounded trite, Sarah said, "I did what I had to do. I did what anybody would do under the circumstances."

"Nay, m'lass. A lesser person would have warehoused her after the initial diagnosis, and permit the professionals and quasi-professionals to do as they might. Your strong character, Sarah, resonates loud and clear. Please excuse me a minute." He stood and padded his way toward the men's room.

Sarah watched the regulars watching their sporting events. She and her mother had liked figure skating. They'd enjoyed it for different reasons. For Mother it had been the artistry, for Sarah fascination in a sport that seemed equal parts beauty and corruption. The political judging. The relentless ambition of the athletes and their parents. The fanatical devotion of the skaters who performed to classical music they wouldn't be caught dead listening to had they been normal teenagers.

Neil returned from the restroom carrying a new drink he'd picked up at the bar. He slid in on her side, nudging her, reeking of cologne.

Cologne from a vending machine aside a condom dispenser?

Sarah was beyond uncomfortable. "Thank you for the coffee, Neil, but I have to run. If it's out of your way, I'll call someone."

He didn't move. "Sarah, I shall come directly the point. That is the person I am. My bluntness is reflected in the raw power of my narrative. Misinterpretation and rudeness by incompetent editors and literary agents stunted my career."

"Neil."

"Your coffee is getting cold. Irrelevant. Why don't you have what I am having? Nectar of the juniper berry. It is happy hour, doubles for the price of a single, my treat."

The creative writing instructor drank with one hand as he took hers in his other.

"Neil."

"Hear me out, Sarah. You must encourage the blooming before the blossoms drop."

"What?"

"Sarah, I do not mean this derogatorily. I am an admirer. I have patiently, agonizingly, bided my time. You deserve better at this stage in your life than spinsterhood."

"Neil."

"You are jolted by my words, yes, and m'dear. A human reaction. You are not a beauty in the artificial Hollywood sense. I do not mean 'not a beauty' derogatorily. Your distinguished nose. The effervescent green eyes, their spacing, wide and thoughtful. The silvery strands in your hair you do not vainly mask with chemicals."

"Neil."

"You are a living, breathing pleasance. You know not how lushly womanly you are."

"Neil, my hand."

"You are slender and petite and supple. Your breasts are not outsized, not bovine. They are enticingly spherical. Your loins are tantalizingly firm. Orgasmic. Your extraordinary arse, pardon the Anglo-Saxonisn, is remarkably tight and globular for a woman your age."

She was too angry to laugh. "You sound like a restaurant critic."

His sour gin breath overwhelmed the cologne. "In that regard, Sarah, I am an oral person. Proficiently oral. I shall rocket you to the moon."

Sarah tugged. "Neil, give me my hand back."

"Your velvety luminous skin," he said, stroking her arm.

She flinched.

"Nurture that bloom. The sterile, desiccated existence of a spinster does not flatter you."

"My life is none of your concern."

Neil pulled her hand to his crotch.

She tugged again. "Neil."

"Feel my desire."

"Neil."

"How can my ardor not concomitantly inflame yours?"

"Neil."

"Allow me to nurture you, Sarah. Allow me to awaken that dormant womanhood within. We only go around once. Ah, never has a hackneyed truism from a beer slogan been so apropos."

"Let me go, Neil."

"Sarah, there is a motel next door. The venue is unworthy of you, albeit convenient. The rooms provide the bourgeois amenities. Playpen-sized beds and a minibar. Fear not an indiscretion. My circuitous route here was designed to throw off prospective busybodies."

"Neil."

"Tell me that you are not aroused too."

Sarah Ann Hilyer had slept with four men in her life. She had loved two of them. Neil Jasons would not be Number Five.

"Last warning, Neil."

"Videos are available in the rooms, my Sarah. Admittedly vulgar and absurdly acrobatic, they do unleash inhibitions and they are instructive. Tell me you are not aroused. Tell me."

Sarah told him nothing. She squeezed. She squeezed and

twisted and squeezed harder until Neil tensed and howled and his eyes rolled into the lids. When he released her, she elbowed him and shoved until he staggered out of the booth in a groaning crouch.

Bar customers had swiveled on their stools, backlit by a multiple-image melee, gloves and sticks scattered on the ice, players throwing punches. They blinked, and their mouths gaped at the live action, at the up close and personal, at the agony of defeat.

Neil was on his knees now, clutching himself.

"Bitch," he croaked. "Professional virgin."

To Sarah's surprise and relief, Carla walked in at that moment and stood at the door.

Carla watched, dumbfounded, as Sarah, a little slip of a woman, a fraction her own size, sidestepped her writhing colleague.

"Carla."

"I'm sorry, Sarah. I took the liberty of following you. I had what they used to call bad vibes. When I saw Mr. Suave in action, I considered getting my tire iron out of the trunk."

"I'm glad you did follow me," she said. "I need some fresh air."

Outside, Carla said, "Not all men are like this sleazeball."

"Thank goodness."

Carla unlocked her car. "My nephew, for instance."

9.

While Carla attended Sarah's mother's funeral, Buster and Rob drove in Rob's rented car. Buster was behind the wheel, showing Rob the Seattle sights. Given their limited time before Carla got home, Buster cut the tour to what was visible from Interstate 5 that ran north and south, bisecting the city—the skyscrapers, Elliott Bay and the ferryboats coming and going, and the spectacularly ugly (in Buster's opinion) Space Needle, which, along with rainfall, seemed to define Seattle to outsiders.

"We average less rain per year than Baltimore, Boston and Philly, to name a few," Buster said, settling into the southbound afternoon crawl. "But don't tell anybody. Outsiders thinking every day's a monsoon keeps the riffraff out. So much for my chamber of commerce spiel."

"Do you rehearse in the car, Uncle Buster? I do, sort of."

"Do you rehearse the news before it happens?"

"No, just tune up my voice on the way out to a scene."

Buster said, "Same diff. Rush hour's the best time and place to break in a bit. Nobody hears you and you're going too slow to get yourself killed if your mind and your car wander."

"Let's hear you."

"Are you forgetting? I got nothing to rehearse for," said the unemployed comic.

"Be positive, Uncle Buster. Come on. Whip it on me," Rob said, clapping his hands.

"Aw, what the hell. Okay. Carla's a sourpuss when I do this, rudely interrupting all the time to remind me of my unspiffy driving record and to pay attention to the bleeping road," Buster said, in synch with the syrupy flow, his head on a swivel, a hand up as if holding a mike. "Good to see you nice folks. I just got out of the pen, you know. Sorry about the striped suit. Didn't have time to change.

"They threw the book at me for making copies of rented DVDs. That FBI warning at the beginning often, where the max you'll get is a two-hundred-fifty-thousand dollar fine and five years? I didn't have the quarter-mil but I had five years to spare. I didn't get no mercy cuz I was a two-time loser. Already did six months for tearing the tag off a mattress.

"Jeez, when I was a kid, I thought if I'd survived to age sixty, everybody'd be getting around like the Jetsons, zipping here and there in their bubbletop flying machines, not piloting a roller skate of a rental car, no offense, Rob.

"My '59 Eldorado, that's a different ball game. I had some weight out there in front of me, some heft. Me and my Eldo, we got respect. Rarely did anybody lay on the horn or cut us off. We got thumbs-up from the many, many admirers of prime carflesh.

"Look around you now. We're surrounded by Super Bubba pickup trucks and monster SUVs, their drivers riding up high inside of privacy glass. We can expect to and we will receive no mercy in regards to lane changes or nothing else whatsoever. Ever see any of those veehickles doing any work? Ever see a speck of dust on all that chrome? You could eat off the pickup beds.

"What a joke those TV commercials are for them, winching a load of boulders up the side of a cliff. These fifty-thousand-dollar rigs, they're like the princess and the pea. I'm picturing them driven by an alien race of pinheads, hiding behind that dark privacy glass, plotting world conquest."

Rob laughed.

"Great material, but I can't use it in a set. Half the audience owns one of those damn things, to hell with the price of gas. They'd walk out in a flippin' huff.

"Material I can use, that anybody can relate to, is in each and every household. For example, I tell 'em, hey, go look in your pantry and you'll scare the bejesus out of yourself reading the food labels. Yeah. Pick up anything at random. Take a loaf of bread and all the vitamins and minerals they make a big whoopee out of adding, which they gotta do cuz they processed all the vitamins and minerals out of the wheat. Or pick up a can of soup. Read the fine print on the ingredients and you see yummies like hydrolyzed yeast protein and hydrolyzed soy protein and hydrolyzed wheat gluten and hydrolyzed hydrolo-gies

"What's a hydrolyzed? Animal, vegetable or mineral? You tell me. I dunno. There's vast fields of hydrolyzed in Iowa? High as an elephant's eye? Or stockyards full of hydrolyzed, waiting for that last stroll down the chute after they're fattened up? Why don't they call it hydrolyzed soup? You could have a complete line of hydrolyzeds, like Cream of Hydrolyzed and Hydrolyzed Noodle and Hydrolyzed with Rice.

"Breakfast cereal. That's the worst. They're marketed mostly to the kiddies. The stuff in the boxes, it comes in colors not found in nature on this planet or any other. The way they glow in the dark, they gotta be made in Alamogordo or Chernobyl, somewhere like that. I'm too chicken to read the contents. Gotta be puree of plutonium and radium juice and whatnot. No wonder kids grow up to be mutants who never look up from their cell phones they're playing video games on and text mas-saging and tweet-tweetering.

"When I was a pup, the only thing you weren't supposed to eat was candy from strangers. Now it's some damn thing new each week. Trans fat is the latest deadly poison we been eating for years. Thanks to trans fat, our arteries are pumping lard. Now that we know how bad trans fats are, people are dying of it. Were they croaking on trans fat before they discovered it's killed? Maybe, maybe not. I stopped believing any of that crapola when they said beer was bad for you.

"See what I mean, Rob? Your pantry and the whole world beyond it is potential material. Take this antioxidant flavonoid thing that was in the news awhile ago. They said red wine and dark chocolate give you this flavonoid juju.

"You might get zits everywhere and a liver the size of Delaware from flavonoiding yourself, but, hey, you'll live to be one hundred and one and it beats the hell out of oat bran. And speaking of hydrolyzed and flavonoided and other food, how's about some miscellaneous food for thought?

"We've all seen hockey fights on TV, eh. Both teams altogether, they've got like thirty teeth that they don't take out of their mouth at night. So how come they throw off their helmets and gloves when they start swinging?

"How come shopping carts always pull to the left or right, where the merchandise is? Never straight ahead to the checkout.

"How come on the highway you see signs that say 'Deer, one mile' or 'Elk crossing for six miles'? They got the critters on contract to stay inside those exact bounds?

"How about these nebula words like 'moment,' as in I'll be back in a 'moment'? How long's a 'moment'? Better yet, somebody says he'll be back 'soon'? How long's 'soon'? I know a guy whose dad went out for a pack of cigarettes in 1978 and said he'd be back 'soon.' They're still hunting for him.

"Time for a survey. What's the smallest denomination coin you'd stoop down and pick up off the sidewalk? When I was a kid, it was a penny. Now it's a nickel. Some folks, it might be a dime. These pointy-head economic advisors with their charts and graphs and gasbag speeches on inflation and recessions and upturns and downturns and leading economical indicators, all they gotta do is ask a hundred people that question. Once the bend-over-and-pick-up cut-off is the five-dollar bill, we know we're in big-time inflationary trouble.

"Speaking of big money, ever hear of a book being swiped out of a car, a smash and grab, like for a purse? My lady, Carla, she's a big reader. She's constantly going to and from the li-barry, forgetting to take books out of the car, leavin' 'em in plain sight. Not a problem. The only books anybody'd steal are the Gutenberg Bible or Saburo Taihotsu's checkbook, may he rest in peace.

"You know what else bugs me? Why do superheroes need secret identities? C'mon. Everybody knows who they are. Doesn't this make it twice as easy for the arch villain fiend to get them, being that they're *two* targets for the price of one? Like mild-mannered Clark Kent. How hard would it be to slip Clark a low-fat vanilla kryptonite latté in the morning when he stops off for a caffeine jolt on his way in to *The Daily Planet*?

"I sympathize with Lois Lane, though. She spends a hot weekend with Clark and feels guilty for stepping out on Super-man and vice versa. Lois, poor gal, she feels like she's a slut."

Horns honking around them were becoming more persistent. Buster talked with his hands, even to himself, and had possibly nudged the edges of his lane when he'd released the wheel.

How he yearned for his abducted Caddy! He could be rant-ing and raving, arms flailing, doing eighty, eighty-five, ninety, the top down, the slipstream roaring like the mother of all ador-ing audiences, and all it'd take to maintain the straight and level was an occasional pinky finger on the necker knob. In this rental unit, he was overheating and getting a headache. In the claustrophobic traffic, he felt like spoiled meat, expanding, about to burst.

A sideburned and NASCAR-jacketed putz alongside them in a ratty old pickup flipped Buster the bird and screamed loudly enough to be heard, "Get off the phone and drive, asshole!"

Buster returned the digital greeting and hollered, "You have a nice day too, Gomer."

Buster Hightower believed "have a nice day" was the least emotional, most insincere sentence in the English language. It bordered on heartlessness.

Shaking his head, he looked at a grinning Rob and said, "There is no respect in this day and age for art and the artist."

The pickup scooted forward and swerved ahead of them so tightly that Buster had to brake hard. Until turning off at the Kent exit, they were assaulted by foul blue exhaust fumes and a REAL MEN LOVE JESUS bumper sticker.

"Let this be a lesson to you, kid," Buster advised Rob. "When you're driving, always pay strict attention to the road."

They walked into the Chance-Hightower unit to an alien aroma.

"Spice," Rob said, breathing deeply. "Mmm."

"What the hell?" said an alarmed Buster. "Carla doesn't bake."

They explored further, into the kitchen, where Sarah Hilyer was stirring something in a bowl and Carla was removing something from the oven.

"An old favorite of mine," Carla said. "Carrot cake with cream cheese frosting."

"It is?" Buster said.

"Carrot cake. Wow! It's my all-time favorite," Rob said, eyes wide.

"It is?" Carla said innocently, fully aware from a genealogical organization questionnaire on Rob that it was.

"Our good friend and neighbor across the way is pitching in, giving me a hand," Carla said, resisting adding that it was "therapy."

Buster went into the kitchen and gave Sarah a big hug. "Sorry about your loss."

"Thanks, Buster," she said, hugging him back, looking over his shoulder at Carla's houseguest.

"Oh, by the way, you guys haven't met. Rob Weather, Sarah Hilyer," Carla said casually.

Rob and Sarah said hello and shook hands. Sarah liked his smile and knew there had to be a story behind that hair. Rob liked what he saw, her gray hair the sole indicator that she had a year or three on him. Both instantly realized that the beaming Carla was playing Cupid. Neither minded, and both were willing to play dumb.

Carla watched the pair closely for sparks. She detected none from either. But, well, that love-at-first-sight business was overrated. She'd settle for cordiality.

For now.

Buster watched Carla, thinking here we go again.

10.

Ashley Parker and Brett Steele, co-hosts of *Exclusive!!,* were, in a word, lovely. Brett's hair was just so, and his jaw was out to there. His teeth were whiter than any porcelain.

A former Miss America runner-up, Ashley burst from her short skirt and low-cut blouse. Blond hair sprouted from darker roots, and she had raccoon eyes from the makeup. Ashley and Brett were perched on stools, as cute as buttons, a large screen suspended between them.

They were on-camera after a Saburo Taihotsu special. It concentrated on his playboy days in the late 1940s and the 1950s when his fortune had amassed in earnest. He had been a darling of *Confidential* magazine, the era's leading scandal sheet. They showed several covers, one with him in Acapulco, then a noted celebrity haunt; another embarking his private Douglas DC-6, a state-of-the-art airliner with four piston engines, accompanied by a long-forgotten ingénue; another at an Oscars ceremony, the implication being that he'd bedded two or more finalists for Best Actress.

Ashley and Brett's interview subject on the screen, Juliana VanderVeen, diminished them, and not only because she was sextuple life-size on a smaller model of the Taihotsu Moni-Tron™ that was in many newer football and baseball stadiums. Her sheer glamour simply overwhelmed.

"How fascinating to have been executive chef to the world's richest man, as well as a member of his elite inner circle at the

87

time of his death," Ashley began. "Tell us, what was Saburo Taihotsu like?"

"He was a kind man. He was a fair and honest employer."

"And?"

"I did not otherwise know him."

Ashley sighed theatrically. "This is going to be a short and uninformative interview. Did Mr. Taihotsu have a hearty appetite?"

Juliana VanderVeen glowed above a TOKYO, JAPAN LIVE graphic. A statuesque natural blonde with a sensual overbite, Juliana routinely caused male passersby to walk into lampposts. She was a Dutch citizen who had lived in Japan for a dozen years. Before hiring on at Taihotsu Holding, Ltd., as executive chef, she worked as a hostess at an ultra-exclusive private club. Its primary rule of employment had been that, aside from customer satisfaction, there were no rules.

"Due to illnesses, he ate like a bird. He enjoyed my presentations and the memories they evoked."

"Oh, I'll bet he did," Ashley said, her voice dropping half an octave, harshening.

Brett consulted note cards provided for him and raised a single eyebrow. "Did your presentation really have anything to do with food? Really?"

Juliana smiled sweetly, saying nothing. *Exclusive!!* high bidder for the rights to her interview: $3,500,000. It had been said in partial jest that *Exclusive!!* had an unlimited budget. When it was exceeded, they got more.

Exclusive!!'s typical fare was celebrity misbehavior and bizarre crime. To the point of monotony, promiscuity, spousal abuse, and controlled substances were favored themes. In the name of journalism they followed starlets into abortion clinics. The last episode had featured a transvestite bank robber and a midget who had killed his mother.

For $3,500,000, Juliana VanderVeen was willing to suffer bad manners. In Juliana's opinion, this fare was even tackier than reality TV. Her very presence would elevate their trashy programming a rung.

Ashley did not need note cards. She said, "Saburo Taihotsu in his youth had been compared to Howard Hughes in regard to the Hollywood dating scene. There was an alleged lost weekend with Marilyn Monroe. He was a vital man in all respects until age and infirmities made living a vicarious event. What can you tell us in this regard, Juliana?"

Brett smirked. "So he took his libido with him too?"

Juliana replied with a cold glare.

"You have been quoted as saying that you cooked and served him food while scantily clothed," Ashley accused.

"I was not quoted."

"It was alleged."

"Go ask your alleged."

"By reliable sources."

"Ask them."

"Was the dining situation secondary to the voyeurism aspect?"

"I am a chef."

"Ironically, your culinary résumé does not exist, nor does a cooking school background. You were a flight attendant and then a hostess at a private club. What exactly does a private club hostess do?"

"I am self-taught in the kitchen."

"In his younger days, Mr. Taihotsu threw lavish private parties that included impressively endowed young women."

"I was not acquainted with Mr. Taihotsu in his younger days."

"Exclusively European and American women."

"I trust that was not a racist remark. I trust further that romance to Mr. Taihotsu is not a topic to smirk about in front of a camera."

Brett suspected he had been insulted.

Ashley knew she had been insulted and retaliated, "So, ironically, you were there to stage a titillating performance he couldn't actively participate in."

Juliana shrugged broad silky shoulders. "You are going to believe what you choose to believe no matter what I say."

"I'll take that as a yes. Were you well paid?"

"I was."

"I'm sure you were," Ashley chirped triumphantly.

"Is that not what I said?"

Leaning forward on his stool, Brett frowned and gallantly sought to break up the catfight. "Ladies, ladies, ladies. Ms. VanderVeen, Mr. Taihotsu's death raises speculation on issues that have come to light through a source with access to private papers of General Eisenhower."

"General MacArthur," Ashley said. "General Dwight D. Eisenhower was the commander in Europe."

"Same war," Brett said.

"It has been alleged by our sources that Saburo Taihotsu didn't in reality wage a guerrilla campaign in Hawaii during the Second World War. Our vast team of researchers is uncovering evidence that he hid out under circumstances yet unexplained, harbored by person or persons unknown, evidence that the Mongoose persona is a myth."

"I wouldn't know."

"You didn't talk about it?"

"No."

"What did you and Mr. Taihotsu talk about?" asked Ashley.

"How he liked his cheeseburger prepared."

Brett laughed.

Ashley and Juliana didn't.

Brett cleared his throat and said, "The overriding issue, of course, is the Taihotsu fortune, in the neighborhood of a hundred billion bucks by most accounts."

"A mighty fancy neighborhood, Brett," Ashley said.

"That's putting it mildly, Ashley," Brett said, then reading from a card." The eccentric Mr. Taihotsu, over a period of months as he knew death grew near, did one of two things. He sold off his companies, liquidating his assets into relatively insignificant increments, thousands and tens of thousands and hundreds of thousands of dollars and millions, converting them to cash and transferring that cash to destinations unknown. Ironically, essentially, he decimated his assets undetected. Or either he converted the assets into cash and burned it to the last yen in his Taihotsu Iron Works blast furnaces. Or some combination thereof."

"I would not know."

"Did he even hint of his plans for his vast treasure?"

"No."

"Ironically, he didn't even own the penthouse he died in. He was renting monthly," Ashley said.

"I would not know," Juliana replied.

"Cash on the barrelhead," Brett said, hoisting both eyebrows. "Or in a sense, ashes to ashes."

"The reality of the situation, the bottom line, is that you were the person who discovered him dead."

"Yes." Juliana dabbed more tears. "I went to his suite to prepare his meal. I was the only person who had permission to enter at that particular day and time."

"A meal he was incapable of eating, by all medical reports," Ashley said, raising an index finger.

"You discovered something else besides his body, didn't you, Juliana?" Brett said.

This was her cue, the raison d'être for her appearance and the fee. Juliana held up the parchment-like paper and its shaky calligraphic string of numbers.

The camera zoomed in to: 122318--------------141522.

"You found this piece of paper with him, these numerals on this unique form of stock?"

He is manipulating me from his grave. He knew I would discover it first. He must have known the petty jealousies I aroused.

"Yes."

"It had to have been a terrible shock," Ashley sympathized.

"It was."

"Don't you imagine that this mysterious document was left for you and you alone to find?"

"I do not know that it was."

"But you took it."

"I believed it was possible he left it for me."

"Why would he?"

She brushed aside a tear and shook her head.

"You didn't reveal this revelation until now, Ms. VanderVeen. Why?" Brett demanded.

Because her payment for this interview would set her up for life, you moron, she thought. Because magazines that lonely men took into the bathroom were vying to photograph her in the waitress costume; her newly hired agent said there would be a centerfold agreement soon in the mid to high six figures, in *euros*.

"I was afraid," Juliana said in a little-girl voice. "I didn't know what to do. I did not want this secret forever. It might be important."

The paper clutched in his bony hand, held so tightly in a death grip that I had to tug. His lifeless eyes following me around the room like the eyes in billboard photographs. He knew what I would do with it. It was my severance pay, Mr. Taihotsu's farewell gift.

"It certainly might be. Has anybody seen this piece of paper before you brought it to *Exclusive!!*?"

"No."

"What do the numbers mean to you, Juliana?" Brett asked solemnly.

"Nothing."

"As we speak, thanks to our exclusive report, mathematicians and cryptographers worldwide are already feverishly at work on the puzzle," Ashley said.

"For the sole benefit of *Exclusive!!* viewers," Brett added smugly. "There is the logical assumption that it's the direct route to the one hundred billion bucks."

Ashley said, "Our *Exclusive!!* researchers tell us that these numbers in their entirety could even be a childish alphanumeric code a supercomputer could crack in microseconds."

Brett frowned. "Those maddening dashes."

Ashley said, "That's right, Brett. Our research staff informed us that there are so many unknowns. Only fourteen out of twenty-six make the chances of arriving at the correct solution astronomical."

Brett nodded grimly. "And infinite too."

"Many surmise that this is the pathway to a king's ransom," Ashley said, sitting up straighter.

"Except the bridge is out," Brett said, nodding sagely.

"Wherever the pathway leads."

"King Solomon's Mines, King Midas's hoard," Brett said, "Golly, one hundred billion small bills stacked on top of each other would reach to, would reach to—high in the sky."

"One thousand one-hundred-million-dollar multi-state lotto winners. One thousand people lucky beyond comprehension," Ashley said. "Now a Taihotsu Tidbit. Where are these things coming from? They're growing on the Internet like crabgrass. One hundred billion one-dollar bills spread out side by side and end to end would encompass nearly four square miles. That's four times the area of Monaco and Vatican City combined."

"Why would anybody need to accumulate that much money?"

Brett said. "Nobody can live long enough to spend it, even Mr. Taihotsu. Obviously Mr. Taihotsu."

"Maybe it's ashes, maybe not," said Ashley, looking hard at her audience, relentlessly sincere.

"Ashes to ashes, dust to dust," Brett said.

"One hundred billion dollars, Brett. Whatever its disposition, *Exclusive!!* will ultimately learn the truth."

11.

Sarah Hilyer stayed for dinner. Carla Chance insisted. Really, it was only fair after all her help with the carrot cake. And no, it was absolutely no trouble at all. The meatloaf she'd taken out of the freezer to thaw was way, way, way too much for three people. Honestly, it was.

Following a pleasant meal with a nice merlot that Rob walked to the corner grocery for (it was too obvious even for Carla to shove Sarah out the door with him on the errand), they settled in the living room for carrot cake and coffee. Sarah had mostly watched the cake preparation, but accepted compliments on it from the men.

Again trying not to be obvious, Carla had seated Sarah and Rob across from each other at the dinner table and now on opposite ends of the sofa. She coaxed a conversation between them, though, by mentioning their professions. This seemed to elicit genuine curiosity by both.

Buster annoyed Carla by turning on the television and channel-surfing, his usual postprandial activity. "Buster."

"It's muted, Carla," he said. "I'm ambidextrous. I can socialize and check out BoobTubeLand too."

Carla beseeched the vaulted ceiling.

"Rob, you're in the TV business. What's your favorite show?" Sarah asked.

"Anything but the local news and its stock words I'll never use in speech, strike me dead by lightning if I do."

95

Sarah wondered if he was being flippant. But, no, he was quite serious. He told of his small-town odyssey, of duties in inclement weather, sketching briefly his final assignment, and his sabbatical, his Yucatán trip.

She told hers, of mathematics and teaching, briefly sketching on her sabbatical. "It'll be shorter than yours."

"I'm sorry about your mom," Rob said. "And I'm in awe of your math skills. I hit a wall in first-quarter calculus. I knew then and there I was destined for the liberal arts side of the campus."

"I hit a wall in high school algebra, me and the rest of the guys who transferred out into wood shop," Buster said.

"What stock words are you referring to?" Sarah asked.

Rob ticked them off on his fingers. "Issues. Situation. Decimate. Ironically. Allegedly. And my all-time favorite, ee-legal. Complete declarative sentences spoken by those who should never try to compose one on their own can set me on edge too. Recently, and I swear, so help me Edward R. Murrow, I listened to an anchor on cable news announce that a celebrity whose name I forget 'went ahead and died.' Then there are usages, further versus farther, and—"

"Whoa," Buster said, raising his surfing thumb at the sight of the famed Ashley Parker. A cute little anchorgirl, he thought. As cute as they came, but as tough as a barrel full of nails. "Here's the show everybody pretends to hate."

"*Exclusive!!*" Carla said. "Yuck."

"Hey, snookums, don't knock it. Ashley and that tough-sultry voice, she's like Julie London on steroids," Buster said. "The *New York Times* could learn a few things from these fine folk."

"They do make the rest of us look good," Rob said. "I knew Brett Steele in Terre Haute. He had star written all over him. It took him five minutes to be promoted to weekend anchor, and five more to weekday evenings, and five after that he was off to a larger market."

"Is he?" Carla said, then twisting her face.

"The village idiot? No. He's no Rhodes Scholar, but he isn't nearly as dense as he puts on. Viewers love to believe they're smarter than he is. He gets tons of mail and email telling him so, much of it from people who aren't smarter than he is.

"Brett's a good bowler too, which fuels that fire. He belonged to a league in Terre Haute. Brett's aware of the downscale perception and tries not to disappoint. He's a perfect foil for Ashley Parker, who is as sharp and cold and hard as she appears. She's summa cum laude from an Ivy League school. Ashley has a temper and a foul mouth too. When she goes off, you don't want to be in the firing line."

"I cannot picture that gorgeous hunk in a bowling shirt," Carla said.

Buster said, "Yeah. Shiny with the name of a tavern on the back."

"Brett has them tailored and he isn't a half-bad bowler. A two-hundred game wasn't unusual for him."

Buster said. "Hey, there he is, Daddy Warbucks, may he R.I.P."

Noting the *Confidential* magazine cover of Saburo Taihotsu and a busty starlet in pleated skirt and ponytail, Sarah said, "Speaking of what everyone loves to hate, my mother used to grouse about that scandal sheet, but she read it every week."

"So we got us a historical context here," Buster said, unmuting. "This qualifies as educationalized programming."

"Keep the sound low," Carla warned him.

Buster knew what was good for him and resisted commenting on the hot tomato on the big screen between Brett and Ashley. When they got to the part about the Dutch woman discovering Taihotsu's body, Carla said, "Turn it up a notch, please."

"Jeez, volume up, volume down," Buster muttered, complying, eyes locked on the bombshell as Ashley Parker said, "You discovered something else besides his body, didn't you, Juliana?"

Juliana held up a piece of parchment-like paper imprinted with a shaky calligraphic string of numbers.

The camera zoomed in to: 122318--------------141522.

"Rob!" Carla cried, startling Sarah.

Buster flinched. "Talk about *me* and my loud mouth, waking up the neighbors from the dead."

Rob ran to the futon room for the cryptic sheet of paper.

12.

Simultaneously, two time zones east, in a concourse lounge at Dallas–Fort Worth International Airport, Dr. and Mrs. J.D. (Wally) Stockwall awaited their connecting flight to Los Angeles and home. Wally was forcing down his fourth marginally potable Taihotsu Cellars™ 2005 Cabernet Sauvignon while absently watching a television mounted above the bar, listening with one ear open, looking at old clips of Saburo Taihotsu on a bottom-feeding talk show.

Sally Jo Stockwall sat with her husband at their tiny circular table, on her third lousy, watered-down cosmopolitan. She was curious and annoyed at her husband's goofy behavior. When they'd arrived here two days earlier, he'd suggested they lay over and visit her cousin Luann, who lived out past Arlington.

"Since we're in the neighborhood," he'd said.

"You hate Freddy Bob and Luann," she'd said. "You celebrated when Luann eloped with him and moved here to be near his family and far from us. You cracked jokes about inbreeding on his side of the family. You said going to their 'hillbilly outpost' was like going to an Arkansas family reunion."

"When are you ever going to understand my sense of humor, Sal? I wanted this side trip for you."

"I never wished Freddy Bob on Luann, even though she asked for it. Leaving a nice apartment and good admin assistant job to move out in the sticks with a bozo who works on oil rigs when he feels like it."

"Didn't I make nice?"

Sally Jo Stockwall looked at him, further mystified. She was a former dairy princess from Washington State, with thick hips and a hardened baby face. Sally Jo had gone off to college to escape the farm and to snag a professional man. As her catch sat heavily across from her, a milking barn did not seem like such a horrible place.

Sally Jo didn't much care for her cousin, either. Nor their kids who incessantly picked their noses and did look and act as if they *were* inbred. But she refused to give Wally the satisfaction of admitting so.

"Didn't you also say that Freddy Bob was a white-trash poster boy and that Luann was made for the lifestyle and as a stock-car racing groupie passed around by tobacco-chewing pit crews?"

"It takes all kinds," Dr. Stockwall had said generously. "I had a grand time with them. It's broadening, you know, to interact with people of a different socioeconomic and educational level."

What I was doing was stalling for time with those simpletons, Wally thought as he continued gazing over Sally Jo's shoulder at the tube, at a trio of aesthetically perfect Homo sapiens.

If Jerome (Chicken) Little, Western States Regional vice president and debt counselor for the nameless Las Vegas–based lending institution led by a Sicilian ruffian who went by "Smith," wasn't already at the clinic menacing Janine, his assistant, who was holding down the fort, he soon would be. If she was still there, that is. Janine was his third—no—fourth assistant he'd gone through in the past year.

Wanna know why the Chicken? Cuz if you welsh on me and Mr. Smith, my boss, when I'm fucking done, you'll look like the sky's fallen on you.

"Wally, what's wrong? You look like you're going to throw up."

Wally was staring at the blonde Amazon superimposed on the screen between the two gorgeous ninnies. In equal parts she titillated and frightened him.

"Wally. Wally?"

The Amazon held a piece of paper in front of her flawless breasts. The camera zoomed in on the paper: 122318-------------- 141522.

Those numbers? He'd caught enough of their blathering to know that a numerical enigma was perhaps a key to old Saburo's vault. That unfriendly Oriental half-caste on the plane from Cancun. The bizarre blonde. Those numbers.

Was the rich old bastard leaving behind a clue for that ex–television news reporter? If so, why?

The napkins upon which he had copied Blondie's number puzzle?

Wally patted himself. Was he wearing the same jacket? *Yes.* Fumbling, pulling out a napkin. Just one of them, goddamnit. The other probably left on his tray. He unfolded the napkin.

Five guzzled glasses was enough wine for Mr. Vino Connoisseur, thank you very much, thought Sally Jo as she observed the frantic activity. When Wally had half a bag on, he'd zone out like this, a million miles away. Now scratching and pawing at himself like he had fleas, the slob. Reading scribbling on a funky old napkin. You couldn't get the man to clean out his pockets. She couldn't count the times she'd miss a well-used facial tissue and run it through the washing machine, making a hellacious mess, her mess to clean up.

"Earth to Wally, what the hell is wrong now? What do you have there?"

Wally read: 1223182392211

In his head, he added: 1223182392211------141522

Think, dammit! He had the first fourteen and the final six, lacking only six instead of the rest of the world's fourteen. The implication was that it represented the key to a fortune that rendered King Solomon's Mines a child's piggybank in comparison.

"Nothing, lovie pie. Absolutely nothing. A patient's phone number is all," he said, pocketing the napkin, aware that'd he'd have to be careful with it, given Sal's penchant for snooping through his pockets too when checking his skivvies for suspicious stains. "As a matter of fact, everything is so right, how would you like a bonus, a fitting end to our junket?"

"What?" Sally Jo said suspiciously.

"Las Vegas," he said, thinking how Sal adored the slots, despite pathetic luck. She had never won as much as a piddling jackpot. When she pulled the lever, the machines became as tight and cold as their player.

"Vegas. An early anniversary present, my love."

Vegas.

The word left Sally Jo Stockwall speechless.

13.

"Nature abhors a coincidence," said Buster Hightower.

"Whatever that means, you're right," said Carla Chance.

They retired to the Chance-Hightower breakfast bar separating the kitchen and dining room with Rob's card and their coffee. Buster brought a bottle of bourbon from a cupboard.

"In lieu of cream and sugar," he said "On account of these new developments."

Nobody objected.

"Henceforth, hereinafter, from this time on, from this moment forward, this card isn't mine. It's ours," Rob said, waving it, looking at his companions.

"No."

"Yes, Aunt Carla. Yes. No argument. Sarah?"

"No."

"If we're in, you're in. You're our mathematical genius, dear," Carla said. "You've been placed here for a reason."

Two reasons now, Buster resisted saying.

Rob gave Sarah the card to study.

She pushed it away. "Carla—"

"You know too much," Carla said, patting her forearm. "Either you're in or we'll have to kill you."

Carla went to the hutch and brought out an accordion folder. She got out a blank genealogical worksheet, and the notes and printouts she already had on Rob. "Let us see what we know about you, young man, and what we don't."

Buster ceremoniously sweetened the cups, raised his in toast, and cried, "To the Four Musketeers."

Carla shushed him. "Please keep your voice down. The insulation in these units is so good we sometimes forget we have neighbors just a foot away, neighbors we rarely see. The Newmans on the other side work graveyard at Boeing and sleep much of the day. Grimes on this side is a hermit. In the ten years I've lived here, I've seen Grimes perhaps three times. He was smashed each time. We think he's an early retiree, Grimes. Carpal tunnel or something like that, but he looks healthy enough. Our closest contact with him is a letter he wrote to the homeowner's association complaining about Buster's door-slamming."

"The Four Mouseketeers," Buster whispered.

"I'm an outsider," Sarah protested again.

"You're family from now on, dear," Carla said.

"Like Carla said, you're our mathematicalized wizard," Buster said.

"Absolutely," Carla affirmed, then looking at Rob, "you're in if the principal in this still agrees."

Rob raised his hand. "Aye to Sarah. Aye to the Four Mouseketeers."

"I have an M.S. in math. Albert Einstein I'm not, guys."

Carla smiled and squeezed her arm. "You know too much, dear. Either you're in or we really will have to kill you."

"The principal agrees, whatever *this* is," Rob said. "If I've been anointed, I sure could use the company. Absolutely positively, Sarah. It could be a four-way split of nothing. But if everybody's willing?"

Sarah nodded her assent. Anyone with bills like hers would be a fool not to be. This was a long, long shot, but if it paid off, there'd be ample money to go around.

Buster raised his cup. "I am, and I solemnly swear, I'll be as quiet as a titmouse while you brainiacs do your work."

Cups clinked.

Carla rearranged her paperwork. "You kids get on with the 'how' while I try to figure out the 'who' and 'why.' "

The community college mathematics instructor had been looking above Carla's head at the playing-card eyeball of a Picasso cubist work. The painting provided no inspiration.

She frowned at the card. "That there are twenty-six numerals and that the twelve numerals on the card on television were separated by fourteen dashes may be a teaser that it's a simple alphanumeric puzzle, as intimated on that tabloid program. It may be relatively simple to solve. Rob, you have the complete array, but there are millions and millions of permutations and combinations to complete the array that woman was holding."

"So the important question may not be mathematical, Rob," Carla said.

"It could be a tracking number on a package," Buster said. "Or it could be you need a decoder ring that came out of a box of cereal, 1955 vintage."

"That's a bit too easy. Rob, obviously the key is who you are to Saburo Taihotsu," Carla said. "You have to have some link to him."

"Yeah. Whip your family tree on us," Buster said.

Rob Weather shrugged. "As far as I know, it's a skinny little tree with shallow roots and not many branches.

"Some of this is a repetition of what I told you in the car, Uncle Buster. My mother and father are, were, Sugar Chance Blanchard and Richard (Dick) Weather. They married in 1971, five months before I was born. I wasn't a preemie. I was an only child and am an only adult. I came late in their lives. They were well into their thirties.

"My father had three siblings, my mother none. My folks died in Hawaii in 1991 in a car crash. My dad was driving too

105

fast and missed a curve. I was eighteen then, in my sophomore year at the University of Hawaii.

"Both had drinking problems, especially him. Hers was primarily because of him. I loved my mother. My father was a horse's ass and a leech and a lech. Neither Mom nor I could ever do anything right. I don't know why she stayed. Maybe for my sake, the nuclear family and all that.

"I think he was unemployed at the end. My mom, on the other hand, was great. She worked as an accountant. Had almost twenty years in at the same firm when they were killed."

"Did your father's family have anything to do with Japan?" Carla asked.

"Not that I know of. My parents met when he was stationed in Hawaii in the Army. My mother, yes. She was born there. Her mother, Marie Chance Blanchard, died when Mom was small. Cancer, I think. I have scant knowledge of her. Her parents were Robert and Pauline Chance, our connection, Aunt Carla."

"Rob's great-grandmother Pauline was second cousin to my grandfather, Clyde Chance," Carla said.

Rob said, "My mother had a small framed photo of Grandmother Marie on her bedroom dresser. It sticks in my mind because of the frame. It was ornate and she told me that it was sterling silver. I recall more of it than Marie, other than that she was a big blonde woman."

Buster sweetened his coffee with more bourbon. He offered it to Rob who shook his head, then on second thought nodded, yes, please.

"What do you know of Grandmother Marie?"

"Not a lot. I never saw a birth certificate. I don't remember how old I was when I first inquired or why, but the answer was always vague and evasive, which kept me asking. I thought it was odd until I was older. I'm certain the reason was that my mother was illegitimate. There was a stigma then."

"Marie Blanchard and your blond hair," Buster said.

Rob smiled. "They say it seldom happens, that I'm an ir-regularity. An anomaly."

Carla looked at Sarah looking at his hair. She wasn't looking at it as if he were a freak.

"What else do you know of your Gramma, Rob? Really know," Buster said.

"She passed away when Mom was young. If Mom knew anything about her father, other than the obvious, that he was Japanese, she never said."

"At the end of World War II or shortly afterward, that'd be a big no-no, wouldn't it?" Buster said.

"It definitely would be, as big or bigger than illegitimacy, particularly on Hawaii where Mom was born and lived till her mom died and she was taken to the mainland to be brought up by members of a church group. She moved back to Hawaii as a teen."

"If her father was Japanese and living in the land of Pearl Harbor, he'd be interned, wouldn't he? A helluva thing to do to Japanese-Americans, but it was done," Buster said.

"A male of Japanese origin whose identity is unknown," Carla said.

Sarah looked up from the card. "Rob, which Hawaiian island did your grandmother and mother live on?"

"Kauai."

"And you received this—unique card," Carla said, after a deep breath. "Have a look at this. Some of the dates are guesses."

"Yikes," Buster said.

"Speculative," Rob said. "We're thinking the improbably im-possible."

"Which is a double negative, which therefore ain't impos-sible," Buster said. "Less impossible, I bet, than the recovery of

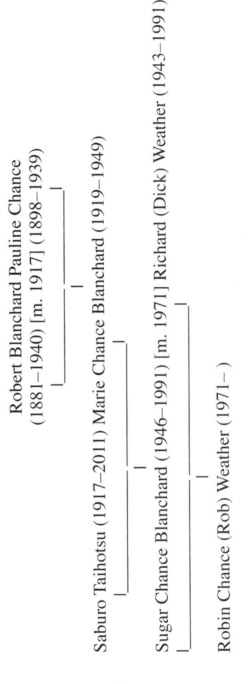

an heirloom Cadillac."

"Once upon a time, I wanted to be an investigative reporter. I'd better give it a serious fling, the subject being myself."

Carla said, "Refresh me. Who else has seen the card?"

"As I said, just Phil and that overbearing guy on the plane. The chiropractor or proctologist."

"Need we be concerned about them?"

"No. I'm sure it's forgotten. Phil had other things on his mind and the guy on the plane was just doodling."

Another glance at the Picasso and Sarah was thinking, well, perhaps geometry. It was a branch of mathematics. Shapes, angles, points, lines. Could the twenty-six numbers be coordinates?

"Sarah?" Carla said.

"Excuse me?"

"What are you thinking?"

"That I'll need an extra pad and pen."

14.

Dr. J.D. (Wally) Stockwall stood at the entrance of the storied Flamingo Las Vegas, punching numbers into his cell phone. He had sent Mrs. Sally Jo Stockwall into its vast slot machine parlor, bankrolling her with a stake that would buy the equivalent of three rolls of quarters.

He told her that while she was gaming he was going to call a couple of adult patients who had moved to this city, see how they were doing, perhaps join them for a drink if convenient, and he'd see her later.

"Contact with these patients will permit us to write off this stopover as a business expense," he'd explained.

As Sally Jo faded into the maelstrom of *chinka-chinka-ding-ding* and pulsating lights, muttering about the last of the big spenders, Wally stammered into the phone, "It's me, Dr. Stockwall. I'm here, Mr. Little."

"Where's here?"

"In Las Vegas. Nevada. Downstairs."

"Where the fuck is downstairs? You got the Strip. You got Downtown. There's downstairs all over the fucking place."

"Downstairs here at the Flamingo casino, sir."

"How come?"

"To do the right thing by you and Mr. Smith."

"Don't move a muscle. Don't even fucking twitch."

In minutes, the most frightening creature he had ever seen was facing him, no less menacing than previously.

"This better fucking be good," said Jerome (Chicken) Little. "You went and saved me a trip to go on out to La La Land and go see you. What's the catch? What's your angle?"

It took Wally a moment to compose himself. Chicken Little was a head taller than the orthodontist. He was pear-shaped and thirtyish, with bloodshot eyes, a weak chin, and a scalp bristling with cowlicks. He smelled of perspiration and fast food. This primordial beast could be a storybook bogeyman concocted to horrify children.

Wally cleared his throat and told the Western States Regional Vice-President and Debt Counselor, "I shall come to the point. You, sir, of course, are aware of the demise of the world's richest man, Saburo Taihotsu, and that cryptic card with those numbers. Interrupted digits, as it were. That enigmatic gap in the center and all it implies."

Little was underwhelmed. Digging in an ear, he said, "How long we gonna stand here with our thumb up our ass waiting for you to tell me what I don't already fucking know?"

Wally withdrew the napkin from his shirt pocket and handed it to Little, who perused the 1223182392211.

Then a slip of paper on which he had written:
122318 - - - - - - - - - - - - - 141522
1223182392211 - - - - - - 141522

"So what's this gotta do with the price of tea in China? I ain't got all day to play some silly fucking game, Dentist. Me and Mr. Smith, we got us a busy agenda."

Wally flinched at mention of the mysterious and ominous godfather, the pseudonymous Mr. Smith. He managed to tell his story of acquiring the numbers from an airline seatmate. "With the last six of the twenty-six publicly revealed, I have twenty. I assure you that they are valid. I'm confident that considerably increases the mathematical probabilities of solving the puzzle."

"I read the papers. You think I can't read?"

"Oh, no no, of course not," Wally lied.

"How do I know you ain't blowing smoke up my dirt chute? How do I know you didn't just go and wrote them numbers down out of the clear blue sky? You tell me your angle now, what you want, is what you are fucking gonna go and do. Mr. Smith, he don't have no patience with con jobs and he's heard 'em all."

"Well, since I hypothetically have the key to one hundred billion dollars, I think my forthrightness, my willingness to include you and Mr. Smith in—"

"Bottom line, fuckstick."

"Forgiveness of my debt and a modest percentage of the manna when the number array leads us to the promised land. Us and our significant edge in the process."

"I ain't no arithmetic genius, but what you got, Dentist, these numbers, even if they're legit and mean what you say they mean, they got a hole in it with them dashes. Small hole, big hole. So long's it's a hole, it's worthless as a month-old dog turd."

"I know who the possessor of the *entire* twenty-six numbers is. I don't know his name, but with what I do know of his recent background and his peculiar ethnicity, he should be easy to trace."

"This ain't no home equity loan you took out. You're in arrears, which makes you a welshing, cheatin' dickhead. Mr. Smith, he don't put up with no arrears. Mr. Smith, he gets his money."

The shortsighted cretin, Wally thought. "I know, I know. I am not a masochist. I wouldn't be here unless I was absolutely sincere, willing to square things. As I said, to do the right thing."

Little said that it was time to get Mr. Smith involved and that they fucking well ought not be wasting his time as he's a busy man. He withdrew a cell phone, turned his back on Wally, had a brief conversation, then led Wally to the elevator.

As they ascended, Little studied the client, attempting to read him and the seeming absurdity of his proposal.

He thought of Ambrose Bierce on absurdity: A statement of belief manifestly inconsistent with one's own opinion.

Jerome Little's Neanderthal demeanor was an act. He was a grad student, not a barbaric thug. Since his job entailed such an erratic schedule, Jerome was currently enrolled in online courses, in quest of a Ph.D. in English at UNLV. His dissertation on Ambrose Bierce, *Ambrose Gwinett Bierce; How the Man and His Acidulous Humor Bridged Two Centuries,* was proceeding nicely and it had been praised by his advisor.

Jerome Little had yearned to teach at the community college level after finishing his M.A., but was never invited back for a second interview. He knew why. It was obvious. It was one thing to motivate the drones in English 101 sections by carrot and stick, and quite another to terrify them into catatonia by his countenance. Jerome continued his doctoral work because he liked the academic regimen and for reasons of vanity, to be a "Doctor" like many of his financially damaged clients.

So Chicken Little he became, capitalizing on his mien and his undergrad drama classes. "Chicken" was an inspiration, a fitting capper to his vocational image. Jerome had to admit that morphing the fairy tale was a masterstroke. However, the role did not come without sacrifices.

Jerome required enhancements, though he did not enjoy eschewing deodorant and making frequent trips to a salon to sculpt his hair into cowlicks. His teeth were not perfect to begin with, but he'd had them yellowed, a coating applied as if they were being whitened. In order to maintain weight, his diet was gross. Oh how he missed a simple luncheon of green salad rich with arugula and bean sprouts and an olive oil vinaigrette, accompanied by a glass of chardonnay! And the eye drops—don't even go there.

They call me Chicken cuz when I'm fucking done, you'll look like the sky's fallen on you.

How delightfully effective. That and his absurd B-movie gangster manners, replete with malapropos and all manner of atrocities committed against his beloved English language.

Not once had he been compelled to resort to physical violence. His high-risk clients were as well educated as he and then some. Jerome Little was a niche lender. He did not seek the middle-class credit card abuser and the degenerate gambler. Leave that flotsam to the payday loan establishments, thank you very much.

Professional people were less fearful of a knuckle sandwich than they were of exposure, subsequent humiliation, and possible loss of credentials. Nothing alarmed an ophthalmologist or patent attorney or senior technology researcher or bond analyst more than the prospect of having his ticket pulled. Consequently, collection methods could stretch the envelope. There was minimal danger of complaints to consumer protection agencies or law enforcement. Most of their clients had assets they secreted from ex-wives and the IRS, so collection percentages were high.

Jerome was generously compensated by the activity. He lived comfortably and easily financed grad school. Jerome's drama background came into play again as he observed his elevator companion. He trusted his acumen at discerning truth from script.

As the cliché went, the orthodontist was sweating bullets. How useful this information was remained to be seen, but Dr. Stockwall was being honest with him. Desperate and honest. The man stank of fear, of insolvency. Five percent of their clients were mistakes. He feared that Stockwall fit in that category.

The elevator stopped. Jerome got out and, with an unintelligible grunt, directed Dr. Stockwall to follow.

Wally obeyed. A third-grade dropout, he thought morosely. My life is in the hands of this congenital idiot.

Little tapped on a door, which opened by itself to a hallway and a golden retriever.

"Wayne," Little said, making a kissing noise like a plumber's helper in action. "Wayne, he got hisself this little button on the wall over by the closet."

"He answered?" Wally said.

"Yeah. She knows my knock."

The tail-wagging animal led the way into a spacious living room, onto carpeting deeper than a lawn overdue for mowing, all-leather furniture, and a floor-to-ceiling window. A high-high-roller suite.

A man in stocking feet came out of an adjoining room. He had an unlit pipe in his mouth and wore a cardigan sweater. He was a dead ringer for *Leave it to Beaver*'s Ward Cleaver.

"Mr. Smith, sir," Little said. "This here's that client we been talkin' about what got hisself in a financial bind and in the hole to us and making me need to go out to see. Mr. Jiminy C. Smith, president and CEO of us guys, meet Dr. Wally Stock-wall, a man with a problem and a way out, so he claims."

"Dr. Stockwall, a pleasure. Please have a seat," Mr. Smith said, gesturing to a sofa.

Wally sat, on the ragged edge of wetting his pants. Little stood alongside him.

Mr. Smith smiled and said, "You were anticipating Don Vito or Tony S., Doctor?"

"Uh, er, well."

"I am disappointed. Such insipid stereotyping."

"I, uh."

Mr. Jiminy C. Smith raised a hand. "No matter. You are only human."

Mr. Smith whistled. Wayne brought his slippers. Smith petted the dog's head, put them on, and said, "Care to guess what my middle initial stands for, Doctor?"

Wally did not want to guess. To guess the obvious would be to utter a bad joke. He shook his head.

"I like to get my unusual name and a sketchy bio covered at the outset of a business relationship. It seems less sinister hearing it from me rather than through the grapevine.

"My birth name is Jiminy Cricket Smith. I was born and raised in Los Angeles, California. My parents were an idiosyncratic mélange of hippie and entertainment industry striver, a schizophrenic combination that proved moderately successful. When I was in my teens, they died in inexplicable circumstances, in our garage, in the front seat of our ultra-classic 1954 Mercedes 300SL, the incomparable gullwing design. The engine was running and a hose connected to the exhaust pipe ran into the cockpit.

"The coroner's report was inconclusive. The Smiths may have done themselves in or they may have been zonked, passed out in the car after an evening of partying, giving a third party an opportunity.

"The gendarmes and the news media put a full-court press on callow Jiminy. He was alleged to be unstable and free-floating resentful. That the lad's mortifying middle name was coined in a haze of parental marijuana smoke was the least of his issues. A 'seething time bomb,' wrote one columnist."

Smith paused to scratch Wayne's jowls. "All the king's horses and all the king's men would not come up with enough evidence to go forward on an indictment. The ruling was double suicide.

"Gosh, Jiminy C. Smith, alleged 'seething time bomb,' was not really and truly so abnormal. If he were filling out a singles questionnaire on likes, heck, he'd say butterscotch sundaes, midnight walks on the Strip, and nudie movies of Eva Braun.

"The Führer hated her doing them, you know. He was a prudish chap, with no bad habits save for tens of millions of violent deaths and genocidal murders. I have the complete collection of the films and regard them in equal parts prurient and wholesome-outdoorsy. Is that so deviant, Dr. Stockwall?"

Wally gulped. "No. Oh, no. No, sir."

"Anyway, when he was orphaned, Jiminy C. Smith inherited a small bundle. He drifted a bit, geographically and emotionally. Before his remittance was completely depleted, he visited Las Vegas, his foolish intent to recoup his funds.

"He became mesmerized by the impulsive behavior that swept across all demographic boundaries. Instead of participating sheep-like, he analyzed the behavior and had an epiphany. A vision.

"The unfulfilled demand for assistance to professionals in financial doo-doo was stunning. Education and sophistication does not render one immune from chasing an inside straight. It was not only those who frittered money away at roulette tables. These proud and conceited people would not lower themselves to seek help from a conventional lending institution, especially since they knew that they likely would be turned down. Alas, the unbearable shame.

"He filled a need, a discreet source. His funds were available immediately, sans formalities. There would be no paper trail. The organization grew. Jiminy C. Smith turned that small bundle into a large bundle. This demi-suite is our national headquarters, as it were.

"Enough on me and my entrepreneurship, Doctor. What do you bring? If not delinquent payments, what, please?"

Trembling, Wally repeated what he had told Chicken Little downstairs.

Smith said, "What you intimate, sir, is spectacular beyond comprehension. One hundred billion dollars is not loose change gleaned under davenport cushions."

"No, sir," Wally said. "It is not."

Smith paused again and sucked on his unlit pipe. He gestured behind Wally, to a wall recess the dimensions of a large fireplace. "Lest I grow too big for my britches, I have set aside a daily time of humility and reflection. Feast your eyes, Doctor. I pale in comparison."

Smith walked to the alcove and knelt on both knees. Wayne went to him and sat at his side, softly whimpering. Little accompanied Dr. Stockwall.

Hung on the wall were black-and-white photographs of a natty, handsome man in his thirties. The largest depicted him in a checked suit jacket, looking sidelong, cigar in mouth, mischief on his mind.

"Wayne is intimidated, is he not? He recognizes the power of Benjamin Hymen Siegelbaum, better known as Ben Siegel, and better yet by that ghastly epithet, Bugsy."

There were candles on a dais of sorts. Smith lit them, saying, "Benjamin Hymen founded Las Vegas as we know it. He designed and built the original Flamingo. Benjamin Hymen died for his sins. In the vernacular, he was 'whacked' for skimming the Flamingo's construction costs. Good lord, he was a gangster. What did they expect?

"Benjamin Hymen died for *our* sins, past, present, and future. He died for creating a Las Vegas that has permitted, is permitting, and will permit into all eternity the rube from Dubuque and Fargo to jet here and sin in virtually any manner that meets his corn-fed fancy.

"Our hotel management erected a tribute to Benjamin Hymen in the garden for public viewing, but it is pathetically inadequate. He deserves far more, here at ground zero of the Las Vegas we know and love-hate."

When Smith bowed his head, Chicken Little patted Wally's

shoulder, which was akin to dropping a concrete block on it, and winked at him. The pudgy, catatonic dentist impressed Little. Men of greater physicality and integrity and resolve had wilted in tears at the conclusion of Mr. Smith's autobiographical outpouring and the Siegel shrine, the psychotic icing on the cake.

Mr. Smith's third-person narrative always augmented the dread, Little knew. They came expecting John Gotti and got instead a 1950s sitcom apparition who sounded like a game show host. Chicken saw the orthodontist squeeze his knees together.

Smith rose, inhaled his cold tobaccoless pipe, and faced Wally. "You also alluded to an individual who is a custodian of the magic string in toto. Now, sir, by gosh, by golly, we need to hear your complete story, our pathway to that pot of gold. While we check it out, we are delighted to comp you and your little woman with a per diem and gambling allowance. Keep in mind the words of the cartoon Jiminy, 'I'm no fool, no sirree.' "

Ambrose Bierce's quotation on money came to mind: *Money, a blessing that is of no advantage to us excepting when we part with it.*

Thinking that they were prisoners without bars, Wally began. Thanks to an overdose of adrenaline, he had total recall of the encounter with Blondie. Several times, when the spoken word eroded into babbling, Smith had to halt Wally and ask him to please slow down. Wally withheld only Blondie's last name and his destination, a community near Seattle named Kent where his aunt lived.

Information in reserve was a potential bargaining chip.

It was something to run with.

It could save his life.

Downstairs on the casino floor, Sally Jo Stockwall was having a blast. A jackpot on a quarter machine encouraged her to move to the dollar machines. A jackpot on a dollar machine sent her to five-dollar machines that were also compliant.

Whatever the hell Wally was doing that was taking so goddamned long, he could just stay there. Her fabulous luck would be her little secret.

15.

Unable to get Rob's airplane seatmate out of his noggin, Buster said, "I have a logically pathological fear of dentistry, Rob. You can't depend on this periodontalitic seatmate of yours to forget and ignore your chitchat on the plane. Dentists of any breed, if that's what he is, they ain't that dependable. They never forget to send their bill. Chiropractors, I can't vouch for them either way."

"As Buster likes to say," Carla Chance told Sarah and Rob, "getting him to a dentist is like pulling teeth."

Buster said, "Rob, you need to be—whadduyacall the buzzwords?—preemptivated and proactive. This story on the numbers is getting harder and harder to avoid. It's every headline, on TV news and in the papers. Our boy on the plane who scribbled them down has probably seen it and put two and two together, equaling $100 billion. With the help of your old buddy Brett, everybody in the world's gonna know soon."

"Proactive how?" Rob said.

Sarah looked up from a tablet filled with numbers and filled the silence. "I'm sorry, but I must repeat, where am I in all this? Four Mouseketeers vow or not, I do feel like I'm intruding in a family matter."

"Sarah," Rob said. "It's not like we're triplets and you're an outsider. I'm maybe the great grandson of Aunt Carla's second cousin. Maybe."

"Yeah," Buster said. "Me and Carla living in sin without

benefit of clergy, that makes me an eleventh shirttail cousin, umpteenth removed."

Carla squeezed Sarah's wrist. "Dear, you are absolutely invaluable."

"Indispensable," Rob said.

Carla said, "You're our Bletchley Park code breaker."

"Some code breaker I am," she said, tearing off and wadding the top sheet.

"Proactive how?" Rob asked again.

"The proctologist on the plane might not remember the numbers, but he sure as hell remembers you, no offense," Buster said, looking at Rob's hair.

"I don't think I gave him my last name," Rob said.

"You aren't certain?" Carla asked.

"No."

"Don't you ordinarily introduce yourself with both names?"

"Yeah. I do."

"It's makeover time," Carla said.

"Aunt Carla," he pleaded.

Carla held thumb and forefinger a hair apart. "Young man, you're this far from becoming famous. And/or infamous. Lose your vanity. That gorgeous mop is your trademark."

Rob nodded meekly.

"Let me. I did Mother's hair in the past few years," Sarah said. "I'll try not to be the beautician from hell."

Buster was dispatched to a twenty-four-hour drugstore with a list: flat-lens glasses, clippers, scissors, and hazardous hair chemicals.

"The good news is," he said to Rob upon his return, "I couldn't find a Botox kit."

In a chair in the kitchen, towel around his neck, Sarah asked, "Buzz cut or just shorter, sir?"

"Just a *little* shorter. Please. You know, with the dye job next, as Aunt Carla ordered, you're doing what no news director could make me do."

"Not us, Rob," Carla said. "Whoever placed that card in your possession and whoever else knows you have it is making us do it."

Sarah plugged in the clippers. She saw no boy-girl twinkle in Carla's eyes. This project was about preservation.

"Sigh," Rob said, as she started on the back. "Heavy sigh."

Rob got out his laptop and dusted it off. The Taihotsu Cerebrum 1500™ was so old it had a floppy drive.

"It's pre-Columbian, my gold watch from the last station. Account execs used them," Rob said. "They were trading them in on new models anyway, getting zip, so I grabbed one on the way out the door. It comes with a wireless card that's still on their billing, which I seldom use. It got lost between the cracks, but I don't want to alert anybody by using it too often, surfing. They screwed me out of a week's pay, so we're even."

It had been Carla's idea to put the laptop on his lap to keep him occupied, so he didn't think too much during the makeover, so he wouldn't, as she said, "Regard the snipping of each individual strand as an amputation."

On Sarah's instructions, Rob typed the twenty-six numbers and separated them with slashes: 1/22/3/18/23/9/22/11/12/23/13/6/14/15/2/2

He winced theatrically as golden tresses fell to the floor. As she snipped, she mentally calculated the tonnage of $100,000,000,000 in gold at $800 per troy ounce: roughly 1,000,000 pounds.

Gold fever, she thought. The last thing these people needed.

If it wasn't a Taihotsu Tidbit yet, it would be.

Then Sarah asked him to change the numbers to match the letter in alphabetical sequence.

A/V/C/R/W/I/V/K/L/W/M/F/N/O/B/B

And then—

AVCRWIVKLWMFNOBB

"Nothing?" she asked. "No word recognition? Abbreviations? Anything?"

Nobody replied.

Then she had Rob separate the numbers thusly:

1/2/23/1/823/9221/1/1/2/2/31/3/6141/5/2/2.

"First time in my life I ever saw a laptop sitting on a laptop, used as a laptop," said the computerphobic comic. "Carla has one of the wretched gizmos too. It sits on her desk where it belongs if you insist on having one of the things."

"We got nowhere with a simple alphanumeric approach," Sarah said. "What we're doing now is breaking it down in numbers between one and twenty-six, arbitrarily in groupings that are prime numbers. Prime numbers are important in cryptography."

"Makes sense to me," Buster said.

Carla said, "I don't know what a prime number is either, Sarah."

"A prime number is a whole number that can't be divided evenly except by the number itself or the number one. One, two, three, five, eleven and thirteen are prime numbers."

"Why are they important?"

"I don't know if they are," Sarah said. "I suspect that the code writer's base or key is more complicated than progressive alphanumeric. Oh damn, 6141 isn't a prime. Three into 6141 is 2047."

Yikes, Buster thought. She did it in her head.

"This could be maddeningly complex," Sarah said. "You mentioned Bletchley Park, Carla. In World War II, the Germans sent coded messages on their Enigma machines, which were keyboards linked to scrambling units.

"Enigma had three or four rotors, each containing twenty-six letters. The position of the rotors was changed daily, completely changing the codes. There were one-hundred-fifty-nine trillion combinations on the four-rotor Enigma."

"So there could be three or four other pages like Rob's," Carla said.

"I'm afraid so. Much more than our laptop can process even if we had computational software for the other pages. Rob, I'll comb in the color and we're done."

No hurry, Rob thought. If he didn't like the hairstyling deed, he liked Sarah's proximity, her hands on his scalp. Aunt Carla's Cupid's arrow had winged him.

He said, "Once upon a time, I kind of sort of used a laptop on an assignment for a week."

"Kind of sort of used?" Carla said.

"Kinda sorta out there in blizzards and tornadoes?" Buster said.

"No. Strictly as a prop. I got to be a studio reporter for a week while somebody was on vacation. We sat and stood in front of laptops and did our pieces as if we were taking news right from the machines. They weren't even turned on."

"You're making me into a cynic," said Buster.

"Ratings had been falling. They thought they had the perfect gimmick. Ratings did not improve. They fell a point or three. There were other cynics out there in the viewing audience, Uncle Buster. The laptops went bye-bye with the news director. I was tossed over the side with him."

"I'll bet you were good at what you did," Sarah said. "There will be news jobs if you want to get back into it."

"Thanks. I was good. I avoided clichés like the plague."

After laughter, Sarah said, "Let me have this for a minute. Let's take a different tack."

She put the laptop on the counter and typed: $x^n + y^n = z^n$.

"Where x, y and z is a Pythagorean set, most commonly three, four and five, and n is greater than two, it supposedly couldn't be solved. It's called Fermat's Last Theorem, named for Pierre de Fermat, a seventeenth-century French mathematician. His proof, should it have existed, died with him. Mathematicians have been trying to duplicate it for centuries. But about fifteen years ago, an Englishman finally did."

"Pierre Ferment's probably dead," Buster said. "He can't help us."

"Besides unsuccessfully hunting for Pythagorean sets, I'm searching for friendly numbers. For instance, 220 and 284 are friendly numbers. That's because the divisors of 284 are 1, 2, 4, 71 and 142. They add up to 220. It works vice versa. Correct me if I'm wrong. One, 2, 4, 5, 10, 11, 20, 22, 44, 55 and 110 tally up to 284.

"Only zero is lacking in the twenty-six on the paper. The absence of zeroes might mean the absence of spacing between the numerals, indicating the complete array is a single entity that must be dealt with as such, as opposed to our presumed separation.

"The number twenty-six is unique in another way. De Fermat noted that it's between twenty-five and twenty-seven, a square and a cube. Twenty-five is 5^2. Twenty-seven is 3^3. He proved that no other number is sandwiched between a square and a cube. Twenty-six could be the key."

"Twenty-six, it could be a bucketful of red herrings stinking up a fish market," Buster said.

"Very true," Sarah said. "Perfect numbers are a possibility. A perfect number equals the sum of its divisors. Six can be divided by one, two and three. Twenty-eight is another. One plus two plus four plus seven plus fourteen equals twenty-eight. Twenty-eight isn't in the array, but all the others are."

"Like friendly numbers that got perfected," Buster said.

"Not bad," Sarah said.

Buster said, "So you weren't wasting ink, huh?"

"Just thinking out loud on paper," she said, examining the bottle of Taihotsu Daz™ hair color rinse.

"If this thing's so all-fired complicated, how come Rob here got twenty-six and the rest of the world got twelve? A fourteen-digit head start on mathematicians and puzzle nerds and computers. And if the dough's burned up, there ain't nothing left except ashes," Buster said. "If you ask me, a decoder ring's still the way to go. If we only had three box tops from 1956-model corn flakes and a buck, we'd be all set."

Everyone stared blankly at him.

"Just thinking out loud," Buster said.

After Rob's makeover, they watched more Saburo Taihotsu, channel-surfing through hastily cobbled retrospectives to endless analyses of the Dutchwoman's discovery to speculative sound bites on the missing megafortune.

Photos of the deceased, the youthful fighter pilot strapped into the cockpit of his Zero, canopy back, steely resolve in his eyes. The Mongoose, the solitary guerrilla fighter. The rising industrialist behind a desk, pen in hand. Newspaper headlines and statistics on the ever-rising fortunes of the Taihotsu empire as he gradually burrowed into reclusion. Clips of blast furnaces, the wide-eyed smarminess on how he conceivably, allegedly, possibly Took It With Him. There were no revelations, no insights, no meaty updates.

Carla, Sarah and Buster could not help stealing glances at the transformed Rob, seeking hints of Saburo Taihotsu.

Rob caught them and smiled, "Genes or chromosomes or a mailman. Whichever, my blond hair leapfrogged a generation. Give it up, guys. Unless you can tell me who I am."

Buster said, "Besides tracing Rob's ancestors and deciphering the card, what's our game plan?"

Nobody had the foggiest.

"DNA," Carla said.

"My folks were cremated. There's nobody else but Aunt Carla."

"Taihotsu's DNA would settle it," Carla said. "But forget that. One of the stories was that he demanded a speedy cremation, perhaps already done."

Then what, Rob thought? If the card was a direct path to the money, if the money had not gone into blast furnaces, neither a sure thing, did it mean that $100 billion was his? It was incomprehensible.

I'm Rob's only known living relative and therefore second in line, Carla wondered. Did that mean I was an heiress of sorts? It was unfathomable.

In a flush of guilt, Sarah, still feeling like much the outsider, once more thought of unpaid bills on her mother. Above all, co-incidence had brought her to this table. It was inconceivable.

Okay, bottom line, if a chunk of 100,000,000,000 smackers landed in my lap, Buster thought, would it add longevity to my sixty years? Unflippinglikely.

OC1 and OC2 ran into the room.

"Them and their hearing," Carla said, getting up. "I thought I heard someone at the door too."

"You cats solve mysteries, like they do in mystery novels?" Buster asked them.

The orange cats glared at him from the upstairs landing. No comment.

Carla came back. "Nobody's there but this was."

Inside a blank white business envelope: CADILLAC RANSOM PRICE IS THAT MAGIC CARD. DETAILS ON TRANSFER SOON.

16.

Like its owner, Mrs. Sally Jo Stockwall's purse was pleasantly plump. Even though the slots had cooled off, she was still having a blast. She'd dropped a few hundred of her winnings into dead machines, then a few hundred more chasing that few hundred. But she could take a hint. She quit while she was far ahead. Sally Jo hadn't counted her winnings—the very thought made her hands tremble—but guesstimated that they were in the five digits.

To calm her nerves, Sally Jo sat primly on a stool in an adjacent lounge and ordered a cosmopolitan. She could've stayed out there on the floor and saved a few dollars on booze. The more you won, the more the casino thrust free drinks in your face.

No, thank you. It was said that in this town a winner was only a temporary custodian of the house's money. This gal was through playing their little game. Had she done so, she'd be half-looped and every single dollar would have gone right back into their one-armed bandits. She'd buy her own drinks.

The cosmo went down easily. Sally Jo ordered another. She looked at her watch, wondering where the hell Dr. Wally was. Finishing the second, she decided, well, wherever he was, doing whatever he was doing, he could just take his sweet time and find her.

There were televisions all over the bar. Most showed horse races and sports, the object being to send you hurrying to the nearest sports book with your money and your latest stupid hunch. Nine out of ten American males were convinced that they were Nostradamus in that regard. Thank goodness, that was one of the few weaknesses her husband didn't have.

The TV above the back bar directly ahead of Sally Jo was an exception. It was devoted to news bulletins, to tornados and mass murder and war casualties as if they were buffet munchies. The news hang-up lately had been the death of that crazy old Japanese moneybags who either hid all his money or burned it to a crisp. Billions and billions and billions.

The story was everywhere, and here it was again, a big Dutch blonde who had high-priced hooker written all over her, and numbers on a piece of paper: 122318--------------141522.

Why was that so familiar?

Wasn't there a feature on the late news last night, how it was thought to be a secret code to all that money? Half asleep, Sally Jo had scribbled the numbers and the fourteen dashes that separated them, just in time before a commercial.

It was dawning on her. Oh, God, could it be?

Sally Jo went through her purse, careful of the stack of currency, but of nothing else. A lipstick went flying. A nail file too.

Here it was, the other numbers she'd written on a sticky note: 1223182392211.

Wally had made such a production of hiding that cocktail napkin. Naturally she had become suspicious. Him thinking he was twice as smart as she was had its advantages.

Sally Jo had found it inside a shoe before he'd gotten up in the morning. She routinely went through his pockets, checking his skivvies for foreign stains, on the alert for lipstick and se-men, the result of activities he rarely participated in at home.

She'd written down those numbers for a logical reason. Two reasons, actually. Her Wally might have a Swiss bank account and this could be the access number. Business at the clinic was not wonderful. He said it was fabulous, but she could tell from his sneaky, wouldn't-look-her-in-the-eye behavior that it was rotten.

He might be squirreling away what he could overseas, taking large payments from patients' parents, with no intention of finishing the work, bleeding the business dry, figuring to leave her with a killer debt when he had a nest egg. She wouldn't put anything past him.

Or he had a phone number buried in the digits. What was that word? Paramour? No. Not that. She was confident he couldn't score without paying for it, and he was too cheap. He could deny it all he wanted, but she strongly suspected that several of the assistants who had left the clinic had done so for him playing grab-ass, brushing by them in tight quarters and so forth, saying, "Oh, gee, excuse me."

Wally was fortunate he hadn't been sued. No, if this was a phone number for some action, he was paying for it, in a massage parlor or cathouse. For God's sake, they had them throughout Vegas. There were fliers in sidewalk boxes, like they had at home for auto ads.

She willed herself to stop straying and compared the numbers:

1223182392211

122318--------------141522

Shakily, she filled in the sticky note: 1223182392211------141522

Oh, Lordy, how she'd misjudged her man, Sally Jo thought, open-mouthed, as she compared the numbers again. She did the math. Wherever dear Dr. Wally had acquired the numbers, he had the first six and last six like everybody else did, *and* eight more.

Twenty out of twenty-six if you could believe the fourteen dashes like the experts did. If they were what they were speculated to be—

She scribbled twenty divided by twenty-six, did the math and came up with almost seventy-seven percent of the complete thing. Either Wally was being conned, or he'd blundered onto the genuine article. He was a sucker for the stupidest get-rich-quick schemes, the kind you attended at airport-area hotels. They fed you a free lunch and "cash flow seminar" hogwash.

Wally's secrecy bordered on paranoia, so maybe he'd finally struck a gusher. Sally Jo belted down the remaining cosmo and signaled for a third. The booze was hitting her. They mixed potent drinks in Vegas, all the better to make you feel lucky.

A Taihotsu Tidbit scrolled by on a sports station's ticker. The $100 billion would buy every NFL, NBA and NHL franchise, with money left over for a new stadium or three.

Dr. Stockwall, you greedy bastard. Wally, fast on the fast track to $100 billion, had no intention of sharing one penny with his bride. Not one fucking red cent. Even for him, this was chintzy. Her slots windfall seemed less than pocket change.

Where the hell had that son of a bitch gone? Oh, speaking of the devil, there he was in the mirror, outside the bar, his head swiveling, looking for her. He was with an extremely large man whose arm was on Wally's shoulder. Even through the mirror, it was obvious to Sally Jo that the arm was not an act of friendship. It was ownership.

The numbers? What else could it be? Wally did not pay friendly calls on patients. Their attorneys called him.

Sally Jo was tempted to duck into the little girl's room, to think this through. But there was something about that big man, something that went both beneath and beyond the towering mass and bizarre hair, something she couldn't quite pin down.

She swiveled on her stool. The man and Wally were walking away, toward the tables. Then the man stopped, effortlessly halting Wally.

He turned toward Sally Jo Stockwall as if reading her mind. They locked eyes as Wally continued to scan the throngs for her.

Telepathy, thought the former dairy princess, shivering.

She fluttered her fingertips at the big man. He was so Frankenstein-gross he was kind of cute. Exotic-ugly, if there was such a thing.

Mesmerized too, he came forward, eyes fixed on Sally Jo, jerking Wally along as if a recalcitrant puppy. A piano rendition of the theme from *Love Story* tinkled between his ears.

If she were truly telepathic, an Ambrose Bierce quote would have beamed from him to her: LOVE. *A temporary insanity curable by marriage or by removal of the patient from the influences under which he incurred the disorder.*

17.

"You're not you," Dave Snider said.

"Then who am I?" Rob said.

"Damned if I know, Rob. You wearing a Mariners cap like you're a Seattle native. Black hair sticking out."

Robin Chance (Rob) Weather had left the phony glasses at Aunt Carla's and done his best to hide his new hair without being obvious. Uncle Buster had protested when Dave had returned Rob's call and said, yeah, we're always in the market for a human interest piece, so long as it's whimsical, off the wall, and cheap to cover.

Buster had said that, yeah, recovering his carnapped Eldo was important, but keeping Rob underground was super-duper important. And don't forget the connection between the Caddy and the psycho carnapper and his second ransom note.

That was when Carla had dropped her bombshell.

"Buster, I must apologize to you for—"

"You apologizing to *me?*"

"I know it's a first," Carla had said. "I'm actually apologizing to your car, apologizing for calling it a hunk of junk and various obscenities. I looked it up online. In average shape, they sell for eighty thousand dollars."

"Yikes! I knew it was priceless but not that priceless."

"Yours may be rated above average too," Carla had said.

"Hell yes, it is."

"You wax it monthly and use cleaner on those hideous wide

whitewalls. Chrome cleaner too. You're not fooling when you say it has more chrome than a showroom full of Toyotas."

Rob had countered that a commitment was really a commitment now, so here they were, at noon, on a busy highway in south Seattle. Besides, after putting out online feelers to the stations, Dave Snider and others knew Rob was in town. Rob also felt that Buster going public might temporarily drive Buster's tormenter underground. This character knew too much about both of them.

Rob shrugged and told Dave Snider. "I'm searching for my inner self."

Snider laughed, eyebrows raised. He was daytime anchor, field reporter, and chief cook and bottle washer for a local cable station that specialized in reruns of old sitcoms, even older movies, and public access forums where kooks denied a forum elsewhere could vent and babble their proof of UFOs. It was the best Rob was able to do. Rob and Dave had worked together in Utica.

"There was always a running bet whether you were a natural blond. Which is the real you?"

"Only my hairdresser knows for sure. I appreciate you coming out, Dave."

Dave Snider, a one-man band, had brought a video camera on a tripod. No whirlybirds. No vans with antenna booms for Live Instant Eyewitness Breaking News. He gestured at the used car lot behind them. A sign on the windshield of one vehicle: $999. NO MONEY DOWN.

Most of the merchandise was a purchase away from being put to sleep in a crusher. On the porch of the office, a single-wide mobile home, pot-bellied salesmen in mismatching clothes smoked cigarettes.

"In the parlance, this is a 'beater' lot, a metaphor for our station," Dave said. "I was thinking a contrast between a classic car and a rogue's gallery of shitmobiles would be, um—"

"Artsy," Rob said.

"There you go. Artsy we can do on a zilch budget."

"They gonna run us off?" Buster asked, eyeing the sales staff eyeing them.

"Nah," Snider said. "They have consumer protection issues and don't want any more bad publicity."

"Which one of these pigs you want him to stand in front of, Rob?"

"Let's pick the oldest and rattiest one," Rob said. "Okay with you, Uncle Buster?"

"This piece of guano will do," Buster said, album in hand, walking near an oxidized, eleven-year-old Taihotsu Orion™, a subcompact with red cellophane taped over a broken taillight. "They all pale in comparison. Hell, you could roll that tin can up inside my Eldo's trunk."

"I'll plug in an intro later, guys," Dave Snider said. "Go whenever ready, Buster."

The comic told his sad, strange story, then held up the first ransom note: BE PREPARED TO PAY BIG RANSOM. MESS WITH US AND YOUR CAR WILL BE RETURNED TO YOU ONE PIECE AT A TIME. WE WILL BE IN CONTACT. The second note would remain their secret.

Buster opened his 1959 Cadillac Eldorado convertible album. The thick, overstuffed book drove Carla to distraction, her often asking him if devoting a scrapbook not to a family but to a machine wasn't just a little sick. Not to mention that the pictures of the car were of a better quality than those he had of her.

The camera zoomed in. Buster turned the pages, narrating close-ups of intimacies such as the necker knob, bechromed tailfins, snow-white cloth top, and the wraparound windshield.

"That's good, Buster," Dave Snider said. "We have enough for—"

"That old saying, the greatest thing since sliced bread?" Buster interrupted, grinning at the camera. "You're out there in BoobTube Land, thinking that my Caddy's the greatest thing since sliced bread. I hope it's greater than that. What's so great about sliced bread, even if you've troweled on peanut butter and jam.

"Speaking of treasured and priceless antiques," he went on. "One day I had nothing to do, I browsed the Yellow Pages. Fascinating reading, they are. Yeah. I counted stores that sold new furniture and came up with two-hundred-seventy-five. Then I counted antique stores. When I got to two-hundred-and-five, my fingers and toes were getting sore and I had to quit. I could still do the math and, I tell ya, it's a scary trend.

"Which is, nobody'll have any furniture anymore? It's dumped on antique shops faster'n it's sold new. What're you gonna sit on? It's all in an-tee-cue shops."

Snider held up his forearm, looking at his watch. Buster ignored him. He couldn't stop. He couldn't.

"Hey, we're in Seattle, right? Great town. But, jeez, this addiction we got for coffee." Buster shook his head. "We've heard of demon rum, which is one thing the abolitionist spoilsports called drinking, whether it be social or antisocial drinking. Madge, my second ex-wife, said I drank too much. I reminded her that she drank twice as much as I did. So what, she said? You drive me to it.

"Let's forget demon rum and Madge. I'm trying to. You wanna talk about a monkey on your back? Let's talk demon coffee.

"We're Seattleites, right? We've seen what a caffeine jones can do. Not a pretty sight. Seattle's the coffee capital of the universe. We Seattleites can't grow our own up here in the Great Wet

North, but we do everything but mainline it.

"In Seattle, there's an espresso shack on every corner and every one of them's got a long line stretching outside, day or night, rain or shine, people impatiently waiting for their quadruple tall low-carb vanilla raspberry frappacappuccino latté that costs as much as a six-pack of microbrew, for crying out loud.

"Once, my girlfriend and I were driving through the roughest toughest area of Seattle. It's so mean and nasty there that they got a block watch committee that goes out checking on tattoos. You ain't wearing enough of them, they boot you out, make you move uptown or to the burbs before you get hurt.

"We realized we hadn't had a cup of java for almost an hour. We were jittery and jangly and twitchy. We were in the grip of demon coffee. It didn't matter where we were. We needed our fix.

"We stop at this coffee stand and get in a line that goes around the corner. Not five minutes later, these two cars come roaring by doing ninety, blasting away at each other with machine guns. We're in the middle of a drive-by drive-at drive-on shooting. Bullets were caroming and zinging and ricocheting and swooshing.

"What did we do? Run for it? Dive for cover?

"And lose our place in line?" Buster screamed at the camera. "Are you crazy?"

Dave Snider made a slashing gesture that Buster took seriously.

"Okay, boys and girls. Gotta close with a stale lawyer joke. It's a city regulation. How can a pregnant woman tell she's carrying a future lawyer?"

Snider lowered the camera and popped a cartridge out.

"Hey, don't you wanna hear the punch line?"

"Irrelevant. You ran me out of tape."

18.

The Stockwalls and the big man, who introduced himself as Mr. Little, were joined in the cocktail lounge by a Mr. Smith, who reminded Sally Jo of a character from an old 1950s black-and-white sitcom she couldn't quite place, a series running all day long on a telethon. It'd been ages since she'd seen a cardigan sweater on a man.

She thought Mr. Smith was a sweetheart with his nice manners, asking her if she was enjoying Las Vegas, his fair city. She said she was, although she wasn't telling a solitary soul how much she *was* enjoying his fair city, it and its loose-as-a-goose slot machines.

Mr. Smith was treating them with such respect, Wally had obviously fibbed about who and what they were. Big surprise. For one thing, he wasn't a Wally patient. Mr. Smith's teeth were perfect, not Dr. Wally's handiwork. Mr. Smith could star in a toothpaste commercial.

Mr. Little, on the other hand, may've been a total stranger to dentistry. Those oddly sensual lips. The dull, watery eyes, too. Eyes that somehow weren't what they seemed. Eyes that didn't stray from hers. There was an air of mystery to the man as well as an air of something else. Mr. Little made Sally Jo tingle, and she hadn't the foggiest why.

After a drink, Mr. Smith invited the Stockwalls out for a meal. No, not here in this touristy hubbub. Somewhere subdued, where they could converse without raising their voices.

Lo and behold, just as they stepped onto the sidewalk, a stretch limo, a gleaming black Taihotsu Executive™, pulled up. Sally Jo was dazzled, even before Mr. Little rushed ahead and opened a door for her.

Mr. Smith's restaurant was off the Strip. It was Italian, cavernous, quiet and dignified, maybe to an extreme. There was a tad too much dark wood and red velvet. The white-aproned waiters were too discreet. The mood music was the theme from *The Godfather*. In the style of everything on the Strip, it was an exaggeration of real life. Sally Jo thought the restaurant was trying too hard, like Mr. Smith was.

Mr. Little, bless his heart, moved those intriguing lips as he read his menu. Mr. Smith ordered the gutbomb lasagna special for Mr. Little, as if father and son. Wally chose it, too. Sally Jo had what Mr. Smith had—a green salad and a glass of Orvieto Classico.

Sally Jo couldn't help but see Mr. Little looking almost as longingly at her lunch as at her. Sally Jo wasn't going to be able to finish her salad. After all these years, she had a reason to put down her fork, to once again be attractive, to be desirable, to be a dairy princess.

There was no conversation until dinner was underway. Finally, Mr. Smith said, "Mrs. Stockwall, the good doctor's ruse that we are orthodontic patients of his was well intended. Of course, you are not buying that deception for a microsecond. You are too perceptive."

Duh, Sally Jo thought. "Gee, wow, thank you."

Now it came to her, the ancient sitcom character he resembled: Ward Cleaver of *Leave it to Beaver*. Mr. Smith was talking to her as if she were Wally or Beaver Cleaver, who'd brought home a good report card.

"You must have had an inkling."

"I kind of guessed," she said modestly. Whatever this bullshit game was, it had to do with the number.

Mr. Smith said, "Your husband is an entrepreneur. We are entrepreneurs."

Entrepreneur? A dental clinic in a seedy strip mall wasn't exactly Microsoft, Sally Jo thought. "Oh?"

"Us guys, we ain't just that entrée thing. We're businessmen too," Chicken Little said, mortified that he had to maintain his village-idiot persona in the presence of this lovely woman. In the parlance, there had been vibes. Instantaneous vibes. Very good vibrations.

But when she smiled a smile that was not indulgent, and when she extended her leg so their toes touched, he thought he'd swoon and keel over in his cholesterol- and sodium-laden goop.

Mr. Smith took a delicate bite of salad, sipped his wine, smiled warmly and said, "Dr. Stockwall had the foresight to answer our query in a professional journal. I believe we're close to a franchisee agreement. He wanted to surprise you."

By the bewildered look on Wally's face, a mouthful of pasta giving him chipmunk cheeks, the surprise was mutual.

"That is *so* sweet of you, darling."

"Ummoomph," replied Dr. Stockwall.

"A revolutionary product for dental professionals," Mr. Smith went on.

"How exciting," Sally Jo said. Her shoes were open-toed, and Mr. Little's scuffed sandals were lightweight. They made toe-to-toe contact, flesh to flesh. The intimacy flushed her.

"We offer an advisory instrument for investments by dentists. The clients access online, so there is no physical start-up cost in the trifling franchisee fee. Through his networking and social contacts, Dr. Stockwall provides the service for colleagues in and around his Beverly Hills complex, then branches out from there. The subscribers have full access to my financial people.

"Since Dr. Stockwall is an early subscriber, as a bonus we're giving him the rights to the Pacific Northwest too, a territory not yet exploited. We're treating you fine folks to a few days up there so he can test the waters, so he can garner a foothold."

Wally looked at an equally puzzled Sally Jo, thinking that he had to give them something more on Blondie now, something they could home in on. For all intents and purposes, he was their prisoner.

"Your man is a formidable negotiator, Mrs. Stockwall. He drives a brutal bargain," Mr. Smith told her.

She replied with a distracted smile.

Mr. Smith smiled in return. He had detected in the woman from the outset a cauldron of barely repressed anger and frustration toward her husband.

Chicken Little already had a man chasing after this Rob (no last name, per the orthodontist) individual, an Asian with bleached blond hair and a television news background, who had been bound from Dallas–Fort Worth to Seattle to an unspecified destination in the Pacific Northwest.

His bloodhound, a client, was into them for an impressive nut. The client, a gastroenterologist, had assured Little that he had topnotch gumshoe resources, the best private investigation firm in town. He would utilize them in exchange for forgiveness of a portion of the debt.

Sally Jo couldn't summon a response to the hogwash. Her folks lived in the Seattle area. She was not on the best of terms with them or the rest of her family in that region.

Her parents had sold the dairy farm and were retired now and lived in a condo, complaining of claustrophobia. They didn't understand why their only daughter couldn't visit more often than every five years, why she complained of money troubles. After all, she'd married a *dentist*.

A dentist with whom she had not provided a household of

grandchildren. Unlike her two brothers, who bred like hillbillies and Mormons, she thought. Among Wally's deficiencies in that regard was the world's lowest sperm count, but that was none of their goddamn business.

"A few days?" she asked with a gee-whiz expression, no longer dubious that this nonsense was about anything else than those numbers on Wally's napkin. It couldn't be anything else. Dr. Wally had plunged into a get-rich-quick alliance that might cost him dearly. But not her too, if she had anything to say about it.

Sally Jo looked at Mr. Little, who had not stopped looking at her as their footsy intensified. Whatever happened, she sensed he'd keep her out of the crossfire.

"If the good doctor can clear his calendar," Mr. Smith said genially, knowing that Stockwall was holding out on them, details that would greatly accelerate their manhunt. There were better ways to skin this cat than sheer terror.

"It shouldn't be a problem," said Wally. Zeroing in on Blondie and that card wouldn't be either. On his own, if humanly possible.

"Mr. Little and I will accompany you, to volunteer our input whenever useful."

"Me and the boss, him and me, we gonna be there for you."

A squadron of butterflies launched in Sally Jo's stomach.

Lunch nearly launched from Wally's.

They separated. Mr. Jiminy Cricket Smith and Jerome (Chicken) Little took an elevator to Mr. Smith's suite. Inside, they each gave the tail-wagging Wayne a pat on her head.

Little went into a bedroom and came out with a plump business envelope. He gave it to Mr. Smith, how it was done on *The Sopranos,* and said, "Nice job, Jack. It's all there plus a bonus. You followed the script perfectly. I took drama classes in college and know talent when I see it."

Jack Armstrong said, "Thanks, Jerome. Much appreciated. We really are going to Seattle?"

"We are."

"I'll still be getting Actor's Equity scale?"

"Plus travel time and expenses."

Wayne rubbed against her fictional master. "I'm getting attached to her."

"How long till her rental is up?" Little asked.

"The end of the week."

"I'll renew her. She needs to come along. You and her as Jiminy Cricket Smith and faithful pooch are a remarkably wholesome duo."

Armstrong said, "I'm getting into that character, you know. Playing a whack job like Jiminy Cricket Smith is great fun. If you don't mind me asking, how did you dream him up? You never told me."

Jack Armstrong, his actual name, Jerome thought, named by his parents for the all-American boy of 1940s radio serial fame. He wondered if they were proud of their son and his third-rate thespian career, relegated to infomercials and reality TV gigs.

Armstrong had been playing the Jiminy Cricket Smith role for weeks and had kept his curiosity to himself. Jerome supposed he was entitled. "I've admired your restraint, suppressing your curiosity. I know by now you have a good feel for my business plan."

Armstrong shrugged. "I'm paid to play a part."

"Confidentially?"

"I swear."

"The dichotomy," Little said. "Turning their expectations upside down. They're semi-prepared for a swarthy gorilla with a pinkie ring. They expect another monstrosity like me. Instead, they get you, clean-cut, yet psychotic and potentially deadly. Any resistance folds, any idea of shenanigans abandoned. The

Bugsy memorial down below gave me the inspiration. I built the memorial in the suite and it went from there."

"It certainly does the trick, Jerome."

"Today is ultra-confidential, Jack."

"I know, I know."

"Let's not let assumptions spin out of control. If Stockwall is putting us on, the likeliest scenario, he is creative. If the number does hold merit, we shall cross that hackneyed bridge when we come to it."

Armstrong nodded. The magic number the orthodontist had attempted to use as a bargaining tool, that was a new twist. The others hauled up here caved in without argument. Whether Stockwall's number string was genuinely connected to the day's biggest news story remained to be seen. Either way, Armstrong was along for the ride. He'd get his.

At the door, he said, "When do we leave for Seattle, Jerome?"

"I'll make reservations and let you know."

When Jack and the rented dog left, Jerome Little fixed a watercress and cucumber sandwich and kicked back in a leather recliner that he'd had specially made for his length and girth.

Two hundred and eleven clients, he thought. Professionals in over their heads to *him*, not to the fictional Mr. Jiminy Cricket Smith. He had a file on each and every one. In his head.

Just a few more unfortunates on his rolls and he'd have what he needed to be permitted to teach on his terms. Perhaps they wouldn't hire him, but they'd have to let him teach whatever he wanted if he endowed an entire English department.

And if the orthodontist's number wasn't a con job or a fantasy, goodness, the potential was staggering. He'd have the world in his hands, everything anyone could want.

All but the client's wife.

Was she feeling what he was feeling? Was she possibly attracted to him?

When their toes had touched, so much blood had rushed to his penis that he'd nearly lost consciousness. Then as now.

19.

They had broken up the meeting and retired for a good night's sleep, thinking they'd tackle the puzzle and the second ransom note fresh. None of the four slept well, if at all, and they were not fresh the next morning.

Buster left Rob and Sarah in the kitchen, to finish breakfast, good luck with the problems. Carla was already at her agency, but had done it up big before leaving: bacon, sausage, eggs, potatoes, toast and fresh fruit. It was like a fancy-smansy restaurant Sunday buffet.

She'd gone to the trouble, she told Buster, because you can't break perhaps the most important puzzle in the history of the world—solve it fast with everybody and his brother breathing down your neck—without a hearty breakfast, the most important meal of the day.

Buster didn't think that was all there was to Madame Cupid fixing the spread, but kept his trap shut when he wasn't shoveling food into it.

Afterward, they stared at the demand notes:

BE PREPARED TO PAY BIG RANSOM. MESS WITH US AND YOUR CAR WILL BE RETURNED TO YOU ONE PIECE AT A TIME. WE WILL BE IN CONTACT.

CADILLAC RANSOM PRICE IS THAT MAGIC CARD. DETAILS ON TRANSFER SOON.

"Mean, vicious and evil," Buster said.

"And clairvoyant," Sarah said.

147

"Do the walls have ears?" Rob wondered.

"Not as heavily insulated as these are," Buster said. "How about a listening device in this card like in spy movies?"

Rob held the card up to the light. "That's a good possibility. They can make those things smaller than the head of a pin. It could be woven into this strange paper."

Buster took his plate to the dishwasher. "So it won't help if we whisper."

"No."

"We could burn the card."

"Don't ask me why, but I can't part with it."

Before heading out the door, Buster peered over Sarah's shoulder, seeing what she'd neatly written.

$$1 \times 8 + 1 = 9 \quad 3 \times 37 = 111 \quad (1)^2 = 1$$

$$12 \times 8 + 2 = 98 \quad 6 \times 37 = 222 \quad (11)^2 = 121$$

$$123 \times 8 + 3 = 987 \quad 9 \times 37 = 333 \quad (111)^2 = 12321$$

$$1234 \times 8 + 4 = 9876 \quad 12 \times 37 = 444 \quad (1111)^2 = 1234321$$

"I'm doodling. For a math geek like me, this is play," she told Rob, who nodded.

Buster nodded too, thinking that what he considered play was watching somebody else play on TV. Looking at her version of play was giving him a killer headache.

"I'm attempting to form a coherent series out of a random string," she said.

"How's about a 1-900 psychic?" Buster said.

"We're not that desperate," Sarah said. "Are you familiar with Sir William of Ockham and Ockham's razor?"

"Who? I've heard of Sir Gillette and Lord Schick."

"Sir William was a fourteenth-century philosopher and logician. Ockham's razor states in our vernacular that the simplest solution is usually the best. It's also known as the law of parsimony. Your decoder ring suggestion fits that category."

"There you go," Buster said, raising a fist.

"I haven't ruled it or anything else out yet, Buster," she said as the comic checked his hair in the dinette mirror. "Good luck."

"Yeah, break a leg, Uncle Buster," Rob said.

Meaning his interview at the Purple Flasher Tavern, down at the corner by the car dealer and up the street past the sports bar and the self-storage facility. The station had run the Buster Hightower taping in its entirety on yesterday's five o'clock news, before a *Gilligan's Island* episode. It'd been a slow news day.

They hadn't received a nibble on his classic Caddy, but the station's phone had rung off the hook wanting the punch line to the lawyer joke. They'd also gotten a call from the Purple Flasher. A lady named Mildred wanted to interview Buster for a standup comic job. Dave Snider had passed along the message.

So off he went on a half-mile death march. When Buster had transportation, he'd driven past the Purple Flasher a jillion times, but had never dropped in. The "Purple" bothered him.

As he walked, Buster mulled the ransom notes and his contact with the carnapper in the Nixon mask. First a probable Watergate angle, now Rob's magic number.

Nature abhors a coincidence.

Think, dammit, he muttered to himself. Saturday night, June 17, 1972. Five losers broke into the Democratic National Committee Headquarters in the Watergate complex in D.C. and got nabbed by a minimum-wage security guard. Simultaneous-like, Buster broke in to his chosen profession at a Holiday Inn in Toledo.

So what?

He forgot what his shtick was at the beginning of the Toledo run, but it wasn't long before he was all over Watergate, the hottest story going. Like every comic in the world. Buster thought his Watergate bit was special, standing out from the crowded pack, him doing two characters, two voices. He'd toss the mike from one hand to the other when he'd shift from snarling Senate subcommittee interrogator to weaseling unindicted coconspirator.

It had been great fun, and the audience lapped it up.

The good old days.

So why was the rancid putz tormenting him now?

Was somebody holding a grudge after all these years? The president of the H. R. (Bob) Haldeman Fan Club?

He arrived at the Purple Flasher, his headache in full bloom. It smelled of stale beer. To his left were customer tables, to his right a pair of pool tables. There were a few morning drinkers at the bar and a big gal behind it. He felt right at home.

"Mr. Hightower. Glad you could make it. Let's go on out to the beer garden."

"Is it self-serve while you're out, Mildred?" one of the drinkers joked.

"Pace yourself, Lenny," Mildred said. "Or by noon you'll be needing a seat belt on that stool."

Buster followed her out an opened door to the beer garden, a fenced area with plastic patio furniture. Mildred lit up, saying, "This no-smoking-indoors law they have now. You never know when the Nicotine Gestapo's watching. In winter, you can catch pneumonia out here, which'll put you six-feet-under a helluva lot faster than lung cancer. The law says you gotta be twenty-five feet from the door before you take a puff. They can shove that one."

"I appreciate your interest, Mildred."

"I liked what you did with coffee. I'm thinking that live entertainment will add a touch of class. And, oh yeah, how can a pregnant woman tell she's carrying a lawyer?"

"Cuz she has an intense craving for baloney."

Mildred smiled. "Not bad. Lawyer jokes work in here. DUI lawyers charge an arm and a leg, the shysters. By the cash register, I got business cards of the better ones to give out."

"There's one thing, Mildred. The purple in the name of your fine establishment? That color, you know, well, purple, it makes you think of—"

"That we're a fag bar?"

The comic fluttered a hand. "Not that there's anything necessarily wrong with alternating lifestyles. Different strokes, you know. Live and let live."

"My customers are neighborhood folk. They take you as they find you, although if you're swishy, you might live longer if you took your business down the street. Put a hand on the leg of the same gender and we'll have us some bloodshed. Guaranteed."

Buster was relieved, though he should've known that a neighborhood beer parlor *and* a gay bar were oxymoronic.

Mildred said, "The Purple and the Flasher come from Prohibition days. This stretch of highway was the boondocks then. Trees and scattered homes and not much else. Before the original building on this spot burned down ages ago, it was a roadhouse diner. Nobody remembers what it was called. There were nights when it doubled as a speakeasy. When they had hooch, they'd flash a flashlight covered with purple cellophane at cars going by."

"I like dignified heritages," Buster said. "I can have fun with it."

"Back then, truckers and travelers stopped off for a little nooky too. Where we're standing was an attached building. Young ladies were available in it."

"A historical site," Buster said.

Mildred flicked her cigarette over the fence. "We can afford

151

to pay you fifty bucks a night."

"Jeez, only fifty?"

"And all the beer you can drink."

Buster quickly shook her hand. "Deal."

Mildred led him inside. "It'll be a temp job. You need to understand that."

"Sure. For how long?"

"Till we get a part for the jukebox." Mildred pointed at the Taihotsu TuneSter™. "The part's coming from Taiwan China. Shit-kicker twang is the music of choice. Folks dance in front of it late when they're choosing up partners for the night. Not that this is a singles bar meat market. We're not a sports bar either. The little TVs you see mounted up there, they're strictly for NASCAR. Forget the Huskies and Seahawks. We want to see those stock cars go round and round.

"They'll like you, Buster. And you won't have a lot of distractions like a kitchen and, God help us if we ever do, a salad bar. Our cuisine is free popcorn and hot dogs simmering in beer in a crock-pot."

"Yum." Buster looked at the jukebox with its display and touch screen. "Maybe it wouldn't have crapped out on you if it had buttons and there wasn't a computer inside it."

"There you go. They can have their newfangled digital. But I'm just the manager, not the owner."

Mildred was beginning to grow on Buster. "I'm gonna be where?"

"Beside the jukebox."

"By the dartboard too, on the other side," Buster couldn't help but notice.

"My customers are laid back, but you never know. Tell you what I'll do. I'll make the dart dispenser off-limits when you're on."

20.

Sarah and Rob were getting nowhere faster than fast. He did like the proximity, side by side at the dinette table, rather than across from each other. He liked the smell of her shampoo.

Sarah said she was punchy and needed a break. Rob refilled their cups with Carla's coffee, commonly known in the Chance-Hightower household as Black Death. They went into the living room and switched on the TV to, yet again, Sublieutenant Saburo Taihotsu on the *Akagi* flight deck, standing by the propeller of his Zero fighter, arms folded, grim-faced. The narrator said that Taihotsu's companies had remained consistent bright spots in Japan's periodically slumping economy.

Sarah said, "Taihotsu doesn't resemble you."

"As I said before, genes or chromosomes or a mailman. A wild card in my DNA."

"Regardless, you have to consider the strong likelihood that you are Saburo Taihotsu's illegitimate grandson. No longer merely speculation on the genealogical chart Carla drew up."

Rob said, "The tabloids are homing in on that assumption, as well as the civilized world."

"If this ever blows over and you and that accursed string turn out to have nothing to do with anything, you should get back into news, Rob. Send audition tapes to the bigger markets."

Rob muted the TV. "There's the helicopter factor, I should confess, the reason I wouldn't go to the bigs even if someone up there wanted me."

"Helicopter factor?"

"My deepest, darkest secret, Sarah. Fear of news copters."

"You're pulling my leg."

"No."

"I'm not aware of crashes."

"It's happened before. In Phoenix. The major market network affiliates all have helicopters. If I moved up, I'd be hovering over four-alarm fires and hostage standoffs and meth lab raids. That's where they'd have me. I'm the guy they'd send up.

"Once, from the ground, stuck in traffic, I watched every news whirlybird in town covering a story. There were two jack-knifed semis on the freeway and umpteen smashed cars. Three fatalities. The copters hovered like buzzards, four of them. From below, they looked like they were two feet apart, jockeying for position, though they had trove been spaced farther than that.

"No, thanks. One of these days, They'll tangle rotor blades again. It's inevitable. I pictured myself spinning out of control into a tornado-whipped trailer park. I'd be part of a story for the eleven o'clock."

"Your fears are understandable," she said.

"You bet they are. I know a guy who's weekend anchor at an L.A. indie. He was up in a news chopper. Said the pilot was eating a sandwich, paying no attention to his flying."

"No."

"Ham and Swiss on rye. *Both* hands on it. He was squirting mustard on, out of one of those little packets."

"Now you're being silly."

"Then he sliced a red onion with a pocket knife."

"Really silly."

"Any progress whatsoever on the number? Any hunches?"

Sarah sighed. "What's frustrating is that you might have the only complete number in captivity and I'm banging my head against a wall. It could be ludicrously simple or something the most powerful mainframe computer can't solve.'"

"Numerology or a Ouija Board or tea leaves or all of the above?"

"Employing that logic, why not consult Buster's 1-900 psychic? Rob, if Saburo Taihotsu was your grandfather and he's given you a road map to his estate, wouldn't he design a search within your capabilities?"

"Yeah, I guess."

"In practice, what are your capabilities on the problem? Realistically."

"Same as your average nine-year-old. I have no advanced math schooling and my laptop is no brainiac, even if I had the software and the knowledge to use it."

"The method is in your grasp. Why else would your grandfather give you what he gave you?" she said.

"If he was my grandfather. If he did give me the magic digits. If they are magical."

"Until we have contrary information, let's presume all of the above."

"There are a zillion permutations and combinations, Sarah. You've said so yourself. The odds of winning a six-out-of-forty-nine number in the lotto is like seven million to one. We're talking twenty-six numbers matched to twenty-six letters. We're talking zillions and kazillions."

"Your grandfather knew that, Rob."

"I'm a dreamer who never dreamt of one hundred billion dollars. I mean, unimaginable wealth? What would I do for an encore? That's why I don't play the lottery. It's too hard an act to follow."

"Think of the multitude of new friends you'd acquire."

"Or the money that could've went up the chimney at Taihotsu Iron Works. I won't see a yen even if it exists and is mine-all-mine legally. If so, why did dear old Maybe Granddad provide those teaser numbers to the rest of the universe? There'll be a stampede by my multitude of new friends over my lifeless form to get to them. Finders keepers is how it'll play out."

He hesitated, moved a little closer to her on the sofa, then said, "We appreciate your help, but this thing is wilder and wilder. No sense you having hoof prints on you too, Sarah. Not that I'm trying to get rid of you. You have to remember the risks that are becoming riskier by the minute."

It was funny, but Sarah didn't much care about the money now, whatever slice of it she'd get if this proved to be a cornucopia that overflowed and overflowed. Silly and irresponsible as it was, her overdue bills were in the furthest corner of her consciousness. It was the excitement, the challenge, mathematically and otherwise. To be taken somewhere she's never been, never thought she'd be, wherever that might be. To take her away from the mundane day-to-day and to distract her from her grief. Romance, too, was not an impossibility. Dear Carla and her matchmaking.

Sarah Ann Hilyer, according to Neil Jasons, was a "spinster," she thought.

Bitch. Professional virgin.

Rob unmuted the television.

A headline newscaster said, *Exclusive!!*, the show we love to hate and its scenery-chewing personalities, may have finally gone over the top. Earlier this morning, their producer announced a ten-million-dollar reward for the complete twenty-six numbers attributed to the late Saburo Taihotsu, which allegedly leads to his vast fortune. This is, of course, *Exclusive!!* reports, subject to verification.

"Ten million is one ten-thousandth of one hundred billion dollars. That's a Taihotsu Tidbit if I ever saw one. Is *Exclusive!!* bargain-hunting or is it a stunt to boost their ratings even higher? We'll see."

Rob was holding Sarah's hand now, and she was squeezing it. She was getting more excitement than she asked for.

21.

The Stockwalls and the two lenders flew to Seattle, largest city in the Pacific Northwest. Mr. Smith advised that the core of maximum population density was the logical place to seek entrepreneurial opportunities for Dr. Stockwall's franchise.

At the Las Vegas airport, the Stockwalls had been amazed that security personnel were almost apologetic for scanning the wholesome Mr. Smith (traveling as Jack Armstrong) and the further indignity of requiring him to unbutton his cardigan and to remove shoes and belt.

Conversely, Mr. Little had been scrutinized as if a card-carrying al-Qaeda. When she'd seen him being taken into a room and a security officer snap on a rubber glove, Sally Jo had believed them to be outrageously discriminatory. It was all she could do to restrain herself from giving them a piece of her mind.

Upon landing at Seattle–Tacoma International and retrieving Wayne from a baggage counter, they rode a shuttle across the highway to the Taihotsu Suites™, where Mr. Smith had reserved rooms for himself, Mr. Little, and the Stockwalls.

After they were settled and had a quick lunch, Mr. Smith set out with Dr. Stockwall in a rental car, a top-of-the-line Taihotsu Turbo Zinger 350,™ a hot little copper-colored coupe with leather and a navigation system.

Adhering to the script, Mr. Little had asked Mr. Smith as a huge favor to follow up on the delinquent account, the gastroenterologist, a serial bridegroom with alimony payments that would choke a pasture full of mules. Mr. Little didn't fly well and had a variety of aches and pains from the cramped seating.

Mr. Smith had said he'd be delighted, as it was good policy for the boss to do field work occasionally, to experience it firsthand. Mr. Smith asked Wally to accompany him, no reason given.

Obviously, the orthodontist thought, getting into the dangerously fast automobile, they'd be taking turns keeping an eye on him, working in shifts.

Sally Jo Stockwall was left to her own devices for the afternoon. She sat in the lobby, reading magazines, wondering how stupid they thought she was, them panting like Wayne after that mysterious number, especially her loving and trustworthy husband. Any moron could see that Wally was a virtual prisoner. But she played along, hoping to linger with the intriguing Mr. Little a while if he came back from upstairs.

Why was he so alluring? She desperately needed to know.

Mr. Jiminy Cricket Smith drove the Turbo Zinger with a heavy foot, enjoying the tight handling and the seven-speed manual shifter. This was Jack Armstrong's first steady job in some time. His last gig had not been as a thespian, but as host of *Feedlot*, a reality TV program that was repulsive even by that genre's standards.

Feedlot's object was for the contestants to eat as if aboard a cruise ship. The weekly winner was the one who gained the most weight. Prize money increased from week to week, so it behooved a winner not to lose ground.

Camera and kitchen crews stayed with them throughout, shopping and preparing whatever they desired, recording every gross detail. It was as if every meal was a death row prisoner's last, no expense or calorie spared. Despite growing popularity, *Feedlot* was abruptly canceled after outcries about the vomiting and trips to the emergency room, and instant replays thereof.

Wally was scrunched in the miniscule back seat as Wayne rode up front, her head out the window. Squinting into the slipstream, Wally decided he'd have to dole out a smidgen more on Blondie. Mr. Smith hadn't yet said where they were headed, but anywhere away from Sally Jo was a relief.

She was getting on Wally's nerves, her and her surliness and her erratic mood swings. Add to that the perfume and makeup she slathered on this morning, as if she were bound for the debutante's ball.

He hadn't a clue what was going on inside her head lately, perhaps a chemical imbalance triggered by early change of life. It wasn't the worst scenario to leave Sal to get juiced in the hotel bar and Mr. Smith's Igor off in a corner reading a comic book, moving his lips. If only temporarily, they'd be out of his hair.

Wally alone with Mr. Smith might not be so horrible. He could reason with the man. Cut a deal between the two of them. Two gentlemen, two professionals.

Mr. Smith was presentable and intelligent and rational. So he had a little hang-up about Bugsy Siegel and Eva Braun. Everybody was a fan of somebody—an athlete, movie star, singer. And nobody was perfect, not even Dr. J.D. (Wally) Stockwall.

Sally Jo Stockwall moved to the hotel bar. She had no intention of getting sloshed, at least by herself. She kept an eye on the elevators.

Hoping.

★ ★ ★ ★ ★

Jerome (Chicken) Little was not reading a comic book. Nor had he plans of using this Seattle visit to harass that gastroenterologist or organize a ludicrous franchise. The gastroenterologist was a basket case already. He did not want on his conscience a scalpel nick in the next intestine the doctor encountered. Jack Armstrong would be kinder and gentler. He'd get results too, having been promised a bonus if he did. Mr. Smith did get his money.

Jerome had gone to his room to freshen up, an uncommon event. His previous occupation had not required much attention to personal hygiene either. To pay living expenses and to finance his education, he'd worked part time as a bouncer in an off-Strip titty bar. His appearance usually discouraged misbehavior.

He showered, shaved, tried to do something with his hair, and even brushed his teeth. He returned downstairs, and before he had time to fret over what he wanted to do and lose his nerve, he sat down at Sally Jo's table without an invitation, not that one was required.

"My name is Jerome," he said abruptly, in a totally different voice, a voice an octave higher with a nervous tremor. This from a man who shouldn't be afraid of anything.

Sally Jo put down her cosmopolitan and softly repeated, "Jerome."

"Jerome," he repeated.

"Jerome," she repeated.

"Ambrose Bierce," he blurted.

"Excuse me?"

"Ambrose Gwinnett Bierce was a dazzling humorist, satirist and short story writer who lived from 1842 to 1913 or 1914."

"He was? He did?"

Whoever the hell they were, this Bierce and her Jerome Little,

Sally Jo *knew* somebody was hiding within Jerome. He sounded like a college professor. He was trying to open up to her in his awkward way.

Sally Jo initiated another footsy session. "Please go on, Jerome."

"I'm studying for a Ph.D. in English, Sally Jo. My doctorate dissertation is: *Ambrose Gwinnett Bierce; How the Man and His Acidulous Humor Bridged Two Centuries.*"

She took his hand. "Jerome, that's fantastic. I knew you were acting out a role for whatever purpose."

Jerome brought her hand to his lips and kissed it gently. "Sally Jo, what you know is just the tip of the clichéd iceberg."

He spilled all. What he did to put himself through grad school and to ultimately afford an endowment. He told how they knew her husband. How the number brought them together in a dubious quest of $100 billion.

He ended by begging forgiveness for the ruse and with an Ambrose Bierce quotation. "Don't trust anyone, Sally Jo. Ambrose Bierce says fidelity is a virtue peculiar to those about to be betrayed."

"Oh, Jerome, all's forgiven. I smelled a rat from the start and knew that number and that card everybody's chasing after was the bottom line," she said, gulping down her cosmopolitan. "What does your Ambrose Bierce say about marriage?"

"A one-word definition. Incompatibility."

"Isn't that the truth?" Before she lost her nerve, she yawned suggestively and said, "I need a nap."

Reading her, he said, "I'm a de facto virgin."

"What do you mean by de facto?"

He wished he'd been drinking too. "I—I—I've always had to pay for it."

"Oh, dear."

"At an establishment that employed me as a bouncer, from

female employees."

"Oh, Jerome, I'm sorry."

"They'd give me discounts, though."

He paused. "But never exceeding ten percent."

Sally Jo leaned forward. "How I'd love to change that, Jerome, but we can't use either room. We don't know when they're coming back."

"This is a hotel, Sally Jo. They'll have other rooms."

Sally Jo Stockwall rose unsteadily, more giddy than tipsy. "That's why you're smart enough to be going for your doctorate."

Either showing off or goofing off, Wally thought, Jiminy C. Smith used the navigation screen to find his way into Seattle to meet the gastroenterologist he called Trent. Wally didn't know if Trent was his first or last name, and Mr. Smith didn't volunteer clarification.

They got off the freeway south of the city skyline and parked in a loading zone between the football and baseball stadiums. They were newish arenas, costing $500,000,000 per copy, combined a cool billion dollars of taxpayers' money.

A new 7-series BMW, the big Beemer, pulled in front of them and backed up, bumper to bumper. The kind of automobile I should be driving, the orthodontist lamented, not a four-year-old Buick oil burner with slick tires.

A graying, balding guy in pinstripes wearing a Rolex or the Taihotsu DigiChron™ equivalent got out holding a manila envelope. He looked at Mr. Smith and forced a constipated smile. He didn't look like he was having a wonderful day.

"Dr. Stockwall, prior to Trent and I having a short chat, is there anything you'd like to confide in me regarding our inscrutable blond friend, anything that might be useful in comparison or accordance to Trent's research? Consensus is

163

invaluable."

Research? This whacko and his mind games, he's bleeding my sanity a drop at a time, Wally thought. Sally Jo and he were captives, yet they couldn't run for it, or any chance at the number would vaporize. He'd seen on the morning news at the hotel that that video rag, *Exclusive!!,* was offering $10,000,000.

"The human memory is an odd and miraculous device, Mr. Smith," Wally said, feeling his forehead. "A last name is almost but not quite there. I'm ninety-percent certain Blondie gave me a last name when he introduced himself on the airplane. What is it? Raines? Snow? Hale? I'm sorry."

Mr. Smith opened his door.

"Please don't work yourself into a frenzy. I'm sure you're doing your best for us. The more I think about it, the more I think you and I will make a good team on this project," he said, following Jerome's script verbatim. "You're a fine and capable man, Dr. Stockwall. Consider us an alliance."

"Thank you."

"Benjamin Hymen would approve of you," Mr. Smith said.

Wally relaxed ever so slightly, hoping he passed the test. As Wayne slobbered in the passenger seat, Mr. Smith and Trent had their short chat. Trent handed over an envelope, and Mr. Smith returned to the Turbo Zinger.

An alliance, Wally thought. Just the two of them. It made eminent sense.

To Jack Armstrong it did, too. This clown was holding out on him; he knew more about the magic number than he let on. Jerome was holding out on him, too. He'd find out what and why, and go his own way, to hell with union scale and bonuses.

Jack opened the envelope and let Stockwall read the report page by page after he'd finished, baiting a trap.

"I've lusted in my heart, but never succumbed to hanky-panky temptation," Sally Jo confessed. "It didn't seem worth the trouble. Until now."

"Was I gentle? For the absence of a better term, I was in a precoital frenzy."

They were lying diagonally in the bed now, Sally Jo's head on Jerome's perspiring chest. Bedding was on the floor with their clothing, strewn every which way. After the poor man's premature ejaculation, she'd insisted that he cease apologizing. With her aid, he'd been operational in ten minutes. Unlike Wally's ten-month intervals.

"You were super," Sally Jo said, meaning it. "Wally's five times as rough, as I vaguely recall."

Jerome tenderly stroked her ass. "Sally Jo, let us henceforth refrain from any mention of him."

"I'm sorry, Jerome." She dabbed his tears. "What's the matter? Did I say or do something?"

His head was turned to the television, where *Love Story* was on, muted. There was a vast offering of films. Sally Jo's preference was porn, to help recharge their batteries. The classic *Deep Throat* was available, but Jerome had pleaded for his all-time favorite, which he admitted he'd seen in excess of fifty times.

He sniffled and said, "Please forgive me, Sally Jo. Please allow me a moment to compose myself. This is the part where Ali MacGraw learns she's terminal."

Sally Jo brought him a tissue. "Jerome, you're so sensitive. I like *Love Story* too."

"Love means never having to say you're sorry," Jerome said, weeping.

"Don't take this the wrong way, but you might be too sensitive for where this number business is leading."

He blew his nose and said, "Not if I have you as a partner, Sally Jo."

22.

"How do I love thee? Lemme count the ways," Buster High-tower said, caressing the Purple Flasher's jukebox.

He gave the Taihotsu TuneSter™ a loud smooch on a side. Except for those out in the beer garden having a puff, the packed house howled and groaned. Thirty-five to forty total, Buster guesstimated, a *big* crowd for him. It could be a tough room too, the tavern's patrons not accustomed to standup artistry.

Buster patted the jukebox low and to the back, as if copping a feel on its posterior and said, "Gotta love these state-of-the-art electronical gizmos. Thanks to this plastic sweetie here having the need for a gizzard transplant and awaiting a donor, I got me a gig and I got you nice folks as an audience."

"Out there, that's my best gal." Buster blew Carla a kiss.

She returned it. Sarah and Rob shared her table, shoulders and legs touching, his Seattle Mariners cap pulled low, almost to his flat-lens glasses. Laughing, they looked at her and applauded.

"I don't cheat on Carla aside from machines that have bum organs. I learned my faithfulness lesson when I was married.

"Madge, my numero uno and me, early on we started having what you call your basic marital troubles. Got so that when she cooked me a meal, I'd give the cat a taste first. Went through more kitties that way. I figured I could do better than a homicidal maniac, so I began stepping out on her with June, my next wife. Talk about jumping from the fire into the frying pan."

The comic was screaming now, pausing between thoughts for a long swig of his all-you-can-drink beer. The crowd was cackling and putting their hands together for Buster Hightower, fueling him.

"Yeah. June. Girl of my dreams. June had herself a few kinda sorta teensy little problems, though." Buster fluttered a palm. "Like being a psychotic schizoid paranoid schizophrenic, manic-depressive substance abuser with permanent PMS, whose headache she developed on our wedding night never went away."

Buster noticed two guys at the bar looking at each other and nodding sadly, poor devils.

"Hey, don't get me going on Flo, my last and final plunge into unholy matrimony. The bride from hell. Flo was a kleptomaniac. I'll grant her this, she was good at it. Not once did she get busted. Flo never met a piece of merchandise she didn't wanna swipe. I wouldn't of minded so much if it'd been practical and useful like beer and blue jeans and doughnuts and motor oil and bacon cheeseburgers.

"Nope, not Flo. We had us a garage full of vacuum cleaner bags and canned spinach and typewriter ribbons and cod-liver oil and enema kits and accordions. That's how come Flo wasn't nabbed. She was saving the stores the job of tossing stuff out nobody'd buy."

Buster was winning guffaws, but he had to stop. Had to. He was veering too close to the truth. Memory Lane could be an awfully depressing stroll.

Giving the TuneSter a one-armed hug, he continued, "Hey, from now on, outside of my girl there, it's strictly platonical relationships with machines. No hanky-panky for this boy.

"Speaking of mad science gone berserk, I obviously ain't no kid, okay? I remember those sci-fi movies from the 1950s, when I was a pup. Who else out there?"

Several reluctant hands went up.

"In two outta three, atomic radiation messed up the characters, like they'd gotten into the mother of all bad pizzas, right? That was in the good ol'days when we were testing nukes above ground, setting off so many bombs in Nevada and Utah that the sky looked like a mushroom farm.

"In one flick, some schmo of a lead actor gets a hefty dose of radioactivity and shrinks till he's the size of a cockroach. In another, the star grows to sixty-feet tall. Whadduya think an NBA team would pay to sign him?

"I'm okay with nuclear radiation doing bad things to you. My only complaint is big or small. Huh? Nukes can't do both to you. C'mon. Which is it?"

Buster chugalugged. He planned to wing it for a while, to air out a bit on the correlation of over-education and insanity, a concept he believed in anyway. Even if it had kinks, it'd click in here, a blue-collar joint. He'd go from there to stale material on aging, donut-sized prostrates and to his staple, lawyer jokes.

As he launched into all poets suffering from DLS, Drooling Lunacy Syndrome, Rob and Sarah held hands. Taking note, Carla was as pleased about that as Buster's sterling performance.

In a table near the women's room, Jiminy Cricket Smith and Dr. J.D. (Wally) Stockwall occupied a table. On the unlikely possibility that Robin (Rob) Chance Weather would recognize the orthodontist, Jiminy C. Smith situated him to his direct rear.

Neither man much appreciated the venue or the comic, Mr. Smith because he was envious of anybody with a bona fide entertainment job and Dr. Stockwall because of his myriad apprehensions that were compounded by the tavern's primitive choice of wines, individual-sized plastic bottles that were sold in six-packs in supermarkets, a viticultural equivalent of the medieval rack.

Wally had already answered Mr. Smith's wordless question with an affirmative nod. Hair coloration and eyeglasses or not, it was Blondie.

Sally Jo Stockwall didn't attend, pleading the onset of illness, probably from a bug that was going around. Dr. Stockwall accepted her story with barely a glance. Sally Jo simply didn't take care of herself properly.

Mr. Smith was dubious. If anything, Mrs. Stockwall appeared blissfully invigorated, doubtlessly a component of excessive alcohol consumption. It was preferable that she stayed there at the hotel, one less person in the way. Little remained at the hotel, too. That the boss was there to keep an eye on her and to babysit Wayne was also a plus.

Who was Rob Weather and what did he have to do with anything, the actor wondered? The dentist was holding out, albeit weakening. Jack Armstrong intended to be first in line when he caved.

On the opposite side of the Purple Flasher, at a table on the route to the men's room and the beer garden, a man sat out of view of all the principals but for the performer. Though he had not driven it here, the man possessed a 1959 Cadillac Eldorado convertible, fire-engine red in color, with a pristine white top.

23.

During Buster Hightower's Purple Flasher Tavern act, Dr. Wally Stockwall pleaded sudden queasiness to Mr. Smith, Sally Jo's virus probably passed along to him. Hand over mouth, he hurried to the john, stopping on the way at the pay phone to tear out a Yellow Page, then latched himself into a stall.

On his cell phone, Wally scrolled to the home number of his last chance, Roy Banker, his mortgage banker.

They were more or less friends. At least, Wally had never cracked wise vis-à-vis Banker the banker, and Roy Junior was a patient.

The kid had been a tough sell. Roy and the boy's mother had stared and stared into Junior's maw, seeing pearly whites lined up as if a marching unit on a regimental parade ground. Being laypersons, they could be forgiven for not noticing subtle anomalies. With Wally's insinuations of lifelong difficulties as extreme as an overbite-induced lisp (you know what people conclude when a male of the species lisps), parental guilt carried the day.

"Wally, where are you?" Roy Banker asked. "All the background noise, you sound like you're at a ballgame."

"The great Pacific Northwest, Roy. I wouldn't want to live here, but it's a nice change."

"Rain?"

"Like cats and dogs, Roy."

"Vacationing with Sally Jo?"

"Visiting her folks. It's been far too long. They're like family to me, too. We're having a ball. A second honeymoon, too, if you catch my inference. Listen, the reason I called, we've lucked into an incredible investment opportunity. We need ready cash in order to act. My investments are boffo, albeit illiquid. Speed is of the essence."

"Wally, do you know what time it is?"

"We need a second mortgage on the house, Roy, and we need it yesterday."

"Wally, you already have a second through us."

"A third, then. Semantics. Available equity is the bottom line. What do you say? Can you ramrod it through?"

"Well, we'd have to do an appraisal."

"What's your balance on young Roy, Roy?"

"We owe you thirty-one hundred. Every time I write you a check, Marcia gets on my case about visible results, but you're the doctor."

"Cosmetic tooth repositioning isn't the issue per se, Roy. Functional tooth movement is crucial to a happy dental adulthood."

"If you say so, Wally. I'm not arguing."

"Get this done and wire the money to me before noon and your balance is zeroed out, Roy."

Following a silence that seemed to Wally to last an hour, Roy Banker Senior said, "We can waive the appraisal. It hasn't been that long."

"Beautiful."

"Can do. Wire to where?"

Wally consulted the directory page and gave him a bank branch cattycorner from their hotel, then lied, "The instant it's done, I notify my office to send you a final statement highlighted by a goose egg."

"First thing in the morning," the banker said.

"How much do you think, Roy?"

"I'd have to put a pencil to it, Wally, but off the top of my head, high-four, low five-digits."

Not what Wally wanted to hear, but they lived in a 1970s split-level that wasn't worth a fortune. The amount Roy estimated would be sufficient seed money to escape Mr. Jiminy Cricket Cuckoo and pounce on Blondie if he could delay his captors doing so first. Credible misdirection was the key. One misstep, though, and his reward for the blunder would be the *Beast from 20,000 Fathoms*.

Wally said fine and wished Roy a nice day. He returned to Smith, rasping as if he'd been retching, "I feel better, a relative term."

"That's good," Smith said disinterestedly, wondering what the dentist had been up to. After this length of time, odds were he'd placed a phone call. Jack Armstrong was seriously wondering what Stockwall knew and was keeping to himself.

"I'd really like to get back to the hotel before I relapse. I'm no good to you in this condition."

The comic had ended his set with the punch line to the dangling lawyer joke, the pregnant woman craving baloney, drawing the heartiest laughter and applause of his performance. He was sitting with his three companions. The heavy woman was dabbing his brow with a napkin as he "replenished vital bodily fluids," he'd say loudly, a bottle of beer then going bottom's up. Robin Weather and his female companion appeared surgically joined, Jack Armstrong/Jiminy Cricket Smith observed. But there was something tentative about them, a clumsy and sensual newness.

"We can. We need to cut Mr. Weather from the herd and that apparently will not be possible tonight."

"Tomorrow then?" said a relieved Wally.

"No later than tomorrow," Mr. Smith said, pointing at a

television screen.

Highlights of a stock car race played on a sports news show, a ticker underneath running ball scores punctuated by: *Exclusive!!* ante raised to $25 million on THE number.

24.

Carla was playing with the number string too. She'd written 1:23, 4:56, 7:89, but changed the 7:89 to 8:29, explaining, "There's no such time on a clock as 7:89, but it converts to 8:29. The times are consecutive numbers. Each is three hours and thirty-three minutes apart. There's no seven in the 26 digits either. For what any of this is worth."

"It could be related to time, Carla," Sarah said. "Why not?"

They were at her home after Buster's Purple Flasher performance, seated around the dinette table, paperwork on Sarah's late mother and unopened funeral bills set aside.

Beneficiary of too much free beer, Buster had sat down at the table unsteadily. Sarah's unit was exactly the same floor plan as his and Carla's, but reversed. "Have I ever told you? Your place discomboobalates me. This reversal, it's like stepping into a funhouse mirror. Oh, hey!"

Everybody looked at Buster.

"Reversal. I got it! Big Bill Hockman and his razor."

Carla squeezed his hand and said, "Dear, You're not thinking clearly."

"Snookums, I do my clearest thinking when I'm not thinking clearly."

Rob smiled. "You have to love the logic."

Sarah laughed. "Yes, you have told me, and your unit has the same effect on me. William of Ockham. Ockham's razor. What about them?"

"Lemme see your latest first, see if we're on the same wavelength," Buster said, picking up:

$$81 = (8 + 1)^2$$
$$4913 = (4 + 9 + 1 + 3)^3 = 17^3 = 4913$$

"No offense, Sarah," he went on. "What's this gotta do with the price of tea in Tibet?"

"Point well taken. Probably none. Carla's approach is as valid as any of mine. I yield the floor to Mr. Hightower."

"Okay, let's move on to my boy Bill. Can't hurt, even if it's the beer talking. Me and my carnapping pal, the sooner we get to the bottom of the card, the better. We can give him the card when he tells us where and when, but we'll have the decoding and he won't."

"Very true."

"Sir Bill, wherever he is, approves of my decoder ring theory. This is where the simplest thing first and reversing the simplest thing fit in. We'll go forwards and we'll shift into reverse," Buster said, squinting and slowly writing:

A-1
B-2
C-3
D-4
E-5
F-6
G-7
H-8
I-9
J-10
K-11
L-12
M-13
N-14

O-15
P-16
Q-17
R-18
S-19
T-20
U-21
V-22
W-23
X-24
Y-25
Z-26

Buster copied the numerals on the card: 122318239221112231361415 22

He arbitrarily divided them: 1/22/3/18/23/9/22/11/12/23/13/6/ 14/15/2/2

Then: A/V/C/R/W/I/V/K/L/W/M/F/N/O/B/B

Then: AVCRWIVKLWMFNOBB

"Avcr wiv klwm fnobb," Buster said. "It's plain as day. Doesn't anybody here know what a fob is?"

"What language is that?" Carla asked. "Martian?"

"Nah. Ain't it obvious? One number, one letter. Your basic alphabetaneurotic."

In a few minutes he had:

122318239221112231361415 22 = abbcahbcibbaaabbcac- fadaebb

"Abracadabra in Abracadabran," Carla said.

"Enough already. I actually do remember having a decoder ring, not one that came in a cereal box, the cheapskates. The deluxe model I had to send off for. Cost me *three* flippin' box tops of some unsugared cereal I hated, plus one dollar, which was big money in those ancient times. My ma made me eat every flake. The stuff tasted like tree bark.

"The ring had a complicated twist that'd fool the CIA. You spun the thing in the opposite direction too, which along with Sarah's unit here, locked my mind in reverse," he said, adding a third column:

A-1-Z
B-2-Y
C-3-X
D-4-W
E-5-V
F-6-U
G-7-T
H-8-S
I-9-R
J-10-Q
K-11-P
L-12-O
M-13-N
N-14-M
O-15-L
P-16-K
Q-17-J
R-18-I
S-19-H
T-20-G
U-21-F
V-22-E
W-23-D
X-24-C
Y-25-B
Z-26-A

"Let's try backasswards now."

12231823922111223136141522
1/22/3/18/23/9/22/11/12/23/13/6/14/15/2/2
ZEXIDREPODNUMIYY

Buster took a tongue-twisting stab at pronunciation, spitting more than speaking, gave up, and said, "Speaking of Martian, this sounds like an alien warlord in a sci-fi show who's come to Earth to eat us. Bon appétit! I'm throwing in the towel, gang."

Sarah said, "We've separated the number just one way. Why don't we try using Buster's key in different cuts, to arrange vowels and consonants to make syllables?"

"And possibly make words from there," Carla said, her turn at the scratch pad:

12231823922111223136141522

It took her half an hour to arrive at:

12/23/18/23/9/22/11/12/23/13/6/14/15/22

ODIDREPODNUMLE

"I'm counting six vowels and eight consonants, so we can't alternate them. Still, almost pronounceable," Carla said.

Carla yawned and said, "All this brainstorming is exhausting. I think it's time for us oldsters to call it a night." ·

Buster yawned too, thinking she was being about as subtle as a sledgehammer. And what do you know? When they got up to go, Rob and Sarah stayed put.

Sarah made popcorn to have while watching TV. Most of it went untouched. They muted the television and turned out the lamp by the sofa.

They were making out like teens at a drive-in movie, all over each other, she thought, his hand inside her blouse. Whether this was right or wrong, whether it was happening too fast, it felt right to her.

It felt right to Rob from the second they'd first held hands, and corny as he might sound, that's what he'd told her.

It went on until he fumbled for her zipper. It would have gone beyond that if it she hadn't glimpsed the TV out of the corner of her eye.

"Rob, oh my God!" she said, pushing away from him and unmuting.

It looked like the reception was bad, as if the cable had unplugged, but the snow was real. Microphone in hand, Robin Chance Weather leaned into the blizzard.

"According to the sensationalist news magazine, *Exclusive!!*, this man may be a factor in the life and death of billionaire industrialist and reputed Mongoose, the legendary World War II guerrilla fighter."

They went to an SUV commercial and Rob said, "Cedar Rapids. I'm out there reporting that the windchill was minus-thirty-seven."

"What do these tabloid people know that we don't know, Rob?"

"That I'm the kind of story they'd never in a million years let me cover."

25.

Next morning, Dr. J.D. (Wally) Stockwall awakened, Sally Jo beside him, arms around her pillow as if embracing it, snoring loudly enough to wake the clichéd dead. Thanks partially to the racket she made, he'd spent a fitful night. He touched her forehead. She didn't feel feverish, but evidently the virus had exhausted her.

He looked at his watch. Two hours until the banks opened. He steeled his nerve and climbed out of bed. Today was the day he'd have to make his move, to be proactive. It was now or never.

Mr. Smith would have his way with Blondie if Wally didn't move quickly. He realized it was a fantasy that they'd be partners. Just the manner in which he'd been treated, him a professional man, a licensed dental professional, was ample proof he was not regarded as an equal. This despite Mr. Jiminy Cricket Smith allowing him to see the private investigator's report that pinpointed Robin Chance Weather as Wally's seatmate on that fateful Cancun to Dallas flight.

We need to cut Mr. Weather from the herd and that apparently will not be possible tonight. No later than tomorrow.

He'd get to Blondie and explain the facts of life. Robin Weather had been agreeable and intelligent enough on the airplane. He'd listen to reason. A bond would be formed, a bond that ensured mutual prosperity and survival.

Wally showered and dressed. Sal, poor girl, still in her one-hundred-decibel coma, had an insipid smile stuck on her face like a decal, a component of her delirium. She was probably dreaming about her cosmopolitans, which were becoming a serious addiction of late. He dearly hoped she hadn't passed her bug along to him. The timing couldn't be worse.

Smith's creature was in the lobby, facing the elevators. He lounged half asleep in a chair, one reptilian eye open, his extremities spread to a three-chair radius. He acknowledged Wally with a glare. The orthodontist shrank toward the restaurant.

Jerome (Chicken) Little thought Sally Jo's husband was cowering on the high side of the norm. The rascal was up to something. Little had posted himself here following Mr. Smith's and Dr. Stockwall's outing. Also, something about Jack Armstrong's briefing had felt wrong, incomplete. The PhD candidate was on the alert for treachery.

Jerome Little, Chicken's alter ego, did not for an instant take his mind from Sally Jo. He was now her Jerry, she his Jo. The diminutives had come to them while entwined in each other's arms.

"Did they ever call you Jerry?" she had asked him.

"If I'd had any friends, they would've called me Jerry."

"Did you?"

"No."

"Ever?"

"Never."

He'd told her that at ten pounds, eleven ounces, he had been a difficult birth. His mother doubtlessly had called him names throughout, none of them Jerry. As a kindergartner, he'd weighed one hundred and four pounds. Throughout school, because of his bulk and grim features and the straight A's he'd carried, familiarity seemed unnatural. Classmates had kept their distance.

Sally Jo related to Jerry's loneliness. She'd told him that she'd forever been Sally Jo on the farm and at school. To her spouse, she was Sal, a tag she thought better suited to a mare. She'd said that her dairy princess victory had been by default, the prettier girls wanting to shake the rural image, competing ferociously to be cheerleaders. She'd always wanted to be *Jo*.

Jo was a yell queen's name. Jo implied vivacity. Girls named Jo had fun. Girls named Sally Jo milked cows after school.

So Jo it was, Jerry's beloved Jo, he thought dreamily.

Jo and Jerry.

Jerry and Jo.

Love means never having to say you're sorry.

In a Taihotsu Suites™ café, in the company of bleary-eyed diners in rumpled clothing with suitcases on rollers, Dr. Stockwall perceived that circadian rhythms had been checked at the door. They were air travelers to whom breakfast, lunch and dinner had no chronological meaning. They were hither and yon, merely tending to bodily requirements, refueling.

Ergo, a glass of wine at this hour was not inappropriate. With burritos, Wally had an overpriced California cabernet that was surprisingly ripe and toasty. Then another and another. He had to occupy himself before the bank opened. Not to mention steeling his courage for what he planned to do.

More news bulletins on the television. The price of the card was raising wildly, now up to $100 million, one-thousandth of the missing $100 billion. *Exclusive!!* was raising every penny.

"Chump change," said the barkeep. A Taihotsu Tidbit was on, informing them that the reward would buy only ten Malibu mansions. "The whole shiteree would buy ten thousand of them. Can you imagine the real estate taxes?"

Relaxed now, Wally smiled indulgently at him. He believed that $100 million was not excessive for the card's recovery.

After all his grief, he was entitled. He was not greedy. He'd settle for relative peanuts if that could be the end of it.

More news bulletins. *Exclusive!!* had purportedly recovered a bag of Taihotsu's cash bound for the furnaces. On an upcoming special, they promised to unveil its contents.

Wally checked his watch yet again. Two minutes till nine. Nearly tapped out, he left a two-dollar tip that won him a last-of-the-big-fucking-spenders look. He went into the lobby, not quite as frightened, and told his captor, "I'm out for my morning constitutional if that's all right."

Chicken Little grunted his acquiescence. The dentist departed unsteadily. He reeked of alcohol. If Stockwall bolted, he wouldn't get far, Little thought. He dug out his cell phone and contacted Mr. Smith, who was outside walking Wayne.

Jack Armstrong was beginning to live aspects of the role. He'd spent the night watching DVDs he'd bought of the nude, frolicking Eva Braun, surprising himself at his arousal. She wasn't movie-star gorgeous, but the Führer, who could have had his pick, chose Eva. There was something about her.

Jack had masturbated his member raw.

Jack/Jiminy asked, "Where is he going?"

"Toward the highway," Chicken Little said, fantasizing the orthodontist blundering into busy traffic, transformed into a grease spot by a succession of SUVs and eighteen-wheelers. Jerry was getting an erection, picturing his Jo in tight black at the memorial service, a ravishing widow.

"I see him. If it's okay, sir, Wayne and I shall divert in that direction," Mr. Smith said.

Little said it was.

Stockwall crossed the highway without incident and entered the bank branch. Roy Banker, bless him, was true to his word to the tune of ninety-three fifty. It was on the low side of Wally's approximation, however. He wondered if Roy had gouged extra fees because of the urgency. You couldn't trust anybody in this day and age.

Wally cashed the check and exited the bank, a roll of fifties and hundreds in his pocket, thinking it'd be adequate for start-up costs. His head was beginning to throb. Typhoid Sal and her flu, damn her, she was passing it along, one of few things she'd given him recently.

Wally went southward, through the first intersection and into a convenience store, to buy aspirin and to phone for a taxi. At the counter to pay, he interrupted the clerk. With a multibladed pocket knife, he was cutting twine and tape on a shipment of canned goods.

Inspired, Wally asked, "How much for that knife?"

"Not for sale, sir. Is gift from my son."

The shopkeeper was a subcontinent type with a British colonial accent, one of the hordes of them who had come to this nation to make their fortunes. Wally knew what lighted their fires. He laid out two fifties.

The clerk smiled and shook his head. "So sorry."

A hundred dollar bill too.

The clerk shook his head.

Wally doubled the pot. The clerk wordlessly handed him the Taihotsu Survivor™. Wally recalled that it had been described as a device that could do anything except toast bread, a Swiss Army knife on steroids.

He was not a violent man, but he required an advantage should Blondie prove recalcitrant and/or Mr. Smith and Mr. Little picked up his trail. He required protection. He could not conceal a saw or an axe under his shirt, let alone wield one. Any one of the Survivor's seventeen blades and pincers should suffice.

"For that sum, order me a taxi too," Wally said.

The clerk did so, the taxicab came, driven of course by a

brethren of the store clerk. Wally hurried into it.

Two blocks distant, Mr. Smith and Wayne observed Dr. Stockwall's deceit.

Wayne growled.

A devoted student of Bugsy Siegel now, Jack Armstrong conceptualized Benjamin Hymen's response to perfidy, his fury. The wrongdoer would be in for a hard tribunal.

Mr. Smith scratched under Wayne's collar.

"Easy, girl, easy. Everything will be hunky-dory."

26.

"Ain't this what you wanted, snookums?"

Carla sighed and looked at the kitchen clock, thinking it was and it wasn't. The result of putting two lonely people together should be a gradual romantic growth that would flower and endure, not a crazed hormonal override of common sense.

Shouldn't it?

Which it most often wasn't.

"Yes, Buster, for them to appeal to each other and to become friends and in good time to perhaps become more than friends is what I wanted, if it turns out to be what they want."

Buster was finishing his eggs and toast. He said, "So Rob didn't come home. They broke a curfew you set? They gonna lose their allowance? They're consenting adults, you know."

She said, "It never lasts when the consenting part happens so quickly. This is a fact."

He reached across and squeezed her hand. "Hey, it did with us. We're doing okay."

Carla had no rebuttal.

There was a timid knock on the door.

Mr. Sheepish coming home to roost, Carla thought.

Buster read her expression, uh-oh, and sprang up to answer.

"Sorry, Uncle Buster, but we fell asleep working on the number and watching TV," Rob said, Sarah at his side, holding a greeting-card-sized envelope. "After I change, we'd like to invite you guys out for breakfast."

Bat guano, Buster thought, grinning. Sarah's crimson face confirmed Carla's suspicion. A forty-eight-year-old gal blushing was endearing, as sweet as pie, but Buster knew they all needed to get off the subject of Carla's cupiding gone berserk into unconnubial bliss.

"We've eaten, thanks, but why don't we give the number a whirl?" Buster rapped his forehead. "I don't know about you kids, but the ol' gray matter is at its bestest in the morning. My Black Death is still hot and even I can make you guys toast."

In they went to the dining area. Carla, trying to be a good sport, was all smiles as she cleaned breakfast dishes.

Sarah sorted through the papers and organized last night's efforts. She knew Carla well enough to know what was going through her mind. To be technically correct, they had fallen asleep with the television on. It wasn't a complete falsehood.

After the clip of Rob in the blizzard they had clung to each other. By and by, Rob fumbled for her zipper again. This time she assisted.

Clothes strewn, wrapped in a blanket, Sarah and Rob had been awakened at dawn by a foaming-at-the-mouth evangelical preacher and his 1-800 number for donations.

Sarah was grateful that Carla declined eye contact. Rob was, too.

"First, have a look at this," Sarah said, handing Carla the envelope. "We found it on my front mat."

"There's been an epidemic of that lately," Buster said.

She removed a flowery and scrolled card, saying SORRY on the face. She opened it to "Neil."

"That repulsive Romeo in the sports bar?" Carla said.

"Yes."

"Are you thinking what I'm thinking?" Carla said.

"Somebody set him up to get us together?" Sarah said. "A long shot."

"The past few days have been a long shot," Rob said.

"Neil never looked at me twice. Suddenly I'm the object of the crudest form of attention."

Buster said, "We're maybe *all* being puppeteered. If that's a verb."

Carla did not appreciate somebody doing her matchmaking for her, providing romance and/or mathematical support. "Let's change the subject and have a fling at sudoku. I play it in the paper. If the numbers give us a winner, we may have solved the larger puzzle, too."

"I do have a serious sudoku jones," Sarah said.

On a lined pad, she sketched a box with eighty-one squares and filled in the twenty-six numbers at random:

After attempting several solutions, Sarah said, "Impossible, Carla. We can arrange the numbers a million different ways and still arrive at nothing."

"Forget it. Let's start where we left off."

"Okay," Sarah said in a few minutes. "Here it is."

12/23/18/23/9/22/11/12/23/13/6/14/15/22

ODIDREPODNUMLE

"This combination of vowels and consonants at least gives us syllables," she said. "But I'm afraid it's still gibberish."

"Let's give backbackasswards a spin," Buster suggested after a moment's study.

"What?" Carla asked.

"Why not? Backbackasswards is frontasswards if you wanna get technical."

Carla stared at it and said, "Sarah, can we reverse the letters, which I think is what he said? We've tried everything else imaginable. My man's illogic can be scarily logical at times"

Sarah agreed. Her arithmetic gymnastics had gotten them nowhere, and the author of the card apparently wanted Rob to solve it on his own, certainly without the aid of a supercom-

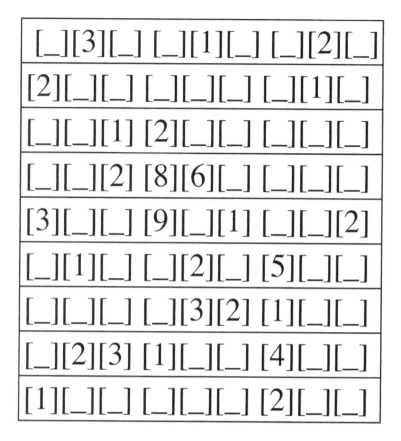

puter or an advanced knowledge of math.

She wrote: ELMUNDOPERDIDO

"Hmm. Elm Undop Erdido," Buster said. "Is that some form of tree fungus?"

"Oh my God," Carla said. "Your pen, please."

She separated the array of letters: EL/MUNDO/PERDIDO

"If the message is in Spanish, I think I have it. El is 'the.' Mundo is 'world.' Perdido is 'lost.' Adjectives follow nouns *en español*. The lost world. Does that mean anything?"

"Name of an old-timey movie," Buster said.

"I think you're thinking of Lost Horizon, where they crash in

Shangri-la," Carla said.

"That's what I said. At the end of the Shangri-la is the hundred billion smackers."

Rob had been quiet, too quiet. He finally said, "Aunt Carla, Uncle Buster, Sarah, the Lost World complex is one of the major sites at Tikal."

Buster punched a fist in the air. "Yes! Me and Sir Bill of Hockshop, we solved it."

"You did, Uncle Buster," Rob said, high-fiving him.

"Tikal. In Guatemala. Where you just were?" Sarah said.

"Where deranged people were tidying up after you to and from," Buster said.

"Yes."

"Rob, your late grandfather is sending you back there," Carla said.

Head on a swivel, Rob said, "Is sending us all there. Partners. Sarah?"

"They should know something, Rob."

"They should," he said, telling of seeing the clip of Rob last night. "They know or think they know who I am, Uncle Buster."

"You're definitely a person of interest on their radar screen."

"I am. I could be unpleasant company."

"How close they are is anybody's guess, how many and whoever *they* consists of. Rob's got a half-lap on them is my uneducated guess."

"Buster, this isn't a track meet," Carla said.

"Oh, yeah? Tell that to them bozos nipping at Rob's heels."

Gold fever, Sarah thought, but kept it to herself.

"Partners?" Rob said, looking around. "The Four Mouseketeers?"

"Hey, Rob, look, I dunno," Buster said. "I got a gig now and my Caddy's in some hellhole of a greasy garage, blindfolded and chained to the wall. It's your money."

"I have an insurance agency to run," Carla protested. "And it is your money, dear, should it be there for you."

"Sarah?" Rob said.

"If you want me along, Rob. Whether you do or not, I'm with the consensus. It is your money."

Buster and Carla looked at each other.

Awakened by the noisy debate, OC1 and OC2 appeared at the foot of the stairs, ears perking.

"Aunt Carla, didn't you say you have a crackerjack assistant named Maureen who'll step in whenever needed?"

"Well, yes," Carla said as the phone rang.

She picked it up, listened, and gave it to Buster.

"Uh-huh, sure, that's okay, no problem," he said and hung up. "That was Mildred from the Purple Flasher. The jukebox part is in. I'm out."

27.

The wretched turban-headed cabby got lost, found his way, then got lost again. The opened map book on the seat beside him seemed to be a prop. It might as well have been written in hieroglyphics. If there was a God of Stupidity in the crowded Hindu pantheon, Wally thought, He was a busy deity.

Finally, after interminable meandering, they went into the condominium complex, located the building in which Robin Weather stayed with his Aunt Carla Chance and his uncle, the comedian Buster Hightower—per Mr. Smith's gastroenterologist's information.

He was just in time to see the remade Robin Chance Weather, his aunt and uncle, and Weather's woman pile into a taxicab with luggage.

All had packed lightly and were in an obvious rush.

"Follow that car," Wally yelled.

"I hear that in cinema," said the laughing cabby.

"Now!"

"I am not understanding if you are serious, sir."

"I'll pay you double what is on your meter to stick on their tail without being seen."

"Pay double I am understanding," said the driver, accelerating, throwing the orthodontist back in his seat.

"Atta boy. Don't get lost again unless they do."

"Know Seattle like the back of my hands, sir."

28.

At the airport, in line at the ticket counter of the airline with which he'd flown home, Rob decided that they should go into Belize City and rent a car. "The fastest route is to fly to Flores, Guatemala. It's less than a couple of hours' drive from there to Tikal. From Belize City it's over twice as long, but on better roads and more places to duck in if we're forced to."

"Duck in" gave Buster the heebie-jeebies. You duck in when you're being hunted like a quacker. "If we have us a welcoming committee, it'll probably be at Flores, huh?"

"That's my theory."

"Heading us off at the pass," Buster said.

Sarah said, "But if somebody is waiting for us, won't they go directly to Tikal? What else is around Flores?"

"Good point," Rob said. "But if we arrive at Belize City, it'll be easy enough to pick up a paper or turn on the TV and find out the latest."

"Then what?" Carla asked.

"Belize is a great place to visit any time of the year. The beaches out on the cays are fantastic."

"Fun and sun and nervous stomachs," Sarah said.

Rob said, "Have I told you about all of Belize's Technicolor bird species?"

"Yeah?" Buster said. "Do they have the cooked goose and the gone gander and the dead duck?"

193

29.

The doubled fare magnetized Wally's taxicab to Weather and company. The driver expertly maintained a two-car interval. It was affirmation to Dr. Stockwall that money talks in Hindustani and any of the planet's hundreds of other languages. He imagined the driver's past life in Calcutta or Bangalore, running hashish and opium, one step ahead of drug enforcement police he hadn't bribed.

Wally queued up in the ticket line, three parties behind the slippery foursome. When they purchased their tickets and moved along, he cocked his head toward Weather and requested, "Another economy fare where they're going, please. I'm late."

Wondering why he didn't come forward with his companions, the agent asked, "The people ahead of you?"

Giving her a look saying, are-you-blind, how-stupid-are-you? Wally replied, "Of course."

The agent gave him the onceover, thinking that anybody could wind up sitting next to you on an airplane these days. Rumpled clothing, carry-on luggage, free-floating rudeness. How things had changed in her twenty-seven years in this crazy business.

Her husband referred to current air travelers as the unwashed masses, literally and figuratively. She was looking forward to retirement in four months, one week, two days, and six hours. They had travel plans, yes, but on highways and waterways and railways.

If this character was dangerous, off his rocker, TSA would detain him. It was their job, not hers, and they were damn good at it.

She processed W.D. Stockwall's ticket, presented him her sweetest smile and asked, "Luggage to check, sir?"

Luggage?

"Oh, yes. As I said, I'm running late," Wally extemporized. "A sudden business conference was called. A long story. I work with the woman's brother. These people don't know me. It's an anniversary bash. They went on a spur of the moment. They didn't tell us. We plan to surprise them, those of us in the family and some friends and—"

She interrupted the babbling. "Luggage, sir?"

"Luggage, yes. My wife's packing and will drop it off to me at the curb. May I check it before I board?"

"Certainly, sir. Your flight doesn't leave for Houston until shortly after midnight, so you should have ample—"

"Midnight?"

"Yes, sir. Our other daily flight departed at six A.M."

"Midnight!"

Was he deaf, too?

"Yes, sir."

The customer sighed, paid, and lumbered off with his ticket without a word. She thought: four months, one week, two days, and six hours, less five minutes.

A red-eye, Wally thought. Why does everything always happen to me? Can I ever have any luck at *anything?* He felt in his pocket. The Taihotsu Survivor™ rested heavily in it. He couldn't carry it aboard for the flight to Houston and he might need it later. He'd have to pack it in luggage he didn't have and check it.

The gift shops were all inside the concourses, so he went

down an escalator to the baggage carousels, to appropriate what somebody had failed to pick up.

30.

In high school, Sally Jo Stockwall had yearned to join the drama club. Alas, its schedule conflicted with 4H activities. But now, today, Sally Jo performed as a real-life thespian. She was having a blast.

Per the script updated by eye contact with and nods by Jerome (Chicken) Little, Mr. Jiminy C. Smith told Mrs. Stockwall how annoyed he was at her husband.

She should feel lucky that his lecture would be verbal, the unknowing Jack Armstrong thought. Benjamin Hymen would be in a homicidal rage and who could blame him.

"If he is given to capricious behavior, his timing could not be worse," Mr. Smith said in a soft, even, congenial, unsettling tone. "If he gave in to an impulsive urge to sightsee, I am very disappointed that he did not first inform us."

Mr. Jerome (Chicken) Little stood behind Mr. Smith, hands on hips, glowering theatrically at Mrs. Sally Jo Stockwall, thinking of another Ambrose Bierce definition of marriage: The state or condition of a community consisting of a master, a mistress and two slaves, making in all, two.

Jerry did an adorable job at feigning anger at his Jo, she believed. Her feelings at the moment about her husband, well, if she had a nickel for every time she'd been peeved at Dr. Wally, she wouldn't need that magic number. Running out on her, the cowardly bastard, this took the cake.

Flinching in terror, Jo looked at her Jerry. She wanted to fly into his arms and smother him with kisses. She wanted to jump his bones.

"Wally didn't say a word to me," she truthfully replied.

"I've managed to cobble together a luncheon conference at a midsized clinic of ten dental professionals," Mr. Smith said. "That they are excited about our investment tool is an understatement. Dr. Stockwall's presence is crucial."

Sally Jo sighed helplessly. This Jack Armstrong fellow of her Jerry's should be up for an Oscar.

"Do you and your spouse carry cell phones?"

"Yes, we do."

"Do you have different numbers?"

"Yes."

"Please call him on yours."

"Now?"

Eyebrows almost imperceptibly raised, this stern sitcom dad didn't have to answer in words. Sally Jo reluctantly took the telephone out of her purse and punched in his number. She was looking forward to having Dr. Dickhead out of her hair, fortune or no fortune.

"Sal?"

"Where are you, Wally?"

"Out and around. I'm on my morning constitutional."

Saying "morning constitutional" as if it were a regular activity. Sally Jo Stockwall heard people noise and loudspeakers in the background, making announcements she couldn't understand. Wally had gotten to be such a lazy liar, insulting her by not even extending himself to be creative.

Jo didn't give a hoot. She was with Jerry, wherever he and the situation led them.

"Wally, why is it so noisy?"

"We live in a busy, congested world, Sal."

Oh, that explained everything.

"You're missing an important business conference Mr. Smith arranged, Wally."

Meanwhile, Wally watched a green case on wheels rotate out of sight again. It was perfect, anonymous and small, evidently abandoned or forgotten.

He suspected they were putting her up to this, the brute threatening to dismember or strangle her or worse—rape. He felt for his Sal.

"Sal, are you alone?"

"Yes," she said. "Mr. Smith ordered me to call you. I'm in our room by myself. They're giving me two minutes."

"He's not listening in, you're sure?"

"Absolutely, but please talk fast. They'll be banging on the door any second. I'll have to tell them something."

Wally had to trust his lawful spouse at some level. When he zeroed in on his fortune, there'd be no way he could deny her a share. Better that she be on his side.

"Wally, please speak to me. They'll hurt me, I know they will!"

"Sal, this has to be between you and me. There is no franchise, no advisory instrument for investments on the part of dentists. It is a ruse."

"Oh God, really?" Sally Jo said, hoping she wasn't laying it on too thickly.

"What it is, Sal," he said, his voice lowering. "It's the pot of gold at the end of the rainbow and Fort Knox and King Solomon's Mines rolled into one. I can say no more other than it is rightfully mine."

"Yours?"

"Ours, Sal. Ours."

Looking at her Jerry, she said, "Please, Wally, what on earth are you talking about?"

"Sal, they can't listen in, correct?"

"That's what I said, Wally."

"All right, you absolutely have to stall them, divert them. Do *anything* to give me a head start."

"To where? I have to know where you're going. If I don't, I won't be able to sleep, I'll be so worried."

"Very well." He studied his ticket carefully for the first time. At a glance, he'd seen that it was to Houston. No, wait. Not Houston as a destination. Houston was a stopover for a connecting flight to Belize City, Belize. In Central America, isn't it? A flyspeck of a banana republic?

He read the flight information to her.

"Why Belize?" she asked, looking at Jerry.

"I don't comprehend the big picture myself. Not yet. Trust me, Sal, and misdirect those gentlemen any way you can. You'll be glad you did. Unimaginable wealth awaits me. Us. Promise me, you'll do as I say. Promise."

Her darling Wally was in full-flight mode. She hadn't the foggiest if he was going to Belize or the Sahara Desert or Greenland, but she had a hunch Jerry and his connections could clear up that issue.

"I promise, Wally," she said, certain that this performance would have won her an A+ in drama class and a starring role in the spring play.

After extracting a second solemn promise, Wally hung up.

The green suitcase was coming around, nobody in sight. He snatched the Taihotsu Vagabond™.

As Sally Jo gave Mr. Smith and Mr. Little his itinerary, Wally went into the closest restroom. Inside a stall, he checked the case's outer pockets for identification and for tape and decals, to make it easier for the owner to pick out on the carousel.

No identification or conspicuous features. Good. Wally slipped the massive pocketknife inside the case and went back to the unfriendly ticket agent to check it, thinking that the woman badly needed to attend a customer-service seminar.

31.

At dawn, having deplaned in Houston at George Bush Intercontinental Airport, Buster Hightower shambled side-by-side with Carla Chance, crankily following Rob Weather and Sarah Hilyer, who were hand in hand. Buster was stiff and sore from lack of leg room. His eyes stung from lack of sleep. It was like playing till two A.M. in an unappreciative beer parlor. More than once, he'd whined his complaints to Carla.

"Bitch and moan all you like, Buster, but please maintain the pace."

"Lookie, kiddo, the kids, they're jogging, for crying out loud. And see how long this ramp is. We're halfway to Dallas."

"Buster, we have less than an hour to make our connecting flight to Belize City. We can't dawdle."

"It is big here, Texas big. Houston's the seventeenth busiest airport in the world," Rob called back to them.

"That makes me feel better."

Buster shut up until they passed a statue of George Bush the Elder, the airport's namesake. It was bronze, the former president youthful and heroic.

"They oughta put it outside so the pigeons can appreciate it, too. Him and one for that boy of his, too."

Dr. J.D. (Wally) Stockwall stayed ten paces behind the foursome. Despite the close proximity in the Sea-Tac terminal and on the aircraft, too, there hadn't been a hint of recognition on their part. Wally had taken no risks, had avoided eye contact.

202

Belize might pose a greater risk. He'd found an article on it in the forward seat pocket. The nation was underdeveloped and sparsely populated. One could rattle around there. By then, though, with any luck, he'd have the magical card and what it promised.

At that very moment, the pilot of the chartered Gulfstream nudged the copilot and pointed out his window. She looked at the sunrise that plated the Caribbean copper. It was time to radio Belize City's Philip Goodson International Airport, to request approach and landing instructions.

"Ever been here before?" he asked her.

"Twelve or fifteen years ago. I remember one runway and no taxiway. According to our charts, there've been changes. Improvements."

"We can hope," the pilot said as he adjusted the elevator trim. "We're nose-up a degree again. It's as if we have shifting cargo."

The copilot shivered. "It's *him* going to the aft lavatory, throwing off our center of gravity."

"You're probably right. Are you feeling turbulence?"

"Now that you mention it, I do. It's like a cadence. Rhythmic. What could it be? The air's been as smooth as glass."

The pilot shrugged and got on the horn to Goodson International.

Of the three human passengers on the manifest, a Mr. Smith, the man who ostensibly paid for the charter, dozed in his seat, a golden retriever curled up at his side.

Jack Armstrong knew his fixation on Bugsy Siegel was getting out of hand, but that wasn't an unhealthy thing for an actor. He could play the role if another movie was made. The one starring Warren Beatty was acceptable, but he could do better if he'd ever get a fair break. But he wouldn't, par for the course.

Fully asleep now, he dreamt of Prohibition and Tommy guns blazing from black Ford sedans that careened around corners on two wheels. He dreamt of Benjamin Hymen Siegel mowing down his rivals, stogie wedged dapperly in a side of his mouth.

He dreamt too of Eva Braun sitting on a dock at some idyllic retreat she shared with the Führer, Berchtesgaden or one of those. He dreamt of Bugsy, a Jew, having his way with her, taking what he wanted right there on the dock, Hitler helpless, frozen in place, screaming like a demented rooster.

Jack Armstrong had an erection.

The copilot's *him* was in the aft lavatory, standing. He also sported an erection. The third human passenger, a woman, was there too, legs wrapped around him as he cupped her bare buttocks, thrusting inside her.

32.

They were drinking Belikin, a mellow Belizean brew.

"It's the national beverage," Rob Weather said. "We'd be rude guests in this country if we didn't partake and help out their balance of payments."

They were lazing and drinking in a gracious, decades-old, wooden house. Their rented four-wheel-drive Taihotsu Mountain Goat™ was parked out front. Their plan was to get a good night's sleep, then drive straight through to Tikal.

The couples occupied two rooms. There was no more pussyfooting. There were larger concerns than Victorian propriety.

Lovingly restored and divided into a five-unit hotel, the house featured gleaming hardwood floors and original furnishings. Sarah and Carla supposed it had been built by a sea captain or a colonial merchant.

This Belize City house also offered hanging swings on the front porch, which were too conspicuous to enjoy, despite the absence of air conditioning inside. Ceiling fans in rooms paddled slabs of warm, humid air that oddly seemed to scoop away Rob's and Sarah's galloping paranoia, their sense of a smothering conspiracy. They felt isolated, safe, incubated.

Sarah was reading Rob's guidebook, *Central America Travel* (Taihotsu Press, $16.95), astonished at the here and now. She was thousands of miles from home, with a lover and near-stranger.

Further, she was drinking the beer like a sorority girl, and she didn't especially like beer. She and her mother had enjoyed an after-dinner glass of good dessert wine, a Porto port or Andalusian sherry. But the Belikin was going down so smoothly, deadening her nerve endings. The dubious power of alcohol and lust and satiation and danger and being smitten.

She began reading aloud, "Belize was a British colony. Belize, formerly British Honduras, the smallest country in Central America, is the area of New Hampshire and half as populous as Wyoming. Following independence in 1981, the Queen remained on their currency and their tongues, although Creole and Spanish pour forth as naturally, all three languages in the same train of thought."

"Population?"

"Two hundred and eighty thousand."

"Belize isn't a big haystack to be needles in," Rob said.

Sarah read on, "One Belizean in four lives in flat, steamy, ramshackle Belize City, which juts into the Caribbean, as if sticking its chin out at Mother Nature, who periodically obliges with a punch in the form of a hurricane.

"The federal authorities, weary of being pressure-washed by tropical storms, created an isolated, humdrum seat of government fifty miles inland. Belmopan is more hurricane resistant, though not as colorful, charming, lively, raffish and exotic as is its predecessor."

"That settles it. No night out on the town for us," Rob said. "We've had our fill of lively, raffish and exotic."

They put the guidebook aside and watched Mexican soap operas and Argentinean *fútbol* and get-rich-quick infomercials in two languages.

They saw Grandmother Marie Blanchard's photo twice; a shot of Grandfather Saburo at the wing of his Zero, bandanna around his forehead, the red meatball and Japanese writing on it; a clip of MacArthur, the famous one where he's wading ashore in the Philippines, keeping his I Shall Return promise; several interviews of Saburo Taihotsu's executive chef, the Dutch woman's skirts progressively shorter, a centerfold deal with a beaver magazine paying her six-digits finalized. Good for you, Grampa, you dirty old man, Rob thought fondly.

Mathematicians and statisticians and code-breakers and computer nerds and jackass moderators postulated on the broken number array. At a computer-generated domed football stadium, there was a Taihotsu Tidbit. A caricature stepped off the stadium's uppermost seats, the 300 level, making a soft landing in the 200 level, on 100,000,000,000 simulated greenbacks.

Wally had taken a ground-floor room, in an old house that'd been remodeled into a small hotel. Adequate lodging in this dilapidated little town was in short supply, and this dump was across the street from Blondie and friends.

They seemed to have gone in for the day, so he took down their license number and went for a walk in search of toiletries. He wondered yet again what a tiny Third World backwater had to do with a treasure that was fifty times its GDP. Had Weather and his female companion thrown a dart at a map?

Wally came to a druggist shop. Its sign advertised LICENSED TO SELL DRUGS AND POISON. A strange nation this was, minuscule and broiling and winterless. He went in and purchased toothpaste, deodorant and shaving gear. He asked where one might find a decent meal and an acceptable wine to accompany it. He was simply advised that there was a bar down the street.

The bar was full of native people. Some were crying, some were laughing through tears. The majority were Negroid, the remainder half-castes of some ilk. Most were youthful. The sadness in this barroom was thicker than the humidity.

At the rear was an open and empty and flower-filled coffin. A grief-stricken, chocolate-brown girl clung to a coffin rail, wailing nonstop. Nobody could comfort her. Wally realized that he was in the midst of a wake, that the majority of the bar patrons were mourners.

Wally sat at the bar and asked for a wine list. The bartender said he hadn't seen one lately. The orthodontist considered a local rum, then thought better of it and dubious sanitation practices in the impoverished tropics. He ordered Taihotsu Select™ vodka on the rocks.

These Belizeans spoke English, so he struck up a conversation with a husky young black on the stool next to him. He wore a Real Madrid soccer jersey and his hair African tribal-bushy. He was drinking Belikin beer out of the bottle.

"Forgive my curiosity," Wally said. "Who died?"

"Marty. We're friends saying goodbye to him. Marty just graduated from the University College of Belize. He was going to teach school up at Orange Walk. He took a holiday to Cancun to celebrate with friends. He had so much going for him. It was not fair for him to end up like this."

"How'd he die?"

"Acute alcohol poisoning is the official cause."

A primitive in over his head at a party scene and drinking himself to death. Picturing Chicken Little, the image giving him goose bumps, Wally knew there were worse ways to go.

"I'm terribly sorry for your loss."

"Thank you," the boy said, extending a hand. "I'm Philip."

"Dr. Stockwall, a dental practitioner specializing in orthodontics," he said, taking it. "My clinic is near Beverly Hills. I straighten the teeth of the stars. Please don't ask for names."

"Okay, man, I won't."

Miffed, Wally asked, "Philip what?"

Philip shrugged. "Just Philip. We're casual here."

So, Just Philip it would be. "What is it you do?"

"Drive taxi."

"Interesting. Are you available for a charter fare?"

"I am. Where to, sir?"

Wally sipped his vodka, grimacing at the burning in his throat. "Well, that's the thing. I'm surprising some dear friends. They're celebrating their twenty-fifth wedding anniversary. They're in town now with her younger sister and her husband. It was spur of the moment, so nobody knows for certain their itinerary. I know they're going to inform us when they get home, but I want to surprise them and make their celebration unforgettable."

This rich, shifty-eyed dentist was talking to him like he was a child, obviously lying through his teeth. His reasons were none of Philip's business.

"We're going to follow them? It's hard to do out on the highway. Not many cars on the road after you leave Belize City. This ain't Santa Monica."

"They have a Jeeplike rental vehicle," Wally said, handing him his notation of the license plate and rental agency. "What can you learn of their destination?"

"Let us see what we can do," Just Philip said, flipping open a cell phone, mildly curious now.

Wally listened to laughter, and English slipping in and out of an aboriginal patois, "fock" this and "focking" that, with the occasional "mon" and "bwah" and other fractured syllables.

Just Philip hung up and said, "Tikal."

"Excuse me?"

Just Philip looked at him. "My car rental friend says Tikal. You know Tikal, man. The incredible ancient Maya site. It's one of the wonders of the world."

"Of course I do," Wally lied.

"Since it is across the border in Guatemala, most rental companies don't allow you to take their vehicles there. This one does, but you have to pay extra and fill out papers, proof of insurance and things."

"Tikal would be an ideal setting for my surprise," Wally said, signaling the bartender for a refill. "Do you go to Guatemala?"

"I can do, but it is expensive," Just Philip said, smelling the dentist's money.

"Price is no object. Within reason."

"When?"

"Dawn."

"No problem, boss."

They agreed on a fee, double what Just Philip normally asked for a Tikal round trip. Wally had another vodka, bought Just Philip another Belikin, and listened to a boring travelogue on the wonders of Tikal. As if piles of old limestone were a fraction as intriguing as $100,000,000 at the very least. If the boy only knew.

Back in his room, Wally tossed the stolen suitcase on the bed. He hoped he'd get lucky and find clean clothing his size. He was a bit ripe.

After removing and pocketing his Survivor, he unzipped and unfolded, revealing a naughty lingerie shop full of unmentionables. They were rather large, though, his size if he were so inclined.

Fully aroused for the first time in ages, he laid a G-string and a skimpy bra out on the bed. At the bottom of the case were black leather boots and a whip. Wally conjured a big girl named Trixi, who knew what she wanted. Trixi who was rough and impatient, who wouldn't take no for an answer.

He unzipped his pants, thinking what was the harm to let one's imagination progress to fulfillment?

Then he spotted a card taped to an inside flap of the case,

identifying its owner as Edward D. Hoopsma, a sales representative for an industrial fastener firm.

Wally yelped and stepped back. A degenerate carrying who knows how many diseases. He'd gingerly repack, drop the filth out the window, and scrub his hands until they were pink.

He turned and yelped even louder.

Chicken Little stood in front and over him.

"How did you—?"

"All you gotta knows we're fucking here, turdbird."

Fumbling, Wally zipped up and cocked a thumb to the bed. "It's not what it seems."

"We ain't got no interest in your hobbies, what kind of fucking prevert you are. Mr. Smith, what he wants to hear outta you is your yesterday, today and tomorrow."

Wally did not omit a single detail.

In bed, Rob and Sarah snuggled, flicked on the *Exclusive!!* special, sound low. Above NAGOYA, JAPAN LIVE, Brett Steele and Ashley Parker stood outside a Taihotsu Iron Works™ mill, a duffel bag between them.

"—miraculously escaped the molten steel inferno," said Ashley.

"Ironically, this is the plant operated by Saburo Taihotsu's father when father and son made the ill-fated trip across the ocean to garner business for the firm," said Brett.

"Why do they constantly say ironic and ironically, along with decimate and decimated?" Sarah asked.

"They have to."

"Why?"

Damned if Rob knew. "They just do."

"—provided exclusively to *Exclusive!!* by an anonymous source," Brett crowed. "Ashley, would you do the honors?"

"I'd be delighted," she said, taking a large knife from an

unseen hand.

"If you want irony, Sarah, how about me being pursued by the media for a story when they weren't exactly pursuing me for employment."

"You aren't the self-pitying type, Rob."

"Ironically."

Not delicately, Ashley stabbed and slashed the bag.

"Ouch," Brett said, wincing at the camera. "You decapitated a big bunch of Ben Franklins."

Ashley knelt, cleavage at the fore, and ripped it open wider. She reached in and yanked her hand out, as if she had disemboweled it, holding a fistful of cut-up paper. "Are you really surprised, Brett?"

"Not really, Ashley. It merely confirms the life of Saburo Taihotsu as a sham. He as the legendary Mongoose, protected by this woman (inset of Marie Blanchard). And now having incinerated his fortune, taking it with him, if you will. We'll return in a minute after these important messages, at which time I will present a challenge to the person who may be key to the mysterious and missing one-hundred billion."

During the commercials, Sarah asked, "How much of anything on this show can we believe?"

"They hire people by the carload as fact checkers and researchers. It's information and advice they often ignore. A story of this magnitude, I don't think they'd tamper with it."

At the end of the break, Brett pointed a finger at his audience. "I have a blockbuster of an important announcement, ladies and gentlemen. It is as explosive as the Enola Gay. Robert Weather is a former colleague, who I consider one of my closest friends."

"Barf, puke, retch," Robin Weather said. "He can't even get my name right."

"You're a respected professional, but through no fault of your own, you're at the center of this vortex. Your grandfather was a prankster of enormous proportions and you, we can assume by your sudden disappearance, hold the complete number string and therefore the key to this unimaginable fortune.

"Do the right thing, Rob. Come to us."

33.

After breakfast, as Carla packed, Buster paged through the Belize telephone directory. Besides keeping his mind off all the bad things that could happen to them, phonebooks were a good source of material.

"One phone book for the whole, entire country and it ain't a third the size of the Seattle White Pages. I tell you that, snookums?"

"Yes, I believe you did. Please get off the bed so I can lay out our suitcase."

Buster obeyed, saying, "I love this. There's less than a hundred attorneys in the Yellow Pages and they don't have 1-800 numbers or advertise. This country would be a helluva tough house to play if you do lawyer jokes."

"Rob and Sarah weren't at breakfast. I hope they're getting ready too."

Or doing something more fun than packing, Buster didn't say. "Lookie at this heading. Offshore Financial Services. Yikes. Talk about a Yellow Pages logjam. Where you go to hide a lot of money, huh?"

Carla stopped and looked at him. "Buster, I'm afraid for us. All four of us."

He got out of his chair. "C'mere."

She did and they had a long hug.

"We'll be okay. I know we will," he said.

★ ★ ★ ★ ★

Sarah and Rob had finished what Buster guessed they were doing and were also packing. Rob was lacing up a size 10 1/2 DD Taihotsu XCountry™ hiking shoe, watching the news on a Mexican station. There was a photograph of a large, pretty tomboyish woman who looked back at him from the 1930s or 1940s, a better shot than on *Exclusive!!* Hands on ample hips, she wore a man's shirt and was trying her best not to smile. The photo was black and white. It tinted her long wavy hair platinum.

"This is the picture in a silver frame on my mother's nightstand. I remember her saying it was a distant aunt. After they died, I packed it away. I don't remember where."

"*Exclusive!!* does, Rob."

Sarah followed what she could with her undergrad Spanish. "The woman was identified from unnamed sources as Marie Chance Blanchard. There's an unspecified link between Marie Chance Blanchard and Saburo Taihotsu and . . . oops, there's your name."

"I heard it."

"I wish they wouldn't talk so fast. They're saying that Saburo Taihotsu, the Mongoose, could have snapped this photo of her while she was harboring him during World War II."

"Reportedly, supposedly, allegedly, ironically," Rob said. "Legally or ee-legally."

Before Carla and Buster left their room, she finished her family tree project:

She showed Buster, who said, "Looks like I'm your dangling participle there."

Wally got into Just Philip's taxi, a 1980s Oldsmobile sedan, a shoebox the length of a city block. It had a cracked windshield and upholstery that was as much duct tape as vinyl.

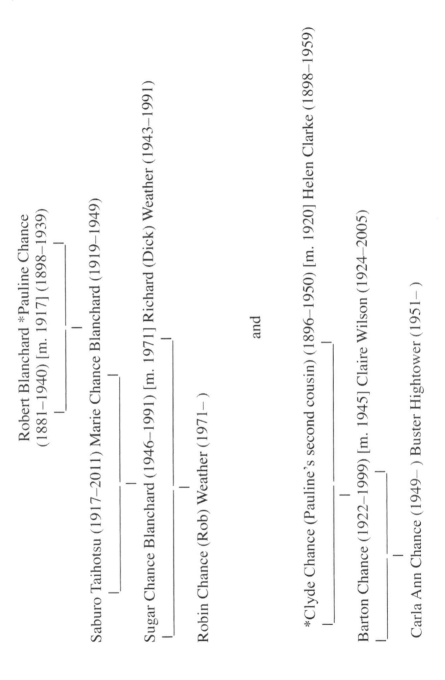

Robert Blanchard *Pauline Chance (1881–1940) [m. 1917] (1898–1939)

Saburo Taihotsu (1917–2011) Marie Chance Blanchard (1919–1949)

Sugar Chance Blanchard (1946–1991) [m. 1971] Richard (Dick) Weather (1943–1991)

Robin Chance (Rob) Weather (1971–)

and

*Clyde Chance (Pauline's second cousin) (1896–1950) [m. 1920] Helen Clarke (1898–1959)

Barton Chance (1922–1999) [m. 1945] Claire Wilson (1924–2005)

Carla Ann Chance (1949–) Buster Hightower (1951–)

After Wally had spilled all to Chicken Little, the beast had
not offered to further the alliance with him and Mr. Smith.
He'd merely stuck an index finger the size of a club in his face
and said, "Don't fuck up no more, as Mr. Smith, he gets his
money." Wally did not think an offer this morning was forthcom-
ing.

"Guatemala," Wally said. "We're going to Guatemala. Is it
like Belize?"

Insulted on behalf of his nation and his fellow Belizeans, Just
Philip jerked away from the curb and told the ignoramus, "No,
boss, Guatemala is nothing like Belize, as you'll soon see.
Guatemala has laws like we do and you do up in the States, but
their laws are soft. People there in Guatemala, they behave as
they will."

Swell, Wally thought. On top of everything else, we're headed
for Dodge City.

Meanwhile, on a chartered flight from Belize City, Belize, to
Flores, Guatemala, the town with the closest airport to Tikal,
Mr. Smith sat up front with the pilot. Dressed on the instructions of his employer, he wore jungle fatigues, a bush hat, and a
sense of adventure on his smiling face. It appeared as if he had
an unlimited wardrobe budget for this role, a first in Jack
Armstrong's dubious career.

Wayne the Wonder Rental Dog, as Jack sarcastically thought
of him, was at his feet. The small, four-seat, piston-engine plane
had dual controls, and the big dog interfered with movement of
the rudder pedals. The pilot said nothing, feeling the breath of
the gigantic mutation of a white man behind him. He'd make
do.

Mr. Smith had asked the pilot about Guatemala, specifically
their slant on law and order. He received an answer much the
same as that which Wally had received from Just Philip. Mr.

Smith was delighted. He knew Benjamin Hymen Siegel would be, too. It was his kind of place.

It was Jack Armstrong's too. He'd make his move on that enchanted set of numbers. He was done working sporadic jobs at union scale.

Jerome (Chicken) Little and Sally Jo Stockwall were squeezed together in the rear seats, no hardship for either. She'd catch him catching a glance at her, then quickly turn forward. He'd do the same. They were making a game of it.

"Be careful to maintain the charade," he had warned in the Gulfstream's aft lavatory.

"I'll try," she'd said. "If you'll try."

"I'll try to try," he'd said, before taking her in his arms yet again.

Jo felt secure, bound for the great unknown with her Jerry. But he seemed moody. Oddly, despite their playfulness, there was a hint of sadness in his eyes. That bothered her a tad, but her purse was slung on a shoulder, nestled in her lap, still stuffed with slot machine winnings. If all else failed, if life disappointed her as it so often had, what money she had talked. It opened doors, swinging them wide.

Jerry *was* sad. Attempting to conceal his sadness, he was dying to know if his Jo knew that her husband was a sadomasochistic pervert, a blazing drag queen, a transvestite lacking the physique to carry it off. He felt badly for this lovely, passionate woman, encumbered for years with a degenerate.

No wonder the Stockwalls' sex life had withered. Ambrose Bierce had insightfully and cleverly defined an abstainer as a weak person who yields to the temptation of denying himself a pleasure.

Jerry caressed the top of Jo's delicate palm with his thumb-sized pinkie. Even the most intense of lovers should be permitted a secret.

34.

Just Philip was going to be a trial, Wally realized, him and his wailing about Marty, the dead drunk, and his endless travelogue. Still in Belize City, he stopped at the foot of a malarial waterway he quaintly identified as Haulover Creek. It offered a view of more ramshackle squalor on the other side.

"This little bridge here? It's unique."

Saying it as if the short, narrow span were the Golden Gate. Dr. Stockwall suppressed a sigh. "We cross it to get to the other side, yes?"

Sarcastic asshole, Just Philip thought. "You know why they call Haulover Creek Haulover Creek?"

"No."

"Before the Swing Bridge, the first of the bridges we got over Haulover Creek now, you had to haul stuff to the other side by barge. Now, we got other bridges, higher off the water. Here, still, guys on ropes, twice a day, they swing the bridge open parallel to the creek so boats can pass. This is the world's last swing bridge. I guarantee it. It is a fact. We just missed the morning swing."

Dr. Stockwall knew that the monstrosity and his crazed superior with the Bugsy Siegel hang-up were nearby and anxious. Wherever they were, Wally also knew he was their prisoner.

"Oh, for God's sake!"

Just Philip took the bludgeoned hint, shut up, sullenly drove onto the Swing Bridge, and headed toward the Western Highway, 130 kilometers of blacktop separating them and the Guatemalan border.

Rob's short lecture on the Swing Bridge was met with enthusiasm, but obviously they couldn't stop and wait for the next opening. Fifteen miles out of Belize City, as they passed through the small community of Hattieville, he said, "Named for Hurricane Hattie after it slammed Belize City in 1961. Folks sought refuge and stayed."

When Rob sped up, Carla said, "No offense, but your driving reminds me of Buster's."

"Hey, I drive like a little old lady, like my Aunt Ethel."

"Your Aunt Ethel, who weaved across the centerline."

Buster said, "They exaggerated her blood-alcohol. When they draw blood from a stiff, they can get the numbers wrong."

"There's no speed limit on Belize's highways," Rob said. "And the whole world is gaining on us, you know."

"One of my companies is perfect for you," Carla said. "Mach One Mutual."

"Good luck, Rob. They're picky. Mach One Mutual, they turned me down," Buster said.

"I'm staying out of this," Sarah said, cinching her seat belt tighter.

After an uneventful two-and-a-half-hour drive along underpopulated scrub, Wally and Just Philip neared San Ignacio, population approximately ten thousand, the last major burg before the Guatemala border. They slowed and went around wagons occupied by blue-shirted men and women wearing thick shawls. Except for the straw hats and suspenders on the men, Wally thought, these blue-shirts could be Franco's Falangists.

In an attempt to make up with Just Philip, as near an apology as he could muster, he asked, "I do appreciate your expertise, your insights. I really do. I have a lot on my plate. Who are they?"

"Mennonites. Most are north, up by Orange Walk."

"Fascinating," Dr. Stockwall said, yawning, weary of being diplomatic.

Just Philip stopped at a single-lane bridge as oncoming traffic passed. The fat, smelly white man fidgeted in the back seat, ants in his pants, impatient on account of nothing he was willing to share. When the light changed from red to green—one of Belize's very few traffic lights—they moved ahead.

Just Philip resisted informing him that they were on the Hawkesworth, Belize's only suspension bridge. Fuck him. Let him be ignorant, him who had to get to Tikal, for some reason other than a normal person's reason. The Tikal ruin put Angkor Wat and Machu Picchu to shame, greatness this man would not care about.

"Are we getting close?"

"Closer, boss. A couple of hours. We can stop for lunch? Right here on Burns Avenue, there's Eva's Cafe. Nobody should leave these parts without visiting Eva's."

Wally had no appetite, for food or provincial lore. A combination of stress and climate and that substandard Taihotsu vodka, he believed.

"No stopping and it's time you oriented me on Tikal."

Saying it like "give me my money's worth, boy." Just Philip couldn't argue the money, though.

Just Philip put his pout in abeyance and began at the beginning, at 800 B.C., when Tikal was thought to be first inhabited.

At lunch, Rob started at 800 B.C. too.

After driving farther on the Western Highway, after seeing hideously wrecked cars left at the roadside, as effective as speed limits and nonexistent highway patrols, Rob had eased off the gas without additional encouragement. They went through and by towns named Cotton Tree, Churchyard and Teakettle Village.

At San Ignacio, they stopped for lunch at Eva's, a local institution constructed of wood-frame, make-do and atmosphere. Outside it, utility lines crisscrossed like black spaghetti and dogs snoozed where they pleased, displaying their ribs. Eva's was a café and Internet point and bulletin board and all-purpose hangout.

"In a nutshell," Rob said, laying out a map of Tikal, touching spots as he spoke, "Tikal was inhabited between 800 B.C. and 900 A.D. At the zenith of its power in the 8th century A.D., and supported a population equaling Tacoma, Washington's two hundred thousand. Thousands of structures have been discovered. There'll never be the resources to uncover and restore them all. Archaeologists believe the Maya knew Tikal as Place of Voices, or Spirit Voices.

"Lord Hasaw Chan K'awil was the twenty-sixth ruler in the dynasty that governed Tikal for hundreds of years. His reign, from 682 to 734 A.D., was Tikal's longest. When his wife died in 703, he ordered Temple II to be constructed in her honor. Upon Hasaw's death in 734, Yik'in Chan K'awil, his son and successor, had Temple I built in homage to him. The latter is showing its age. The face is blackened and the steps are too worn to ascend.

"Here," he said, pointing. "The Central Acropolis. Longer than two football fields, it's a warren of stairways, corridors and doorways, probably a residential and administrative center for the upper classes. The Central Acropolis was part of the building frenzy that characterized the rule of Hasaw and Yik'in.

"The son's most ambitious project is west of the Great Plaza. Temple IV. A blockish monolith, Temple IV remains shaggy with vegetation and rises two hundred and twelve feet, a building height not exceeded in the Americas until the advent of elevators in the late 1800s.

"I went up a series of wooden ladders totaling one hundred and fifty steps, then a dozen more on the temple itself to reach the base of the roof comb. The view compensates for the effort. Temples I, II, and III erupt from one-hundred-foot-high triple-canopy jungle.

"I mentally defoliated Tikal. The Great Plaza is mown grass now, but was plastered in its heyday. The temples and lesser buildings were painted. The city teemed with commerce and ceremony and agriculture.

"I tried to visualize a satellite photo of the region snapped in 800 A.D. It might resemble today's central California, a mix of urban centers and intensive farming.

"Tikal's last dated inscription was 869 A.D. Other Maya city-states were emptying out by then, too. Overpopulation, warfare, and deforestation had caught up to them. There need not have been a calamity such as a hurricane or a plague. A couple of years of below-average rainfall could have been their ruination. Anyway, that's my theory. I prefer to think of Tikal as Place of Distractions."

Rob's voice trailed off as their food arrived. "We'll just have to see it to do it justice."

Impressive, Buster thought. Rob was doing it from memory, in a nice anchorman voice, no idiot cards in front of him. The guy was definitely underemployed when he was employed on the air.

Sarah squeezed his arm, moved, knowing what the site meant to him, more than the money.

Carla watched him dab red liquid from a small bottle onto his rice and beans. "What's that?"

"Marie Sharp's hot sauce, Aunt Carla. Locals tell me that no meal is complete without it."

"I'll try a little."

Sarah said, "You didn't mention the Lost World complex."

"It's impressive as all Tikal structures and complexes are, but it's a rung below the list of must-sees, like Temple I and II."

"Ayee!"

"Sorry, Aunt Carla. I should've given you fair warning. The active ingredient is the habanero pepper, the world's hottest. Marie's has a carrot base. I think it's the tastiest of all the hot sauces."

"Yeah, right," Carla rasped, grabbing her Belikin. "Tasty."

Buster smiled. His honorary nephew didn't seem too sorry. "What's the big deal about the Lost World, the Mungo What-not?"

Sarah answered, "Somebody knew how important this was to Rob. It fit the puzzle, you-know-who's conception of him solving it."

Mr. Smith was already at Tikal, in his safari finery, with Chicken Little and the Stockwall woman, waiting for something to happen, for events to unfold. He led his companions and the panting Wayne toward the complex. Jack Armstrong had his Benjamin Hymen Siegel face on, prepared to make his move.

Just then, thanks to high-level, greased-palm clearance, *Exclusive!!*'s production caravan pulled onto the grounds. Helicopters containing, among others, Ashley Parker and Brett Steele, settled to earth.

35.

The change from Belize to Guatemala was economically and sociologically dramatic.

Half a mile beyond the border, they had passed from genial subsistence to tense impoverishment, from decent macadam to potholed roads Rob slalomed when not pausing for stray cattle to cross. Hardscrabble villages were set against the highway and everybody stared. They went by groups of Guatemalan police and soldiers who seemed to be loitering, bored, waiting for something to happen.

"My paranoia bugaboo is making an encore," Carla Chance said.

"It's got company," Buster Hightower said.

"It's up and down my spine too," Sarah Ann Hilyer said. "Is it because of Guatemala per se or hangovers from too much Belikin or are we being followed?"

"Any or all of the above," Rob Weather said.

They reached the Tikal visitor's center and bought a map and soft drinks. Rob rubbernecked the surrounding vegetation—trees tall, bushy and crowded, and the bird and animal sounds within.

There were a few hotels and eateries, or *comedores,* at the site. Ocellated turkeys roamed freely, as tame as pussycats. They were shaped like ordinary gobblers, Buster thought, but they had metallic-looking feathers in all sorts of colors. Coatimundis, long-tailed members of the raccoon family, also had their run of the grounds and tree branches.

A swamp beside the visitor's center sported a sign warning of crocodiles.

"Where are they?" Buster wondered out loud. "Not that we gotta take a closer look-see."

Rob said, "Short of tossing in a tourist as a snack, I can't help you."

"Did you know that many of the coati groups are exclusively female?" Rob said. "Males are invited in to mate."

Carla looked at Buster. "Whatever you're planning to say, don't."

"It's too damn hot to be funny," said the comic.

Sarah touched *Plaza del Mundo Perdido* on the map. "It's prominent, a large complex."

She read from the guidebook. "Named for *Lost World,* the Arthur Conan Doyle novel, where the characters come upon a similar ruin and prehistoric creatures. Except for the absence of dinosaurs, the setting reminded the archeologists of the book."

Sarah squeezed his hand. "Shall we, Rob?"

"Yes, I suppose we shall."

"Cold feet at one hundred degrees and two hundred percent humidity," Carla said, wiping her brow.

"If we got bogeymen around the bend, they're sweating like racehorses too," Buster said.

Knapsacks on, containing bottles of water and valuables out of the Taihotsu Mountain Goat™, they walked three-quarters of a mile to the heart of Tikal.

They were treated to a promenade of birds in the trees and in the air. Monkeys and more coatimundis roamed the ground and the trees like domestic animals. Green parrots zipped and swooped raucously, like swallows at home.

"We're in a zoo and an aviary," Sarah marveled.

Rob said, "My first time here, I hired a guide named Miguel.

He's the legendary *El Pájarero*. The Birder. His list is in excess of four hundred species, impressive considering that he's never been outside the local area. I was fortunate to have been referred to him by a friend in Belize. *El Pájarero* gave me a crash course in bird-watching."

He pointed out woodpeckers, flycatchers, herons, rails and a Baltimore oriole. The others nodded politely, knowing Rob was stalling to encounter whatever awaited. They were in no rush either.

Then Rob heard or saw something they didn't. He darted from the path onto a narrow trail. They followed reluctantly on a rainbow promenade of what he identified as blue-crowned motmots, indigo buntings, crimson-collared tanagers, and yellow-bellied tyrannulets.

He laced his thumbs and forefingers together. "As taught by Miguel, I'm making a 'window.' Windows in the foliage make even the smallest bird easy to spot."

Flora was not overlooked. They came to a tree that had a trunk like a cylindrical porcupine.

"They call it the Give and Take Tree," Rob said, picking a leaf. "If a needle stings you, squeeze the juices from the underside on it to relieve the pain."

"Hey, we'll take your word for it," Buster said, steering wide.

Rob beelined to another tree, a sapodilla, and touched diagonal machete scars in the crusty bark. Once upon a time, a *chiclero* had collected the latex used in chewing gum.

"We're in luck," he said, pointing into trees that shaded the jungle floor.

"See. That yellow-and-black bird with a big, gorgeous, greenish-orange schnoz? I've never seen one outside of a pet store. A keel-billed toucan!"

"Rob, we've come thousands of miles," Carla said. "We should move along."

"Yeah. Maintain our half-lap lead on the bad guys," Buster said.

He sighed. "I know, I know. This way."

They came to a limestone pyramid that had to be fifteen stories tall. It was stacked in levels, like a towering wedding cake.

"Oh wow is an understatement," Sarah said.

"Temple I," Rob said. "It's Tikal's pin-up, the one you see in the travel ads. This is the backside. You rarely see the rear of Temple I."

Before she could reply, he took her hand, marching them onward. Sarah thought of her mother, teaching elementary school early in her education career, before she earned advanced degrees. She had described her students' eyes when she announced a field trip to a fun place like a zoo. Rob had those eyes.

They went onto the grassy Great Plaza and it was her turn to have those eyes.

"Way cool, huh?" he said, loving her reaction as much as the sight.

Temple II, a pyramid nearly as tall as Temple I, bookended the plaza. There were busy arrays of partially restored structures on the other sides—the Central Acropolis and North Acropolis.

Carla pictured the Great Plaza as a bustling marketplace as well as an open-air smoke-filled room. Tikal was the hub of a sphere of influence extending for a 100-mile radius. Like the Roman Forum, there would have been deals cut, alliances made and broken, grudges settled.

The Great Plaza was thick with tourists. A couple sat on a round, flat stone, one of a dozen or so, which their guidebook described as an altar, not a park bench. A uniformed Guatemalan park ranger strode to them, blowing his whistle, waving until they got up, language anybody could translate.

Coatimundis were underfoot, successfully mooching in spite of DON'T FEED THE ANIMALS signs. Sarah shooed one away; it promptly cadged a banana from another visitor.

"Rob," Carla said gently.

"I know, Aunt Carla, I know. I realize we have pressure on us to buckle down, to take care of business."

Buster said, "A hundred billion smackers worth of business."

Rob rocked a palm. "Allegedly, possibly."

Sarah said, "Highly speculatively, too."

"Ain't we tourists, too?" Buster said.

Carla said, "I'll concede that we have time to enjoy, too. We can hope we have the time."

Rob didn't say "oh boy, oh boy, goody, goody!", but relief was plastered on his face. Sarah and he climbed temples and explored the acropolises as Buster and Carla stood below. They walked to the west end of the park, to what Rob called the "big daddy."

"Temple IV," he said. "Two-hundred-and-twelve feet to the top. The tallest building in the Americas until the introduction of elevators in the late 1800s. Sorry about the repetition. I can't stop marveling."

Sarah looked up at a blockish monolith. The bottom half was shaggily overgrown. A progression of wooden ladders provided tourist access to a landing not far from the top.

"Who's game?" he said.

"Speaking of elevators," Buster said. "Where the hell is it?"

"Amen," Carla said.

Sarah said, "Rob, this isn't a Disneyland ride."

"And it's no dry heat we got here," Buster said.

Rob smiled and gestured. "After you."

Sarah didn't protest.

Buster said, "Where's your parachutes?"

"Buster and I will wave to you from down here."

Sarah thought 212 feet was an understatement. Halfway up, drenched with perspiration, she asked Rob, "How many more ladder rungs?"

"Less than a thousand," he joked.

The view after the climb more than compensated for the effort. Temples I, II and III erupted from triple-canopy jungle.

Sarah and Rob watched black vultures circle, gathering and wheeling in a lower and tighter pattern. Some unfortunate creature inside the forest was destined to be a meal.

Sarah looked upward at helicopters descending in the direction of the visitor center. "Is that unusual?" she asked.

Rob said, "It is. We may've had our fun for the day."

36.

Back together on the ground, despite Buster's moaning and groaning, saying he needed a couple or ten beers to replace vital bodily fluids, Rob led them on jungle pathways to the Lost World complex. It was only a few hundred yards from Temple IV, but when they reached El Mundo Perdido, they were more than ready to rest on a lower step of the largest temple.

It was wide, around 100 feet tall, with what appeared to be terraces on several levels. There were a dozen tourists exploring the pyramid. It was massive, flanked by smaller structures. But after what else the foursome had seen, the complex was almost prosaic. Magnificent as it was, El Mundo Perdido was anonymous compared to the Great Plaza.

"Now what?" went unspoken.

"Sarah, ever smooch in public on a fifteen-hundred-year-old pile of stone?"

She backhanded his thigh. "I *do* have a headache."

"You kids behave yourselves," Carla said.

A Guatemalan boy carrying a rolled-up sheet of paper stood before them.

"Hey, squirt," Buster said.

"Hi," Sarah said.

The youngster of seven or eight had materialized unnoticed. Saying nothing, he unrolled the paper, looked at it, and at Rob. He repeated the Rob–paper visual comparison and gave Rob a computer disk. The TaihotsuData™ high-density, formatted 3

1/2-inch floppy diskette was unlabeled.

Rob unzipped his backpack and got out his laptop. "Somebody knew I had this relic with me."

Carla said, "The somebody and somebodies who tidied your clothes and rolled up your toothpaste tubes."

"You got it, Aunt Carla."

Sarah asked in Spanish, "What is this and who are you, young man?"

The kid studied his sandaled toes.

"Pleased to meet you," Rob said. "I don't know if you understand English, but you know who I am."

When he didn't respond, Sarah asked, "May we see what you're holding?"

He gave her a printed photographic collage of Robin Chance Weather. Rob Weather on camera in a parka. Rob Weather getting into a car. Rob Weather standing at a curb. Digitally enhanced head and profile shots of Rob Weather with long and short hair. Bearded and smooth shaven. Bespectacled and not. Blond, brunette, redhead, graying in all hues.

"Who gave this to you?"

He smiled at her and said in a mix of Spanish, Yucatec Maya and broken English, "I was to come here and stay until I could give the disk to this man."

"I do hope they paid you well for your services."

His parting grin as he scampered off told her that they had.

Rob said, "Would you do the honors, Sarah?"

Forearm shading a dull screen, she inserted the disk, clicked on an unnamed file, the only document on the disk. There was no written text and no heading. Sarah scrolled bank names, account numbers and PINs, row upon row of them. Balances were in dollars and euros, six to eight digits at a clip. Rob watched, open-mouthed.

At the end of the file, she asked, "Again?"

"Thanks, no."

She removed the disk and gave it and the laptop to him.

"My alleged granddad didn't allegedly take it with him. He didn't allegedly burn it up in an alleged blast furnace," Rob said. "Did he?"

"Apparently not. What are we going to do?"

Rob stared at the disk, shaking his head. "I haven't the vaguest, foggiest, remotest notion."

Sarah put an arm around him. "Let it sink in."

At that moment, Ashley Parker, Brett Steele, and a phalanx of camera and sound technicians walked into the clearing. Brett was wearing pressed khakis and a shirt printed like an arboretum.

He sat beside Rob. They shook hands.

"Aren't you supposed to say, Robin Weather, I presume? Or Robert if you prefer."

"Great disguise, Rob. You would have fooled me if we were total strangers."

"We are, except for Terre Haute," Rob told Brett.

"What have we here?" said Ashley, looking at the laptop, which Rob turned away from her.

Brett leaned forward. "Ms. Hilyer, my pleasure."

"I don't know if pleasure is the correct word," she said.

Rob said, "Jesus, Brett. 'It will be as explosive as the *Enola Gay.*' Did we really, really hear you say that?"

"It was written for me, Rob."

"Still getting the mail accusing you of having an IQ in the teens?"

"It's all part of the package that I am."

"Speaking of Terre Haute, how goes the bowling?"

"I don't have the time I'd like for it," Brett said.

"You were a good bowler."

"Was and am. I rolled a two-fifty-nine in a six-thirty-six series

Gary Alexander

last month."

"When you lose your looks and *Exclusive!!* dumps you, you'll have a second career."

"Rob, are we small-talking to delay and minimize the impact of this situation?"

"You're decimating it," Buster said. "Ironically."

"Mr. Hightower," Brett said with a curt nod.

"I'm along for comic relief, pal, but you're upstaging me."

"Shouldn't it be the *Enola Gay*'s *A-bomb*, Brett?" Rob said. "The *Enola Gay* didn't blow up. It's in an aerospace museum."

"This is no time for nitpicking, Rob."

The cameras were getting in position, some already rolling. A sound boom was above them, and Ashley, in skintight jungle fatigues, joined them at the ready with a mike.

Rob said, "Brett, have you gone tabloid on me? Oh wait, you are tabloid."

Buster advised, "If you're gonna tabloidize it, do it full-bore. Don't fool around. Bring on the Martians and crop circles."

Brett ignored Buster. "Our sources have advance word on those secret numbers, Rob."

"You people always find a way," Rob said.

Brett said, "MacArthur and your grandfather were as tight as ticks. The general knew the Mongoose was a fraud from day one. They exploited each other to the hilt, the economic recovery of postwar Japan arguably being MacArthur's motivation for their secret partnership."

"You've done mighty fine for yourself since Terre Haute."

"Yeah, Terre Haute. Those were good times, Rob. The best weeks of my life. May we proceed? Please?"

"How did you get so hot on our trail?" Rob asked.

A trace of the Brett Steele–patented smirk. "At Terre Haute we had a zilch budget. At *Exclusive!!*, when I exceed my unlimited budget, I get more."

"I've heard that one, Brett."

"We pulled out all the stops."

"Crack investigative journalism on steroids. Okay, but your bloodhounds needed something to sniff. What was Point A? The MacArthur papers, that amazon on *Exclusive!!*, what?"

"There were many crucial contributing factors."

"What crucial contributing factors, bwana?"

"You, yourself, are the foremost, Rob. Thanks to our Terre Haute days, I know you and I am privy to your background."

"And?"

"We received a call the night Saburo Taihotsu's executive chef was on *Exclusive!!* From Phil, your cameraman."

"Ah."

Brett said, "Ironically, Phil lost his job earlier that very same day. Did he have a chip on his shoulder? I get the impression that Phil carries free-floating anger on his back like a steamer trunk."

"Phil hadn't been completely happy at the station," Rob said. "Phil had issues, as they say."

"Issues. Yes, issues. After his firing, he had a midday cocktail or two. He received a call on his cell, reminding him that he hadn't turned in his field video camera. He had more cocktails, returned to the station, and threw said camera at someone in management or through a wall or he missed a station exec by inches and it went through the exec's office window, smashing into the sunroof of the executive's car parked below. A Lexus, the big model with all the trimmings.

"Phil's call to us was made at midnight, Pacific Time. There was a jukebox twang as mood music. Though unclear on every delicate detail of employment termination, Phil did vividly recall a row of numbers."

Rob said, "Luckily for my old buddy Phil. Guess I can't

blame him. Hey, Brett, tell me where you got the clips of me you ran."

He looked into the middle distance. "I am beholden to my corporate Caesars, Rob. I have an obligation to maintain confidentialities."

Rob laughed.

"You have the skills to be up here with me. If you hadn't been so stubborn and had seen your way clear to make a few compromises."

Rob ran a hand through his darkened hair.

"Much too late to make that makeover. The helicopter hang-up too, Rob?"

Rob looked at him. "I confessed that to you?"

"One Terre Haute night when you were in your cups."

"A hang-up till the day I die. However I check out, I will not be on assignment, upside down in a flaming whirlybird above an overturned semi on an interstate."

"Good for you, Rob. Back on the subject, when we met personally, Phil said he hated himself for giving you up. I have no doubt his tears were genuine."

Rob rubbed thumb and forefinger together.

With her microphone, as Ashley edged closer to Rob to peek at the laptop screen, she said, "May we cease with the memory lane shit and cut to the chase?"

"What did I tell you about her?" Rob said to Sarah.

"Language like that from a pretty girl like you," Carla said, *tsk-tsk*ing.

Ashley said, "Fuck off, Granny."

"Why you little strumpet! You're the granddaughter I'm glad I never had," Carla said.

"Phil's compensation?" Rob said.

"Phil has three kids and an ex who despises the air he

breathes," Brett said. "He's so deep in the hole he can't see light."

"Did you take good care of him? Phil's an okay guy."

"He begins at a network's San Diego affiliate on Monday."

"Bravo for Phil," Rob said.

"Year-round sun and a major market for a man who had rendered himself unemployable. An equitable quid pro quo."

"Are those airborne deathtraps we heard a while ago yours? Your crew's assembling the boom and dish as we chitchat?"

Brett checked his eighteen-carat gold Taihotsu DigiChron™. "Thank you for reminding me of scheduling constraints."

"Holy fucking shit," Ashley said, beseeching the heavens.

"You're too young and pretty to be working yourself into an ulcer and nervous breakdown, dear," Carla told her, approaching closer than the social distance and looking downward. "Furthermore, you need to be taken over a knee after your mouth's washed out with soap."

Ashley averted her eyes, ending the conversation.

"Rob, be a buddy and give me a one-on-one?"

"Getting the story first," Rob said. "What did you once tell me?"

"It's better than sex, Rob."

"This is kind of a bad time for an in-depth interview, Brett. I don't have any makeup on."

"Cut it out, Rob. You obviously broke Saburo Taihotsu's code. That's why you're at this godforsaken place."

"Godforsaken?" Sarah and Rob chimed.

"That youngster with the Rob Weather centerfold and the floppy disk slipped under our radar."

Rob was flipping the disk like a coin.

"Is that the grand prize, the whole shebang?"

"No comment."

"Any insights on Saburo Taihotsu, the man? He's proved to

Gary Alexander

be unfathomable."

Rob didn't answer.

"Assumptions will be made regarding the data on that diskette. You should be careful, Rob. Work with us. We can escort you out of this Third World hellhole in one piece."

"After our on-camera, breaking-news, exclusive interview on your developing story."

"You've gotten cynical, Rob."

"Always was."

"You liked to say you weren't a serious person."

"I am a goof. I yam what I yam."

"You should take yourself seriously. You should, Rob. A purported one-hundred-billion dollars is serious business."

"Screw you, Brett," Rob said congenially. "And the horse you rode in on."

"You have a responsibility."

"I've heard quite enough, Mr. Exclusive," Sarah said. "Look me in the eye and tell me you care about Rob other than for your story, your scoop, if that's what you television people call it."

Rob put his arm around her and kissed her cheek.

Brett said somberly, "Ms. Hilyer, this phenomenon is a runaway train."

Rob said, "C'mon, Brett, whip a Taihotsu Tidbit on us. *Exclusive!!* does its share and then some."

"We haven't today's from our researchers yet. We know it'll have to do with pizza. How many you can buy with one-hundred-billion dollars or how high they'll stack into the ionosphere or how end-to-end they'll extend to the moon and back. Twice. Five times. I don't know. You're adamant we can't talk on camera, Rob?"

Rob raised his right hand. "I am, Brett. So help me, Edward R. Murrow."

238

From around an adjacent structure, behind the camera and sound people, came Mr. Jiminy Cricket Smith, Mr. Jerome (Chicken) Little, and Mrs. Sally Jo Stockwall.

Mr. Smith yelled, "Come to your senses, Rob Weather. There's plenty of cabbage for everyone. Don't you go being greedy on us."

"Who the hell are you?" Brett said to the threesome, then to Little, who was holding Mrs. Stockwall's hand, "What the hell are you?"

"Partners," Little said, looking at Jack Armstrong, to whom he'd given no speaking lines.

"I'm in, Little," Smith/Armstrong said. "I'm not a bit player in this."

"We'll see," said Chicken Little. "As of now, you're off the clock."

Armstrong said, "Fortune or no fortune, I'm filing a grievance against you with my union."

Rob observed the odd trio as he continued flipping the disk. It was growing heavier and heavier.

A coatimundi appeared in front of them, attracted by it, available for a handout. Rob smiled at the coati. It was as cute as a button.

Brett glanced at his watch again. "Rob, how about it?"

Rob flicked the disk with a thumbnail. "Catch, boy."

Leaping as if for a Frisbee™, the animal snatched the rotating floppy in midair, crunched through the hard shell with his powerful teeth, and bounded into the jungle.

Ashley screamed.

Jack Armstrong realized that his scheming may have been for naught. As his employer stood unmoving with his woman, the quasi–Indiana Jones ran into the jungle after the coati.

A pudgy, disheveled man, vaguely familiar to Rob, appeared. "Sal?"

239

"Wally?"

Rob snapped his fingers. "The proctologist on the plane."

Dr. J.D. (Wally) Stockwall pointed at the couple's joined hands, his spouse's lost inside the gruesome giant's. "He's holding you prisoner, Sal?"

A prisoner of love, she thought.

"In a sense, Wally."

"At my earliest opportunity, I'll notify the police, Sal."

"Just take care of yourself, Wally."

Dr. Stockwall looked at Rob and said, "I want my share. I am entitled. I have twenty of the twenty-six numbers."

Sally Jo Stockwall gestured to the jungle and said, "There it went. Go get it."

A darling dog the color of OC1 and OC2 emerged, ran past the catatonic orthodontist to jungle's edge, and hesitated.

"Here, boy," Carla called. "You'll get hurt in there."

"And eaten," Buster said, softly clapping his hands. "C'mon, doggy. C'mere."

"Well," Brett said, "Bill Gates did say some years ago that the floppy disk was dead."

"My story," Ashley shrieked at Rob.

"Yours?" Brett said.

Curious tourists trampled into the jungle too. They didn't know what the object of the hunt was, but they all recognized Brett and Ashley and knew it couldn't be pocket change. Helicopters hovered above.

"Hey, toots," Buster said to Ashley. "You wanna hot story, go find the world's most valuable classic car."

Her eyes perked at "world's most valuable." "I'm listening."

"A dynamite sidebar to this surreal day, Ashley," Rob said.

Buster said, "You people think you're so all-fired smart. Track it down, cutie-pie. Go check with whatshisname, Dave Snider, crack reporter for Seattle's finest zero-wattage TV station. He'll give you all the specificals."

"Cutie pie? You old sexist bastard."

"Sticks and stones, girly," Buster said. "Yes or no?"

"You can take your classic car and shove—"

"There's your story, Brett," Rob said. "It's better than nothing."

"Marginally."

"Tell you what I'll do, Brett. I'll give *Exclusive!!* the exclusive on what went down in the here and now, me and my disk and the coati, providing you find Mr. Hightower's car."

"Jesus, Rob," Brett said. "You throw away a hundred billion dollars, and you're worried about some old beater."

"Watch your mouth, boy," Buster said.

A hundred billion bucks, Rob thought, hearing yelling within the tropical vegetation. *Did I really do that?*

"That's my deal, Brett. Take it or leave it."

"We're on the story," Brett said.

37.

At San Ignacio, inside Eva's Café, the small TaihotsuTron™ TV bolted to the wall above the bar was tuned to the chaos and TIKAL GUATEMALA LIVE.

Over ice-cold Belikins, they watched soldiers swarming in the jungle. Helicopters, Guatemalan military, as well as *Exclusive!!*'s chartered whirlybirds, circled, darting low when someone erroneously caught a glimpse of the animal and the disk.

"How many coatis are in the general area?" Sarah asked. "Approximately."

"Approximately countless," Rob said.

"As many as cats and tiny, yippy, inbred dogs in our condo complex?" Buster said.

"And then some, Uncle Buster."

"You'd think a coup d'état was in progress," Carla said.

"It may come to that if the wrong folks come up with that floppy gizmo," Buster said.

"It wasn't one of my swifter moves," Rob said.

Until now, they hadn't exchanged ten words after their hasty departure from Tikal. Rob was contrite after his disk-flipping impulse, and the others were willing to wait him out.

"You'd like to undo it, huh?" Buster asked. "Like rewinding a TV news tape to where you were flipping the disk like it was a one-hundred-billion silver dollars?"

"Okay, probably, maybe. Hell, I don't know. It's not an easy question, Uncle Buster."

242

"Hey, don't sweat it now. There're two pluses. Talk about your basic misdirection. Nobody's paying us no never mind. The camera-toting posse's tramping through the jungle after that critter. I hope there's snakebite medicine handy. What's the really nasty one?"

"Fer-de-lance. They're large, extremely venomous, and will strike without provocation."

"Yikes."

"Buster's right. The big big plus is that the heat's temporarily off us, Rob. You especially," Carla said.

"The minus is obvious, Aunt Carla."

"We'll be fine in the long term, dear, diskette data and where it leads or not. None of us is starving."

"Speak for yourself," Buster said, slapping his gut.

Sarah said, "How long do we have, do you think, Rob, till we resume being the center of attention?"

Rob shrugged. "A day tops, and that's a wild guess. As long as the disk is out there, it's priority *numero uno*. There's no chance that disk will be usable even if they find it, is there?"

Carla said, "I don't know. I'm no expert. The coatimundi bit through the case and it's been exposed to foreign matter and moisture."

"So it'd be like Humpty Dumpty?" Buster said.

Sarah smiled. "An apt comparison."

"But everybody will assume I'm the heir, legit or not, disk or no disk."

Rob got the laptop out. "I'll have to do this quickly. The battery is almost kaput. I can't believe I forgot to bring the charger or a converter."

"Do what?"

The low late-afternoon sun beamed through a window, so the screen was marginally visible. Rob squinted as he scrolled the bank deposit data, column upon column of account numbers and amounts.

"I'll be go to hell," Buster said.

"Way cool," Carla said.

"Working fast, I managed to save Grandfather's present to the hard drive."

Carla said, "You rascal."

Rob said, "Should I laugh or cry?"

"You decide while I shut down."

Sarah said, "Just a minute. Can you shoot to the top?"

He did.

"Now to the bottom."

He did.

"That's what I thought. There's nothing but data. Nothing else."

"Meaning?"

"No note. No words, Rob."

He said, "No dear grandson-san. No, hi, how are you, kiss my backside. Does that bother me? Maybe. I guess I was expecting some damn thing."

Sarah wrapped her arms around him. "Saburo Taihotsu was a reclusive man, Rob, not remotely a people person. You never knew each other. You're the end result of a deep, dark secret. He was paying an obligation the only way he knew how."

Buster said, "As they say, money is the ideal gift. It don't spoil and it goes with everything."

"What will you do with it?" Sarah said.

"What will we do with it, partner?" Rob said. "Partners. The Four Mouseketeers."

Then he kissed Sarah and said, "You tell me."

"Remember, I don't make out in public," she said, kissing him. "Do I need this trouble?"

"You're obligated on all kinds of levels. Furthermore, I'm flaky. Without your steady hand, I'd piddle one-hundred-billion dollars away in a week, though I have a hunch that nobody but lawyers and the IRS will see much money anytime soon."

"Shall we keep our voices down?" Carla said.

"Help me give it away," he whispered into Sarah's ear.

She cocked her head and laughed when he nibbled. "A worthy cause. Many, many worthy causes."

"A foundation. We'll run a foundation."

"To promote world peace or another worthy cause?"

"Nope to world peace. Who'd we give it to? Who we *don't* give it to is the difficulty. We'd be responsible for starting nine new wars."

"You'll think of something," Sarah said.

"You're on sabbatical. I'm unemployed. I have the time. We have the time."

"We?"

"Yes, we."

"I'm witness to that," Carla said.

Rob shook his head and said, "*Exclusive!!* was totally unaffected, you know. We could've been in downtown Peoria. Tikal, one of the great wonders of the ancient world, and all it was to them was a venue for Getting the Most Sensational Story First."

It would be utterly impossible for Sarah Hilyer to be without this man. Inconceivable. She didn't understand why and didn't want to understand why.

She said, "Am I the only one starving? How does the rice, beans, and stewed chicken special sound? We can eat and be on the road before dark."

Carla had been looking at the laptop screen. "Oops. I'm looking more closely. The sun's off the screen now. The PINs may not be PINs. They're each twenty-six digits."

Buster laughed. "Here we go again."

"Math might be no help this time," Carla said.

"No problem. We'll buy us a warehouse full of decoder rings,"

Buster said.

Rob felt a sharp instrument against his back. It was being held by a plump, disheveled, wild-eyed man.

Buster also saw tweezers, compass, pen and wire cutters bristling on the jackknife weapon. "Bug off, pal. This is a private party."

"Uncle Buster, this feels serious. It's very sharp, whatever it is. Whoever you are, as if I don't know?"

The intruder said, "I am your former seatmate, Blondie. I am a health care professional. I know exactly what to do with this weapon and where to go into your body with it."

Raving incomprehensibly about entitlement and eugenics, the pudgy, disheveled, wild-eyed man grabbed the machine and lurched out the door.

Rob took Buster's arm as he rose to chase him. "Let him go."

Buster sat heavily and looked at him.

Rob said, "It's okay. There's nothing useful on the laptop for our demented proctologist. I just deleted the file."

"Ouch," Buster said.

"Sarah, remember my purloined wireless card that came with the purloined laptop? It works from here. I emailed the file to myself."

Carla refilled a water bowl and placed it in front of the darling golden retriever at her feet that'd gone out of Tikal with them.

Then they ordered the rice, beans and stewed chicken special, and more ice-cold Belikins.

38.

"You gotta love technology," Buster said, caressing the Purple Flasher Tavern's Taihotsu TuneSter™. "That medical transplant operation they were gonna do? They shipped the wrong part from Taiwan. It was the left-side gizzard, not the right-side, so I got me a reprieve, which is your bad luck. You want I should be a cowboy singer instead, like the ones trapped inside this thing, tough bananas."

Mild applause and raised beer bottles indicated that the crowd of twenty or so thought their luck was running okay. On her feet, Carla Chance clapped the loudest, prolonging the applause.

Responding to Carla's hard glare, Old Man Grimes from next door also rose to his feet. The boozy, reclusive Grimes, with his sour expression and pot gut and gray comb-over, the carnapper of Buster's Cadillac, was afraid to disobey her.

"That's my Carla there with Mr. Grimes, our good friend and neighbor," Buster said, blowing her a kiss.

Grimes made a face.

"This jukebox is kinda sorta a symphony in its own twangy way. Not long ago, Carla drug me downtown to the gen-u-ine article, the Seattle Symphony."

A collective groan.

"She might as well've marched me to Gestapo headquarters for a thumbscrew fitting. But in retrograde, it was okay. Couldn't help but notice how they sat on the stage, the fiddle players especially. Carla explained that they had first chair and second chair and so forth, according to who was the best fiddle player or horn tooter or whatnot.

"I had to wonder, is it like baseball, when if you're not up to snuff they send you down to the minors? If you toot or fiddle at the wrong time, are you sent down to the Podunk Philharmonica?"

Buster swigged his free beer, looking at Grimes. While not laughing with the crowd, the old boy finally cracked a smile. *Exclusive!!* came through, by who knows what means, to locate his beloved Eldo right-flipping-next-door in Grimes's garage, inches from its own automotive boudoir.

"Lemme ask you some questions that've bugged the hell outta me. How come out on the highway, when a cop's writing a ticket, everybody slows down to the speed limit. He's already got a customer! You could go ninety and there's nothing he can do."

Another swig and a semaphore wave to Mildred to replace the dead soldier. Grimes, it turned out, was a Purple Flasher regular. Buster thought he'd caught someone familiar in the corner of his eye in his Flasher debut.

Grimes had spilled the beans without resistance to the police, thanks to *Exclusive!!*, which had been there to tape the defiant confession live. Grimes admitted that he was nosy and liked to hold a stethoscope to his neighbor's walls.

Was that a federal case? Hell, no, it ain't, he'd argued.

The more Grimes had eavesdropped on the comic, the angrier he'd become. He'd gotten thoroughly sick of Buster going on and on about his Caddy and how (for the 612th time, per his companion) Buster had broken into the profession on June 17, 1972, the evening of the Watergate break-in.

He had just been trying to shut Buster up, unaware that to do so was a violation of the laws of nature. Grimes had never recovered from the consequences of Watergate to his hero, Richard Milhous Nixon, and his CRP underlings. To this day, Old Man Grimes believed that the Watergate hearings were a communist plot to put a liberal in the White House.

He'd been at the Purple Flasher much of the day, had gone home for a while, put together the first ransom note, taken the bus to the Snickertown Comedy Club with a Nixon mask he'd purchased in the 1970s, snatched the Eldorado, run it to a park-and-ride lot near the Purple Flasher, sat it out until two A.M. bar closing, then drove it home and into his garage so late nobody had been up and around.

He'd written the second ransom note while sloshed too, even though he'd been frightened by what he'd done (when sober) and hadn't known how to collect a ransom. He hadn't the foggiest what the magic card meant either.

Buster and the law had worked out a deal not to prosecute Old Man Grimes, who had a clean record. Grimes had been ordered to wash the Eldo weekly for a year, to wax it *semi*-monthly, and to keep the convertible top and wide whitewalls snow-white. The deputy prosecuting attorney in charge of the case had wanted to include alcohol counseling, but Buster had vetoed the idea, citing cruel and unusual punishment.

"Void where prohibited," Buster Hightower screamed. "If it's prohibited, it's gotta be void, don't it? A great big void.

"Speaking of secret codes. We all heard about Saburo Taihotsu's grandson being given a code to break so he could have the old boy's wampum," Buster said, then lying, "All I know about it is what I read in the papers."

He gulped his brew, thinking how happy Carla and he were that Rob kept them totally out of it. They would've been here tonight, but had commitments involved in setting up the foundation with Sarah. As Rob said, they had $100 billion in the kitty, the goal to make it like Bill and Melinda's, and then some.

"The difficulty of codes to find zillions ain't zilch compared to the codes on bus schedules. You're smiling, sir. Ever try to read one? I'm no spring chicken. I'm not a summer, winter, and fall chicken no more neither, but I'll tell ya, even in my younger days I couldn't solve the cryptoprestidigitation."

Buster produced a bus schedule and let it fall open. "Like a centerfold, but a helluva lot less fun. Lookie at these times and numbers and this map they drew on it. Are you kidding me?

"What if you gotta transfer buses? What you gotta do, you gotta hunt through another one. What they need to do to the sadistic sadists who write them things, they need to put them on buses at random with bags stuffed with schedules and give 'em an hour to get back to the office. If they're late, they're canned on the spot.

"Hey, boys and girls, you been great. Gotta go or I'll change into a pumpkin, but before I do I'm wrapping with a—yeah, I know—a stale lawyer joke. What's the difference between a lawyer and a vulture?"

Pause.

"The lawyer gets frequent flier miles."

Carla jumped up. The crowd joined in. She was glad he was cutting it a little short tonight. This was the first time they'd left the golden retriever home alone with OC1 and OC2. All manner of fur could be flying.

The poor animal had been abandoned at Tikal. Evidently it belonged to somebody who'd chased into the jungle for the floppy disk, one of many who'd joined a hazardous and fruitless game of fetch with the coatimundi. Carla did have a good home for it, though, once the smoke cleared, and Rob and Sarah got settled.

Buster had named it Sir Bill of Ockham.

"A show dog name," he'd said. "Like the mutts who win the ribbons at those fancy-pants dog shows."

Carla looked at Grimes, still seated, arms folded, teeth clenched. Other than being older than dirt, he reminded her of the odd, deranged American who had confronted them in San Ignacio, Belize, with a Swiss army knife. How the wretch had run out of the café with Rob's laptop and his confrontation with a Belizean taxi driver. It'd been a quarrel about money, a refund request or demand for an additional fare, or the American claiming to be without funds.

Whichever, the American had foolishly brandished his absurd knife. The cab driver easily disarmed him, but the laptop had been a victim in the scuffle, smashing on the pavement, smashing further when the American fell on it, driving him berserk.

The cabby and passersby had held him for the police, who took him away, raving. As far as anyone knew, he was in Belize, detained indefinitely at a mental health facility. That or he'd been deported, brought home to a similar institution.

Carla looked at Grimes again, once more glaring him out of his chair.

Now *everyone* in the Purple Flasher Tavern was putting their hands together for Buster Hightower.

39.

Three days later in Las Vegas, Jerome (Chicken) Little and Sally Jo Stockwall attended Jack Armstrong's funeral. Mirroring the city's tradition of instant weddings, it was a quick, efficient service. The funeral parlor was as tacky as any Vegas wedding chapel, too. The artificial scent on the artificial flowers bordered on pungent.

Besides the rent-a-pastor, they were the only attendees.

The Guatemalan authorities had reported that Armstrong (aka Jiminy Cricket Smith) stepped too closely to a fer-de-lance, one of the most deadly and aggressive vipers.

Little had paid for transportation of the body as well as this service and interment.

Outside, after the five-minute service, during which the instant minister shocked them by recognizing Armstrong from *Feedlot,* describing the show as "daring programming," Little said, "How did it go?"

Dr. J.D. (Wally) Stockwall was institutionalized out-of-state in a facility for the insane. Jo had taken divorce papers there and had just gotten into town and taken a taxi from the airport to meet her Jerry at the funeral parlor. This was their first chance to talk.

"They keep him medicated because of repeated attempts to get his hands inside the mouths of the staff and fellow patients," Jo Stockwall said. "He lunges unexpectedly."

"His former profession," Jerry said, nodding.

"He remembers orthodontia in bits and pieces."

"Did he remember you?"

"No, but he signed the papers anyway."

"Great, baby! I have news too," Jerry said.

"On your endowment?"

He'd also gotten into town earlier that day. "Had you heard of Northern Plains College, Jo?"

"I hadn't before you mentioned it as a possibility, along with several others."

"NPC is not exactly Ivy League, but it's my best shot. The upside is that Northern Plains College is small and the numbers work. NPC is strapped for funds, too."

"When you say 'numbers,' you mean revenue from your loan business?"

"Yes."

"If it's what you want, Jerry, it's what I want."

"Do you mind snow on the ground until mid-May?"

She held his hand tightly as they walked. "Not if I'm with you."

"They had an exceptionally rotten winter, far worse than usual," he said. "The worst on record, in fact. The most tragic too. In February, two grad students froze to death on a Friday night. They apparently lost their way in a blizzard."

"Oh, no."

"They'd decided to check on an experiment in the agriculture barn, something to do with hog sperm. They weren't found until Monday, when a snowblower tipped over on a mound on the walkway between the nuclear bioengineering lab and the field house. It was gross. You don't want details, Jo."

Jo paused, halting him and looking into his eyes. "I certainly don't. Are you thinking what I'm thinking?"

Jerry looked into her eyes and knew. He almost quoted Ambrose Bierce on love, but thought better.

Love: A temporary insanity curable by marriage or by removal of the patient from the influences under which he incurred the disorder.

Love means never having to say you're sorry.

"I absolutely am. It's a short flight from there to here," he said.

"To come to Vegas the day my divorce is finalized," she said.

"The instant it is," he said, hugging her.

"This is the luckiest city in the world for me."

"Your slot machine winnings?"

"They're minor compared to meeting you."

Jerry said, "Let's cease the direction of the conversation."

Pushing away from him, Jo said, "We do tend to lose control, don't we?"

"We do. Even Las Vegas has public decency laws."

"To change the subject. Your endowment?" she said.

"We're not going that route," he said.

"I'm not understanding. Northern Plains College won't let you buy a chair so you can teach?"

"They will, but I'm buying the college instead."

ABOUT THE AUTHOR

Gary Alexander is the author of nine mystery novels in three series, including *Disappeared,* the first Buster Hightower novel. He has written newspaper travel articles and numerous short stories. One story appeared in *The Best American Mystery Stories 2010.* Formerly a regional vice-president of the Mystery Writers of America, Gary lives in Kent, Washington. His website is www .garyralexander.com.